ECHO ENCODED

BY

TONI CRUZ

WGWPublishing.com

ISBN: 979-8-9887355-5-7

Editing: Wandah Gibbs, Ed. D.

Cover Illustration: Toni Cruz

Dedication Illustration: Lee Cruz

Printed in the USA

WGW Publishing Inc.
621 Wellington Avenue, Rochester NY 14619
wgibbs@wgwpublishing.com
(585) 245-0285

FOR MY DAUGHTERS: KEEP IN MIND THAT ANY ART I CREATE PALES IN COMPARISON TO THE THREE OF YOU.

TO ROBERT: THERE IS NOTHING I COULD SAY THAT WOULD SUFFICE.

... AND DAD, YOU WERE RIGHT; I WOULD THANK YOU FOR MAKING ME COPY ALL THOSE DEFINITIONS FROM THE DICTIONARY.

Dear Reader,

I want to fill this space with a short note instead of a formal introduction.

The way I figure it, a list of what society deems success will hardly speak for my story. I believe I've written something I can be proud of and that you, the reader, will (hopefully) enjoy, whether you know my personal details or not.

I once heard, "we are all stories in the end," which resonates deeply with me. As a writer, I think it is a beautiful concept; becoming the very thing I've spent my life loving to create.

After all, we are what we leave behind; the memories people have of us and the traditions we share as we cross each other's paths. We are alive in those moments, even when we are no longer physically present.

My book sitting on a shelf is a story. It's a form of immortality I'm honored to share. It's also incredibly humbling as I prepare myself for potential critics.

The thing is, I don't have to be one of the greats to be satisfied because I know that someone, somewhere, will read this, and that---in and of itself is enough for me.

You reading my work brings me joy for which I'm eternally grateful.

If we are in fact what we leave behind, then my best addition to this world will first and foremost be my daughters. After that I'd like to think it will be my writing.

I wholeheartedly thank you for every page you turn.

Toni

BENEATH THE SUNSET

I wanted to make an impression and now was my chance, but it was so hot. I couldn't understand how these people could spend hours beneath the beating sun. Working in this field, the sun felt like it was right on top of me. I was hotter than I'd ever been and every move was draining.

I stopped to close my eyes and catch my breath. It wasn't only the unforgiving heat; it was the blinding light reflecting off of everything and onto my face. I was roasting but determined. I needed to make up for lost time as I only had myself to blame. I'd meant to start earlier yesterday but spent a good portion of the day learning the lay of the land then gathering a few things I required. I tended to the plants, my skin reddening as I did so even though I slathered sun repellent all over myself to no avail. I was blistering already. I worked hard though; carefully, quickly, yet efficiently.

At this point, I was merely perfecting what I had started, but now every detail was of the utmost importance. I felt myself slowing down as the burning persistence forced me to seek shade. I was disappointed in myself for my lack of commitment, even though I knew I wasn't built for such heat.

I laid beneath the wonderfully large tree a short walk from the farm. The green blades, which were cool and moist, felt so soothing on my skin. It was refreshing and calming. I liked it. Without realizing it, I was rolling around a bit, embracing the soft ground. I traced the designs on the stone and found patterns in the bark.

I'd gotten distracted, again. I meant to be productive, but something about this place made me lose myself. Despite everything negative I had heard; I could see how someone could live here. I hadn't been here long, nor could I stay, but I took it all in. Right here below this tree was the best place to appreciate it. The sound of the birds chirping was lovelier than that of the humming insects from the night before. The sky was hypnotic and ever-changing. I'd never seen it like this; so open, so blue, and so bright. It was intoxicating and odd, wanting to look up at its beauty yet be blinded by it at the same time.

I laid there as if I was not under any time constraint. I might very well wander in the magnificence of it all. I took a deep breath. I liked the air out here, so different from the city where I had first been. This air was crisp, still ridden with smog, but undetectable to most. They say fresh air, but I could smell dirt and waste and farm animals in every direction. It wasn't exactly what I would have referred to as fresh, but it was strangely appealing.

I inhaled again, as if I could analyze each aspect of the country air. I caught the scent of flowers in the wind and sweet fruit in the trees. Even the grass had a remarkable fragrance. I watched the sun move in the sky, which seemed like a short distance away, and I became one with it all.

I suddenly found myself holding my breath and I knew why before I felt the footsteps on the ground. I heard them talking and knew they weren't far. Then came the infernal barking of that mangy dog. It shook me to the core. Bruno was easy enough to hate on his own, but the reaction I had to his dander further justified my loathing of him.

I knew when he was getting close because my breaths became further apart or not at all. He was a vicious thing with a slobbering mouth full of crooked, yellow, jagged teeth. He was huge. I did not know dogs could get that big. The scariest thing, though, was that he didn't even need to touch me because merely a whiff of him was enough to take me down.

I was not sure what they were saying, but I knew they were looking for me, though I couldn't understand their obsession with me. I'd spent most of my time working and kept to myself. I think they wanted to scare me away as if I did not belong here, but I had a job to do. I was working my best to make sure that everything grew properly through it all. I most certainly meant well, I really did. They were so quick to prosecute here, which I had been warned about. I'd continuously been warned about it.

I felt them coming even closer, so I laid as still as I could, resting my head on the pretty rock I traced earlier. As they approached, I pretended not to exist. I would say, I was holding my breath, but Bruno's dander was already having an effect on me. I was trembling and concentrating on staying quiet as much as I possibly could.

Suddenly, a rabbit caused Bruno to dart in the opposite direction, barely missing me. Any closer and one of them surely would have stepped on me and worse, I'm sure. One of them ran behind the predictable mutt as I fought to draw in air. It became harder and harder to do so every time Bruno was within range. I hated that helpless feeling. I lay still as the other one lingered behind. Had he seen me? He stared intently, so I closed my eyes, still trying to breathe, while trying not to be visible. Then he took off running too, and I breathed in so deep I swallowed all those tiny bugs that linger in the country air. I didn't even mind though because I was so relieved to breathe freely.

I sat up and headed back to finish up. It was becoming obvious that my time was coming to an end. I needed to get done. I thought it would have been so different coming here. I'd heard so much about the country and all that comes with it. I thought I picked out a small enough and distant enough place where I could tend to my work. It was supposed to be a safe haven.

Walking towards the farm, my fears were confirmed. My time really was limited and watching them destroy my work only emphasized that. I knew I was not supposed to fault everyone for the actions of a few, but I'd thought I would be safe here, of all places.

"You have to admit, it is interestin'," the big one spoke. "Would you quit sayin' that? Ain't nothin' bout this interestin'!" The small one snapped.

He stood there, a tiny package of a man, bald head glistening in the sun. I hid, trying to determine my next move. I was not afraid of either of them. It was that dog of theirs that made me hesitate. I stood there out of sight, waiting, thinking among the stalks. I watched the small one damage my work, destroying what could have easily been restored. I should have shown myself right then and there. Did he not understand the considerable effort required for something so meticulous? Clearly not. I stood still waiting.

Observing had always been my strength, even though I'd been reprimanded time and time again to act without hesitation. My tactics were always best when I carefully surveyed a situation first. With that in mind, I found myself following a few steps behind the big guy, who was also oblivious to my presence.

He was different from the small one and it amused me how such a big person could tread so lightly. I watched him kneel, touching some of my finest work. As he got closer examining it, his cap fell off and a mop of curly brown locks were freed, falling down his shoulders. He ruffled his hair then stuffed it back under his cap again, except this time, the brim was facing backwards so his features were much more visible.

"This really is interestin'," he said again, even though there was no one nearby. Was he talking to me? He couldn't have been. "I mean, wow, I ain't never seen nothin' like this before. It's an odd beauty, really."

I stopped in my tracks while he admired what I had done. He did not seem angered by it, but rather appreciated it like it was meant to be. I was intrigued as I didn't think either of them had the brainpower to appreciate anything so divine. He turned, and I recognized that look. He was taking it all in. I'd often worn that expression. I watched him walk around, investigating. He was so invested that he brushed past me without realizing it. I understood everything right then, and in that moment, I let my guard down.

He looked me right in my eyes. I had never seen eyes so blue. They were like the afternoon sky. We stood there paralyzed, gazing at each other. I'd realized the instant he brushed past me that he was beautiful. I'd never known such a debilitating feeling. I felt my breath grow shallow, not the way it did when Bruno was around, but instead each breath was revitalizing, as though I'd never really breathed until that moment.

He was bigger up close, not in a threatening way, but I could see the evidence of industrious farm life, defined by his thick arms. He was fuzzy and his hair stuck out from under his cap. Most of his soft, inviting face was covered in facial hair. He was sweating, and it beaded up on his nose, shimmering in the sunlight. But those eyes set on me expressed everything with their blue embrace.

We stood in awe of each other.
I knew he wanted to speak, but he didn't need to. I already knew what he was thinking---the same thing I was. His lips parted but his mouth fell agape and I immediately realized why when I felt the air leave my body. I was screaming with all the breath I could muster, as Bruno fell from my torn limb, yelping and quivering. The soft blue eyes turned hard behind a wall of tears as he called out, "Evan!" He looked down at the dying dog as I fled.

Ain't a worse way to be woke up than with yelling and carrying on, but Evan was mad as usual. Most people said it was to compensate for being so small and all, but I knew it was 'cause he missed Pa. He would never admit it, but he regretted leaving the farm and not looking back 'til it was too late. So, walking 'round mad is how he dealt with things.

I didn't know what it was this time but I ran fast to get to him cause I could hear him cussin' and knew it was going to be a bad day. Pa used to say, "the faster you deal with a bad day, the faster it's over."

I ran towards all that foul language at full speed. I found him and right then, without even asking, I knew exactly what was up. I discovered a section of field completely flattened right out. I spun in a full circle, wondering how the heck something like this could've happened.

Evan stood there hollerin', talkin' about those darn security lights again. Only he could stand in the middle of something like this and not be speechless.
It was so interesting, and nothin' interesting ever happened here. Most days were like the one before, schedules and routines and whatnot. I stepped as lightly as I could on the flattened stalks. They was all still green and well alive, but completely folded up like origami.

"Elias!" Evan's sharp tone popped my thinking bubble.
"It's real interestin'," I thought aloud.
"Stop smilin', ain't nothin' interestin' bout destruction of property," he spit out through clenched teeth.

He would have stood there all day cussin' until he ran out of words, but we had errands to run, and nothing gets done when you're standing still. I called for Bruno who, like me, was goin' 'round that flattened field like he was also tryna figure out how it had happened. I had to convince Evan to let Bruno come. He wanted him to stay back and guard the farm, 'til I asked him, "what from, folded corn stalks?" We had a good, rare laugh until he remembered he was mad. We jumped into the truck.

Bruno drove me crazy, but I liked having him around. He made Evan the happiest he could be.
Plus, it tickled me to watch Bruno slowly climb into Evan's lap during those long drives into town. By the time we was there, it looked as if Bruno was doing the driving.

This morning, though, I couldn't stop thinking about the farm. I was still imagining how the stalks got folded and why?

"Damnit Bruno," muttered Evan.

I looked up. "We ought to get 'im a license," I joked, coming outta my own thoughts. But they lingered anyhow in the background while we got what we needed in town to finish repairing the barn. The whole time Evan spoke, I kept thinking, "why?" Why would someone waste all that effort unless it was for good reason?

I found myself thinking of Mama holding my face, telling me that if I didn't have a good reason to do something, then I shouldn't do it. I was no more than four years old and I'd picked up Evan's BB gun and shot a bird square in the chest. I remember it turned stiff and fell and Mama let out a cry. She ran over and asked me, "Why? Why did you do that to such a beautiful creature mid tune?" All I could do was shrug in response. She then cupped my face softly in her hands and looked me right in the eyes and said, "Baby boy, if you do not have a good reason to do something, then you do not do it."
That stayed with me. What could've been someone's good reason? And who was that someone?

I kept thinking. I was still thinking of it on the ride home. The past day and how Evan kept talkin' bout, "Someone been trespassin'." Thought it was his usual paranoia, but this time he might have been right. 'Cept Evan wasn't a wonderer, he didn't really wanna know why someone was there. He wanted them to know they shouldn't be.

It was the darndest thing early yesterday when I was out with Bruno. I had this crazy feelin' I was being watched, but I shook it off, thinkin' Evan was rubbin' off on me. Of

course, no one was watching me. There wasn't nothin'
'round here worth watching.

I musta been thinkin' real hard 'cause before I knew it
we was pullin' up to the farm. Evan was arguing with
Bruno as he got outta the truck. We still had a full day's
work ahead fixing that barn, so we immediately started
unloading the truck. I noticed Evan stop, but before I
could ask why, he was tellin' me to "shut up." But I knew
why as soon as I seen Bruno standing the way he did
whenever he sensed something. Evan crept towards the
crops with Bruno, and I followed close behind. Then
Bruno started barking hysterically, but that wasn't out of
the norm. He was a firecracker and anything could set
him off. He was runnin' all around that flattened crop
like a fool.

We caught up to him running in circles and I stood there.
The area looked bigger, shaped differently even. What a
sight.

"Interestin'," I let slip, riling Evan up even more.
I hated when he cussed at me, but he really never found
anythin' interesting.
I realized and said, "Something is definitely different."
"Nah, it's the same as before," he replied, keeping his
eye on Bruno. He seemed to think it looked the same,
but it didn't. The shape had changed, and I could see the
difference whether he did or not."

It made me wish I had a bird's eye view so I could see it right. Something told me this was a very small piece of a bigger picture that was coming together.

"Bruno sees 'em!" Evan shouted chasin' behind him. I didn't see anything because I was so focused on spottin' the differences. I chased behind so Evan wouldn't be mad. Then we stood still in that space between the farm and Mama's tree.

"Where we goin', ol' boy?" Evan hyped Bruno tappin' 'im on the rear. He was looking towards wherever Bruno was, waitin' for someone to come from somewhere. They was lookin' alright, but they sure wasn't seein' a thing. I thought I did though, right under the willow tree: some funny reflection like upside down sunrays. Then it was gone. I stood there while Evan walked with Bruno, who was sniffin' all around. Then he tore off in the other direction while Evan tried his best to keep up.

Near this tree was my favorite place to be. The least boring spot on the farm. You could catch yourself an eyeful of activity going on from under this here tree. Mama loved lying under it long before it became her final resting place. Like back in the day, I still laid beside her in my still moments. I looked toward her stone, and it seemed like even in the shade it shone, sparkling almost, something magical like. I walked over 'fore I heard Evan callin' after me. I knelt a few feet from her stone, touching the shimmering grass and got that feelin' you get when you rub your socks 'cross a carpet then touch a doorknob.

Evan called me again, and I found myself beside him. I wasn't tryna fuel his flame. He was stompin' around straightenin' out stalks and carryin' on.
"You have to admit, it is interestin'," I said as I tried to lighten his mood.

"Would you quit sayin' that? Ain't nothin' 'bout this interestin'!" He stood there lookin' puzzled and frustrated. He started snapping the stalks tryna get 'em to stand straight, which made it worse since he was breakin' 'em even more. If I didn't know any better, I would've bust' out laughing watching him take all that time to stand them back up to watch them tumble back down.

As he grumbled towards the house, I told him I'd look around, but I didn't say why. I wasn't gonna say for admiration's sake, 'cause he'd' a' lost his mind. I always did like riddles and askin' "why?" So, poking around here seemed like some big mystery needin' solvin'. Something to break up the routine, but even more, something lovely, whatever it was.
I was making my best effort to tread softly. Looked like the stalks could be stood back up if we took the time. They were so neatly folded into each other that I pondered what it meant when suddenly I got that

feeling again, like someone was there. Musta' been
Bruno nearby. I hated when he snuck up on me.

I crouched down tryna' figure out how somebody had
done this? I was thinkin' maybe I could undo it so Evan
wouldn't lose his mind. My hat fell off my head as I got
down real close to the ground. My hair done got so long.
I was way overdue for a haircut, which Evan kept
remindin' me of. Only thing was; since I skipped the last
few haircuts, every time I went into town everyone told
me I looked like Pa when he was younger. I guess I ain't
really realize it 'til then, and I liked it. I shoved my hair
back up under my hat so I could get back to my secret
admirin'.
"This really is interestin'," I couldn't help say.

I moved around carefully, tryna choose good spots to
step.
"I mean, wow, I ain't never seen nothin' like this before.
It really is an odd beauty!"

It was like art or something or maybe somebody was
tryna say something, but what? I knew it couldn't be for
nothin', not something so heavenly. I wanted to really
appreciate it right now, in case Evan tore it up.

I walked along the edge of it when I felt that fuzzy,
static-like feelin' again. When I turned, standing there
from out of nowhere, I saw a young lady unlike anyone
I'd ever seen before. Her big eyes was like shiny dark

glimmerin' marbles. I was frozen in my tracks. I thought I seen the most interesting and beautiful thing I was going to see for a long while and here before me stood a desire my heart never knew it had.

I was never no good with words, but I knew what I wanted to say. I tried but couldn't, yet somehow, I felt like she knew. There was something safe about her eyes. Something comforting and calm like the night sky.

She had an illuminating glow that electrified me, and I was without a doubt, entranced by her. Her ethereal aura beckoned me, and I wanted nothing more than for this moment to last through eternity. My thoughts made even more sense when I looked into her eyes. She stood there, sparkling in the sun. She was nude and not at the same time. Her skin was a deep blue, and she had purple marks along her shoulders and back and the top of her head that reminded me of when Evan got sunburned. Then I knew that's what it was. It was sunburn which was reddening her blue hue to purple. She looked like a sunset I'd watched under Mama's tree.

I was in awe of her. She was incredible. I wanted to tell her what I knew in that instant: that I loved her. I fixed my mouth to say so when Bruno ripped through the stalks and latched right onto her leg. She let out a sound that felt like someone rang a bell in my head and I lost my footin'. Before I could steady myself to help, Bruno dropped to the ground shaking and crying.

It all happened so fast. I saw her. She seen me. Then Bruno bit her and she…what did she do to him? He wasn't breathin' right. In fact, maybe not at all. "Evan!" I called. She left. I didn't even hear her leave. I looked down to see if he was breathin', and in a split second, she was gone.

I was up before the sun most mornings. It was engrained in me, I guess. You can leave the farm life, but it don't leave you. Elias would sleep clean 'til eight if I ain't wake 'im and Bruno was no better. He was out cold after spendin' most'a the night barkin' at whoever been trespassin'.

"Ain't nobody trespassin'," and "What'd they be trespassin' here for, anyway?" Elias kept saying. Boy still couldn't trust my instincts even after all this time.

There had definitely been somebody, and I might know why. See, I paid attention; I was alert, had to be. People had that habit of miscontruin' my alertness for anger. I was focused. I had a lot of weight on my shoulders with the farm and all the responsibilities that come with it. I'd wasted enough time. I came back here for redemption and I was simply waitin' for my moment.

Like every morning, I walked the perimeter. It had to be done and there was always something that needed doing before the day started. I rushed through those kinda days that started off bad 'cause the faster I dealt with 'em, the faster they was over. Most days was the same, give or take what had to be done. Farm life is routine that way. Gotta be organized, gotta put things on schedules. I didn't mind.

The sun was barely peekin' when I was 'bout done with my rounds. Made me wish those security lights was worth a damn. Could barely see a foot in front of me. It was no wonder someone was so comfortable walking 'round; they was under the cover of darkness. Then right there at the edge of the cornfield I froze. I couldn't move a muscle. I knew right then this was my time, my moment.

Looking at the flattened crop, I heard Pa's voice in my head, and I was battling myself, apparently aloud 'cause Elias came a runnin'. I didn't wanna get into it with him, cause he'd never understand the importance of this moment and 'til now I wasn't sure it was even ever gonna happen. I was caught up in it, yet was frustrated 'cause I was up most nights; watchin', pacin'. I shoulda seen something. Damn security lights. I knew they was far too dim to ward someone off. Now I had to add security lights to the never-ending to-do list.

I saw Elias all excited, and it was the last thing I needed. He was like a cat, curious to a fault. Last thing I needed was him wandering around pokin' at things. "Elias!" I called out, distracting him from himself.
"It's real interestin'," he was smilin' like a goof.
"Stop smilin', ain't nothin' interestin' 'bout destruction of property," I told him. It wasn't interestin' and I didn't want him thinkin' it was some puzzle needin' solving. We had a whole lot to get done, and it wasn't gettin' done standin' 'round here.

Of all this, my biggest issue was Elias. I could see him in la-la land, gears turning, steam comin' from his ears. That boy was a wanderer something fierce, always lookin' for somethin' outside this place. He didn't get that there wasn't nothing worth lookin' for out there. I made that mistake myself, chasin' after what I thought was real, true love...

Started off a summer love, but when summer was over, we was just gettin' started, so I followed her home. It was a love like everything I'd ever fantasized about. Worth running away, worth abandoning my responsibilities for, worth disappointing Pa. Every moment with her reassured me I was right where I was 'posed to be.

People in the city ain't caring folks. They don't know your Pa. They don't say good morning or even wave. You're lucky to get a nod. There's no community, no sense of togetherness. Everyone is out for themselves, plottin', schemin'. I dealt with it for her though and it was worth it to me.

She was a born and raised a city girl with no intentions on leavin' and I wanted her to be happy. I knew I was a dumb country boy lost in a big city, but when I was with her, I wasn't lost. With Alexandra I didn't mind the hustle of the big city 'cause things slowed down when we was together. It was us against the world. Her parents would never approve of "some uneducated farmer's son," but she didn't care, we didn't care.

We didn't need anything 'cept each other. At least it seemed so until they cut off her money and she dropped me without hesitation, without so much as an apology. Enough to make anyone retreat home, but I stayed— fool that I was---tryna prove I could be a provider and that love was all we really needed.

I stayed, wasting time rollin' over showin' my belly while Pa lay dyin'. No one knowin' how to get a hold of me. Cruel city livin' was suckin' the soul from me while home was beckonin' me, arms wide open. There wasn't nothin' outside this place worth pursuin'. I been tryna break this to Elias since I been back. Wish someone would've warned me.

I knew somethin' was off soon as we pulled back up to the farm. I burned daylight following Bruno around. We didn't see anything 'cept the biggest damn rabbit I ever seen come from nowhere sendin' him runnin' crazy.

Lookin' at the field, it was different, as Elias had noticed. As much as I hated to admit it, he sure was good at figurin' things out. I played it off, sayin' it was the same, but I could see the fire in his eyes. It made me want to tear the whole thing up right then and there.

I started pulling at those stalks so they would stand upright, but they fell, again and again. I knew there was more to it and I knew I was going to have to go through a bunch of things I'd been putting off for some time now, so I headed towards the house.

I stood in that doorway for what felt like forever 'fore I stepped in. Hadn't been in here since the last day Pa was. I could see it; me looking down at him in that bed, lookin' nothing like I remembered him. The once strong, capable, active, independent man I knew had become a frail, weak, withered shell of himself. I could barely make eye contact with him 'cause of my own guilt. I couldn't believe I'd let so much time pass 'fore coming back.

His time had come days ago, and he was barely holdin' on. He was clingin' desperately to life so he could deliver some sort of message to me. I sat there cringing inside, as I watched him use every ounce of energy he had left to sit up. He spoke and even his voice was strange to me; shaky, hoarse.

"I knew you'd come home. I waited for you."
I was ashamed of myself. I'd abandoned him and had nothing to show for it. I was far more than remorseful.
"Pa, I'm sorry, I..." I started.
"We're not here for apologies, son. Don't you ever be sorry for living your life."

He grabbed my hand and squeezed with more strength than I would've thought he'd have left. Perhaps he'd been more lucid than everyone had let on. "Been waitin' on you, " he told me, eyes glazed, looking less at me and more lookin' straight ahead. "Could only ask this of you; only you."

"Pa?" I called as if he was far off somewhere, and I was leading him back. He was staring off into nothing. "Ethan West!" I hollered, first time callin' 'im by his full name, like I was the Pa. He looked at me.

"Only you, Evan. I was a fool, you know? A damn fool... Love is blind, ya know?"
I did know that.
"Love will make you think you can change someone when you can't."

I knew that too, but how did he? He'd only known Mama, and they was happy. He looked at me right in the eyes. He was there for real now, and he insisted, "You'll protect him, I know it. 'Specially now, you're lookin' for redemption." He drifted off...

"Pa," I started. What was he talking 'bout? Who was he talking 'bout? "Pa, you mean Elias?" He was worrying me.

"Of course, you won't let 'em take 'im. You'll protect 'im."

Perhaps he wasn't lucid after all. "Yeah, Pa, okay," I agreed, saddened by his state.

"Don't you patronize me, boy," he reprimanded, sittin' straight up without effort. He was lookin' me square in the eyes, gripping me strong like the Pa I knew. I saw him sittin' there like the day I left; tall and strong. "You'll protect 'im, you have to," he demanded. "The boy's a wanderer like his Mama. A different kinda thought process, not like you and me. See, Evan, your ma, she…" he stopped staring off into space. I missed her too. I had those moments.

"Well, your Mama, she… she was somethin' otherworldly," he finished.

Yeah, that's what I saw too. I thought of her as a goddess, glowin', floatin'.

He grabbed my face, "I mean it Evan, otherworldly for real, not just an expression. You know what I mean? Do you KNOW what I mean?"

Did I? I seen her in my memories. She was something special, beautiful… blue? I was only a kid with an overactive imagination.

"Pa?" I was racked with guilt. I should've come sooner. "You know, I've made note. You'll know."

He was ramblin' now. I wasn't even sure he was talkin' to me anymore. "Don't let 'em signal. You can't, okay?"

He was breathin' heavy, "Son, trust me. Go through it all and you'll know, ok? I've made note. You'll know."

Then suddenly, the Pa I knew was gone again, replaced by that sad, old man gasping for breath. He was irrational. I was too late to get my real final words.

"You'll know, you'll know soon as the crop is all folded up. That'll be your moment, son. You'll stop that message. That's why you came back. I kept note."

He was wheezin' something fierce, shakin' even. I'd missed him. Before me was a man holdin' on far past his time. It was my fault. Whatever he wanted to say came out all jumbled up and crazy. I was too late; I was too damn late. I hated myself for it.

I stepped in; I wasn't sure what I was looking for. Pa's room was tidy the way he'd left it and neither of us had dared come in since. Whether he was here or not, it was still his room and we treated it as such. I started shuffling around, part of me feeling guilty like Pa could walk in at any second givin' me that look. I was ready to give up when I discovered a set of stairs in Pa's closet. I went up to what was obviously the closet he shared with Mama; women's clothes and shoes filled most of it, a small vanity in a corner with a dresser and a few stacked boxes behind it.

"Baby Clothes"

"Extra Sheets"
"Odds and Ends"
"Ethan's Notes"
"Picture Books"
"Keepsakes"

Ethan's notes? *He made note.*

I tore into the box, revealing a stack of notebooks. They
looked like the journals Pa kept.
The ones I read through and through thinkin' they'd tell
me something. The notes I thought he was talkin' 'bout
at first. I'd read through 'em revealin' nothing 'cept what
I already knew; what he had already told us about him,
about Mama, farm life, us. I'd even given 'em to Elias to
make 'im feel closer to Pa since they was of no use to
me.

These sure was Pa's. I knew by the handwriting, but not
the tone. These wasn't like the others, they was raw, no
filter. He wrote for himself, not like the others I read.
The ones he left accessible 'cause it was meant for us to
find them. They was hopeful and inspiring and
highlighted our best moments, but these, they was
truthful. They told of the struggle of farm life, the
difficulty of fatherhood and long nights awake thinking
'bout the deeper meaning of it all. I finally saw Pa as a
man who worried, stressed, who made mistakes. An
equal.

I don't know how long I was there lost in his words 'fore I heard the worst sound coming towards the house. I ran out to see Elias running full speed with Bruno in his arms. He was blubberin' and whimperin' so much I couldn't tell the sounds they was making apart.

I didn't need no explanation; I knew what it was. Bruno would get so focused he'd chase something off the property. Wasn't the first time he'd tested the electric fence, but never so severe. God damnit Bruno, I loved him in all his stupidity. I would've cried if I had a minute to spare.

Wasn't gonna make sense to try 'n make it to town for him. Elias and I both had plenty of animal experience on the farm. We had done about every kinda' patch up there was. Farm life will teach you a bit of everything from birth to death. We laid him in the barn on clean towels and patched him up best we could. I fought back tears every time he winced.

Bruno was family. It meant everything to me, to us, for him to make it through this. But after a certain point, all we could do was let 'im rest and hope for the best, so I passed the time gettin' to my research.
I had been up reading. Normally would've been pacin' or seein' what Bruno was barking at. I would've been up checkin' the property. Now here I was like Elias solvin' a mystery, figurin' out a puzzle.

The puzzle was Pa. I'd never really known 'im 'til now. Not really, but these journals, these notes, they was sayin' more than giving a realistic perspective on adulthood. I started reading from the earliest date on. I knew what he meant now, everything he was ranting and raving 'bout. I had a feelin' of relief knowin' those final words really was solid and meant for me. I felt a weight lifted.

I knew now. I knew what Pa meant.

Everything about her was everything I coulda' wanted in another, 'specially now. Who was I to look a gift horse in the mouth? To be awarded with two loves back-to-back and deny it? Not I. I mean, what were the odds? I was too busy figurin' out life all over again. It's not exactly like I went looking for love—it found me. I knew I was lucky to have a whole family, no matter how I came by it. It wasn't the way I imagined it would be, but I figure that in life that's often the case. Life often turns out different from what you expect, but it don't mean it ain't a good different.

I was livin' the life like so many before me and farm life suited me. I was a man of routine, grew up that way, and I meant to raise mine the same. Always knew what needed to be done and when. This farm was our home, and I took care of it so it could take care of us, same as I was taught.

That was pretty much how it happened. I was workin' the farm like any other day and that's when I met her. She became everything I could've ever needed. We spent every minute we could together. I didn't get much free time, but when I did, it was hers. We had this unspoken thing where we could sit for hours underneath that willow tree, pinkies barely touchin' and that was enough.

I was a shy man who'd suffered an unbelievable loss. I wouldn't have been able to find words for what I needed even if I knew what it was. I was tryna do the best I could, and she understood that. She understood everything. Touching pinkies became arms wrapped around each other and we laid beneath that tree in a whole different way. She had a way of seein' things. She knew me without effort. She wasn't taken aback by much, but she was often alarmed by how quickly and deeply she'd opened herself up to me.

As much as things change, they stay the same cause I was still a man in charge of a farm, a husband, and a father. We were in love; it happened fast, but we made up for lost time. We spent every free moment fillin' in the blanks.

She was beautiful, but sad. I wanted this farm to be her home too, our home, but she was a wanderer and always lost in her thoughts. I understood part of her was havin' trouble adjustin' to country living, but another part of her tried. She wasn't built for farm work, but she could coax the cattle to go pretty much anywhere and I ain't never seen anyone break in a horse in a softer way.

I knew there was a piece of her that longed for home, but whenever I thought to question her plans, I seen her with the boys, and I felt sure. She might not have been built for farm life, but she was more than meant for motherhood.

Those boys made her happier than anything. I could see her glowin' at times on those rare occasions she'd put her guard down and simply be herself.

I knew she still ached for home from time to time and sometimes she'd mention goin' back, but it was something she went on about in her weakest moments. She knew I couldn't come; I couldn't leave the farm. I don't think she really wanted to either; but I think she felt like she had to. It had been years though, and I watched it become her home. She stopped referrin' to herself as a visitor. I watched her soften.

What she'd told me about her upbringin' was shocking and made me understand why she looked so uneasy when she thought about it. It was in the past, but it held so much power over her. She was tryin' her best to fight it, to be her own kind of person, not influenced by her background.

At times she was sad 'cause she thought she was unlovable. Love was a new concept, and she thought she could never be a good lover or mother. She made me promise to always be a good father to the boys, to make up for what she couldn't give them. She made me promise her so many things when she was swept up in her emotions, so I agreed, mostly to soothe her.

She could be happy. The four of us could be.

This was a second chance for the both of us and I watched her let go and live. We farmed and raised two little boys that couldn't have been more opposite, and we always made time to lay 'neath that willow tree and remember why we loved each other. We was truly happy. It was good; real good, everything a man could ask for.

But our past circles back and one night after rollin' over to an empty bed, I found her outside weepin' hysterically. She managed to let me know she felt she had to go home. She had done everything to fight the urge, but she had to go. She was convinced I would never understand and then she held me accountable to a promise I'd made her years ago. Something I thought she asked of me while distraught, but hadn't really meant...

"You promised," she cried, beating my chest, her words lost in her sobbing.

I could see how blue she really was. Bad emotions always unmasked her. I loved her that way still, always. I held her and looked into her eyes; no words needed.

We walked over to our spot under that tree and laid there lookin' up at the night sky. It comforted her. She loved me; she loved us. We reached a conclusion that night; I did make her a promise. She was right, but I knew she was worried for nothin'. She acted like she hadn't changed. She didn't give herself enough credit. She wasn't a product of her upbringing. She was more than that. She was my love, the mother of my children. She could be who she wanted; she didn't need no approval. I didn't doubt her, but I promised her again to pacify her self-doubt. We put it all behind us and once again we was happy.

She always reminded me that the years go by quick. Things were different here; kids grew up slower, were exposed to less, and she embraced it. Whenever I felt like I could relax, she kept me on my toes by remindin' me of that promise, that damn promise.

Everything was good. Everyday Evan grew more like me while, lookin' more and more like his Ma. I'd stop and appreciate that sometimes. It warmed my heart in a different way. And Elias, he was a dead ringer of me with the personality of his Mama, not quite as poetic.

I never doubted that she was meant for this, and I never doubted her. She knew me from the first moment. She really did, but I knew her too. May have been my intuition, but it was pretty much the same thing to me. Then it was that one night I found myself rollin' over once again to an empty bed. That always got me worried. I ran to find her at the edge of the cornfield cryin' again and I realized what she had done. It was like a punch in the stomach after all this time, after everything.

She begged me to forgive her and told me she didn't have a choice and reminded me again, always beatin' me over the head with the promise I'd made her. Only thing was, this time I realized I was going to have to fulfill it, because this time, for the first time, I doubted her.

I grabbed her but couldn't bring myself to look her in the eyes. I hugged her tightly, despite everything. I was still in awe of her beauty glowin' in the moonlight.
She gathered herself quickly, and we worked the rest of the night undoin' what she had done before the boys, or anyone, got a look at it. Only problem was it mighta already been too late.

We finished as the sun peeked and all necessary farm work was put on hold for me to lay with her a few more hours. We woke the boys and enjoyed the day in that kind of way where you do and say what you want and you ain't got no cares in the world.

That evening, the four of us laid under the tree and watched the sunset, which was the cherry on a sundae. We got the boys ready for bed and I made my rounds. When I came back, she was standing over Evan, all teary.

"He's my boy," she uttered, "my first baby. I don't want him to forget me." She was strokin' his teenage face as if it were the round cheek of a babe.

"I wouldn't let 'im forget you," I told her. I think she thought it'd be easier if he did.

"You're right," she agreed. "I worry too much. We'll be fine, we'll be fine." She was saying one thing, but I knew another. I knew she was tellin' me what I wanted to hear, and I knew why.

I didn't sleep a wink that night. I watched her all night long; waitin' for her to get up, to try to leave, to try to sneak away. I never doubted her, but now, she lay there beside me, almost a stranger as I remembered where we was the night before, cleanin' up the mess she'd made. I knew what it could take from me, and of course I remembered the promise.

My eyes was heavy, but they never left her. Bittersweet keepin' my eye on the one I loved so much and expectin' the worst from her at the same time. I must've drifted off to sleep when I suddenly felt the bed move. I jerked up so quickly that I startled her. She was still beside me; she was still beside me! I was overtaken with guilt.

I'd spent the last night up starin' at her, waitin' for her to give in to that compulsion she thought she could no longer control. I had always told her she could overcome it, yet now I was the one accusin' her of the same thing. I was mad at myself, but happy that I could be mad at myself about being wrong. I kissed her then embraced her.

I wanted to admit it, but she knew. She always did, but she also knew how bad I felt. I wanted to make a gesture, something to make us feel normal again, to put this lack of judgment behind us. I got Evan so we could head towards town and run errands, but mostly pick up her favorite chocolates from a lil shop in town that had a fancy layout.

We got in the truck and had reached the road when we smelled that burnin' smell. It was a good thing we ain't get too far with it breakin' down and all. We was a small walk away. The farm was still in sight. The farm was so much in sight I was able to see something I mighta missed a half mile down the road. Elias was walking with Norma in plain sight, there, clear as day, walkin' across the farm. I was in disbelief tryna keep Evan focused on a truck we had no chance of fixin' while my mind raced. I was panickin'. Damn near had me a heart attack when another truck pulled up. Was a neighbor lookin' to help, so I used it to my advantage.

Usin' more hand motions than I ever did to speak to draw attention to me, I asked 'im if he didn't mind takin' Evan with him since he was already headed into town. He agreed of course, cause that's what neighbors was for. As he got back in the truck, I gave Evan money and a list of things then reminded him to pick his mama up some of her favorite chocolates. Then I joked with him about how she stood in his room last night and called him her baby. He got all red. He sure did love her, and I wanted him to remember that.

I was still hopin' to high heaven they was lookin' towards the road as they drove off. I took off like a bat out of hell, runnin' straight towards our tree and hopin' against all odds that I would make it there in time.

I seen her, my Norma holdin' Elias' hand, and she was movin' forward and he seemed like he was fine with everything, followin' beside her wherever they was goin'. I called to them, screamin' so much my throat hurt and I was runnin' full speed and wishin' I might have run more often, so that this wasn't so hard for me. I ran and I ran.

I passed the barn realizin' the dogs was all out of their kennels and I called to them, screamed for them to follow. They did as I still ran screamin' myself hoarse, beggin' her to stop, callin' after the both of them. I was chasin' behind them, feelin' myself fall apart, hopin' Evan was halfway to town by now.

"Put him down Norma, please," I never wanted to be here. My mind was comin' to terms with the possibility of havin' to keep my promise. The dogs followed me closely and I could see her face, like she was in a trance, gone to me. Driftin', our son in hand, my son. "Please," I begged, tearin' up 'til my sight blurred. I'd caught up, tryna look her in the eyes, but they weren't the eyes I

36

knew. They didn't see me. Whatever they was lookin' at was somewhere far beyond. I grabbed her, pulled her close, Bruno, Becca and the pups waitin' for my command. She held on tight to Elias' hand.

"Let him go!" I pleaded. It took everything in me to keep her there. I finally caught a glimpse of her for a moment. "I can't. I love you, the three of you… you promised."

She was gone, pullin' from me again. I could barely see anything through my tears. I called for my son, and he took no notice of me. I was dyin' inside, but I had made a promise. I cupped her face, and although she pulled away from me, I kissed her one last time."

I seen her flicker briefly one more time before me. "I love you. I promised," I choked on my own words. I stood behind them both. "Go to Mama," I sputtered and the dogs ran over to her. She collapsed and Elias too as I softened the blow by helpin' to lower them both to the ground. I then grabbed our boy and ran towards the house; he was barely breathin'.

I was pacin' and, of course, the one night I'm up, Evan wasn't. Guess my head full of thoughts wasn't gonna let me sleep. I been waitin' for something to happen on this farm forever and now that it has; I wasn't sure I wanted it to after all. Not at the cost of losing Bruno Junior, the last of Bruno and Becca's pups. He was the spittin' image of his dad and Pa loved him, so gosh darn much for that. That's why we loved him; he was one of us, one of the boys who remembered and missed Pa. Bruno was my brother, too. My furry, trouble makin' brother and I was gonna lose 'im, and I wasn't even sure how or why.

Then I started thinkin' about everything that happened. It happened so fast I didn't even have time to take it in or nothin'. Between patchin' him up and cleanin' myself off I hadn't the time to understand what I'd even saw. I didn't eat dinner, which was rare for me as I was mostly always hungry. I was thinkin' and thinkin' and tryna make sense of it all.

Whole time I was runnin' towards the house with Bruno in my arms I was tryna think what I might say to Evan. When he thought it was the fence that got 'im I let it be. How could I ever explain otherwise, anyway?
I started tryin' to wrap my head around everything that had happened. I was there again in my mind; standin'

there, jaw on the ground, starin' at the most beautiful creature I ever did see.

I'd never before felt like I did when I was lookin' in her eyes; smart, thoughtful, soundin' like a book.
I seen she ain't mean no harm, no ill will. When she looked back at me, I knew everything I needed to know. Eyes was universal, Mama said that, cause they was the windows to the soul. I was lost in hers in that moment. Though I was a man of few words, right then, I felt I could've blurted out entire poems.

Then I pictured when she was attacked, and it gave me the chills. I knew he wasn't doing nothin' more than what he's 'posed to be doing. He was guardin' the property and lookin' out for me, but then again, she wasn't doing nothin' really either. So, I wasn't feeling guilty for Bruno being laid up, I was feeling guilty for what he'd done to her. I didn't see no blood or nothin', but the way he bit down couldn't have left her in good shape.

There was no way she could've made it very far. There was a good chance she was hurtin' somewhere nearby. There wasn't too many places to hide. I tried to get in her mind so I could think where she might be, but it wasn't the same without her standin' in front of me.

Mind racin' after a sleepless night, I went lookin' for her anywhere 'round what seemed like some place someone might hide, but I didn't find nothin'. I wasn't sure if I was happy or sad about it, but at that point I thought it was in my best interest to check on Bruno 'specially now. I'd been looking for who-knows-how-long and I was eventually gonna have to sleep 'cause I knew Evan would be up before the sun, real early since he'd been asleep all night, and I never could sleep much longer than him.

I suddenly started running knowin' I was being led by guilt. Here I was, checking on a beautiful stranger instead of checking on Bruno. I ran towards the barn and got caught up in a memory of when we used to keep the dogs in there 'cause of Mama's allergies. When I reached the barn, it wasn't full of happy pups playin' anymore, only poor old Bruno. Then, I thought I saw something... I did. There was someone touchin' Bruno and even though I could see her, she didn't react, nor did I. I never seen her before, but I somehow recognized her.

"What are you doin'?" The words fell out my mouth. She looked up at me and I recognized those eyes. I musta scared her 'cause she moved so fast that she was 'cross the barn in an instant. "Wait," I called. I could see she didn't do anything to 'im, he seemed to be breathin' fine. "Wait please," I caught up as she approached the hole we had aimed to repair earlier. I reached out to touch her, she turned, and I felt something come from behind me and take me down to the ground. It was furry and wet. It was Bruno! There he was playful as ever, jumping on top of me like old times. I hugged him real tight and pet him. I looked up at her.

"He's going to be fine," she spoke softly.
"Don't go," I called out kinda muffled, stilll roughin' up Bruno and lookin' at her between licks. We was rollin' around on the barn floor like nothin' had happened to him. She stood there.

"Come 'ere, he's good, I swear," I waved her over. She smiled; it was weirder seeing her this way than before. She stepped back in, made a sound, and kneeled down. Bruno ran right over to her, ears down, tail waggin'. She pet him the way he liked. Then she looked at me.

"I know he meant no harm. He was doing what he felt he needed to. He had a good reason to do what he did. I understand that. "
I knew that.

She was real sweet to him; think she was talkin' more to him than to me, though. I was still on the ground. I stood up. I was movin' in slow mo, because I was in a daze between Bruno and her standing there that way.

"He'll need rest," she advised.

I got closer, but she didn't move. I was simply gettin' a look at her.

"Bruno come," I tapped the bed we'd fixed 'im. He came over seeming like his old self 'cept suddenly getting real sleepy. He laid down. I looked down at him and he seemed alright. He had seemed so much worse earlier.

When I looked back, she had already left through that worn place in the barn wall. I patted Bruno once more and ran to catch up with her.

"Wait, please!" I whispered. She was real graceful-like and walked as though she was gliding across the ground. She paused for a moment, lookin' back at me, and I felt I didn't want her to go.

"He'll need to rest," she told me again, looking different 'cept those eyes.

I lost my words, so I was noddin' while wantin' to say: "Please stay. I can't quite suppress my urge to be beside you, even if for a moment. Would you allow me the pleasure?"

She remained silent but walked beside me towards the willow tree. I wish I could've said the words that came to mind when I looked into her eyes, but I couldn't get 'em to come out. Thankfully, she still gave me some of her time. Even though I couldn't get myself to say a thing, she sat with me there under that tree, looking up at a sky full of stars. While she was looking up, I was looking over at her. "You was d... d... di... iff... diff'rent when I f... fir... irst saw you." I stumbled over my words, feelin' my childhood stutter. She looked at me, eyes twinklin' same as the night sky.

My tongue couldn't make words again, but I thought about how she'd stood in front of me in the cornfield and how perhaps I mighta imagined it. It was the only thing that made sense. I mean, here she was different than before, but regular. Yeah, she was lovely, and back in that field, she was magic, pure, and took my breath away, all fairy tales and daydreams. Then my breath left me when she sat there in front of me, glowin' in shades of blue and sunset purple. How had she done it?

"I took a form more comfortable to you," she told me.

I gazed into her big eyes. I wanted to tell her that I loved her original form and that she needn't comfort me with a disguise. I wanted to say that, but instead I sighed because that was all that would come out.

"I know," she smiled.

Then I noticed her leg. It wasn't like that before. "Your leg," I blurted out. It was a stump. Her foot was clean gone. How could Bruno have done that? Oh, the pain she must have felt. She rubbed the place where her foot should've been and looked at me. Strangely, even with the way it looked, I knew she was going to be okay.

We sat there. Most people filled time with words, but I liked sittin' and watchin' and she was fine with it. I ain't never sat there like that with nobody before. I loved sittin' under the night sky, these was my clearest moments. I'd come out to sit, looking up, wonderin' what life might be like somewhere else.

She asked me to help her, and I obliged. I went to give her a hand up, but she didn't need it. Although she was on one leg, she was movin' real normal-like. I walked with her to the cornfield, and she started tellin' me a whole lot. I said what I could, and she strung it together somehow. It was the easiest conversation I'd ever had. We was carryin' on til I noticed the sun was due to peek and I knew I couldn't let Evan see her, not like this anyway. She knew too.

It sure was odd Evan hadn't been up yet makin' rounds, could've been 'cause of everything with Bruno. Maybe he needed a real good night's rest, so I made rounds alone. Rare for me, hadn't done so since Pa was here, but did it every morning from when Evan left 'til he came back, so I figured I was due some time off. This mornin' though, even without a wink of sleep, I was more than willing.

I wanted her to walk with me and stay with me, but she was hurt and needed to rest. I wanted to offer her comfort, but I didn't know how I might do that. A place to rest, somewhere safe maybe? She wanted to take care of herself, but she looked like Bruno did, all sleepy suddenly. I scooped her up and ran towards the house, knowin' Evan had to be up walkin' around bout now, but instead he was comin' out the house like it was on fire.

"Why you standin' there like that?" he asked me.
For the second time in too soon, I had my arms full and no way to explain to Evan what was happenin'.
I looked down, and she was there, but gone, like I was holding an armful of glitter.

"Like that," he repeated, mocking me holdin' my arms out like I was holdin' something. Could he not see?

"I, uh... I wa... was go... gonna," I couldn't think.

"You stutterin'? Ain't heard you stutter in a while," he muttered.

I started walkin' into the house keeping my back facing him before my luck ran out. I ain't hear anything else he was talkin' 'bout as I carried sparkles up the stairs. I went into the one room I knew Evan would never go into. I put her down on the bed and that's when I fully saw her again instead of a shimmery light.

"No one comes in here," I told her. I wanted her to be calm, and she was.

I covered her. I wanted to hug her, kiss her maybe. Instead, I put my forehead to hers, then I pulled back and looked at her. That was enough. I knew she'd be fine. I closed the door behind me and felt all kinds of ways and I sure was beat. I snuck off to my own room, hopin' to at least get an hour or two of sleep in before Evan started lookin' for me.

My Dearest Son,

I was so naïve when I first began this mission. It was all I
ever knew, and I believed with every part of my being
that what I was doing was for good reason.
Until I looked at you and knew that you had become my
good reason to do any and everything.

Our prior contact had been minimal and distant, but as
we needed for things, as we adapted, we looked
further. We investigated, as we are those of action.

I had heard many things about the inept, incapable
inhabitants destroying their homes as they went about
things uninformed. Weakened by emotions like
empathy, love, anger, and hate.

We had investigated from afar as Earth had always been
unattractive to us because of the smell of pollution and
war residue, among other concerns. What was once an
inviting green space and scenic beauty had become
poisoned. There was more brick and mortar, chrome,
fiberglass, and cement than there was earth.

We even believed you to be audacious with your space
travel, exploring territories outside Earth, yet barely

knowing about your own home. I was taught and groomed to believe these things to be true.

Upon touching down, your father was simply supposed to be a means to an end. At least he should have been. But he was so much more than an assignment, my Ethan and almost immediately, I began to feel things my upbringing deemed weaknesses. Or as your father put it, "Normal."

I became your mother with the intent of winning his affection, all the while pretending he hadn't already won mine. Continuing to work hard to remain true to the way my upbringing made me: unbiased, impartial, neutral.

I was doing exactly that. I hadn't come to any conclusions solely based on what information I was given, because I also took into account everything I had gathered and learned while here.

I soon realized that my training had not been designed to help me be unbiased in a fair and non-judgmental way, but rather to encourage distance so I wouldn't form any real connections. I was meant to touchdown, find shelter, find a suitable mate, and create a specimen. I was never meant to find a home, fall in love and create a family. I was simply meant to follow protocol, but that's not what happened.

I was not behaving in accordance to the way I had been prepared, which now seemed based on incomplete and unfair portions of truth. I refused to hold your father accountable for the deplorable actions of others. Through him, amongst other things, I learned kindness, respect, and thoughtfulness. I learned that being emotionally moved by someone wasn't a weakness. It was pretending not to be moved that made you weak.

The moment I held you, you embodied what I had already come to love: a family. Your father, your brother and now you, here, looking up at me. I knew right then that disobeying protocol had been the right thing to do, and you were my good reason to do it. I knew my time was limited, but every minute with you made it all worthwhile.

If you are reading this, you're probably pretty confused. Do not fault your father. I made him promise me that he would let you remember me as I am here on Earth. I wanted you to know me like this, the best, happiest version of myself, here with all of you, my family. I made him promise he wouldn't tell you. However, I also warned him to stay vigilant as someone would eventually come to collect "the specimen"---you.

But you are no specimen. You are my incredible, lovely child, created in the image of the man who changed me for the better. He is all you could need in a caretaker and you have an incredible big brother who will never let you down. You are in good hands.

My Elias, you are my good reason for doing anything. May you one day love someone the way your father loves me and the way that I love you.

Love,
Mama

All of last month I was in a haze, and could easily have been functioning on overload with all I'd taken in. Between Bruno's injury and miraculous recovery, Elias's actin' all weird, plus all that I'd learned, I was in a fog. Him tip toein' around and I even mighta heard 'im stutter, which was somethin' he only did when he was real stressed or nervous.

I should've figured it had something to do with a girl. Honestly, I appreciated the fact that he was runnin' around behind her, 'cause I was so caught up with things that I couldn't even begin to explain to him. With her around, he didn't seem to care about what I was up to. In fact, any time I passed them he was showin' her how to do farm work, so she was alright in my book.

We had a quick intro, but I was caught up in other stuff. I gave her a nod and a wave and a very quick glance. I hardly noticed her, wasn't personal. I was deep in thought. I'd lost myself in Pa's journals which had become a puzzle I was piecin' together. A long, elaborate, drainin' one. I ain't never felt so many emotions. I didn't even know I had so many. I learned so much about myself and Elias and the kind of man my Pa was when he wasn't a father or a husband. I realized how much we were alike. All this time, I thought Elias was his favorite when it turns out he understood me most.

These journals was his thoughts, his ideas, his fears and all those things you keep to yourself. When I read 'em it was like meetin' 'im all over again, but for real 'cause I was understandin' him in a way I never could as a kid. It was a whole process, reading 'em, rereadin' 'em, really graspin' 'em and letting it all sink in. There was no particular order to them. Yeah, they was all dated, but some parts was so worn and faded I couldn't tell what was on the page.

After looking through 'em all and tryna establish whatever order I could. I started pickin' 'em up and reading 'em and tryna make sense of what I could. I never really knew if I was reading 'em out of order 'til I read the middle part of a story 'fore I read the beginning part. Then I had to go read the beginning part and then reread the middle part, so it was takin' me a long time to piece things altogether. Not to mention that I was sneaking around doin' it. I could only do it in my quiet moments, which luckily seemed to be more and more frequent with Elias all hot and bothered over that neighbor girl. I sure was grateful for that.

With Elias bein' elsewhere, it meant he wasn't askin' questions about why I was in and out of Pa's room. And he certainly wasn't gonna ask about a secret attic closet that he ain't know about.

I was 'bout halfway done with his stack of journals and I was obsessed; I farmed, I read, I ate, I read, I used the toilet, I read. I was even readin' 'stead of sleepin' then over-sleepin'. I was readin' instead of workin, and I was tuckin' it away whenever Elias came 'round, which was rare since he ain't seem to notice me lately.

Bruno, too, was very active lately. After sleepin' for days, he seemed to have gained years of energy. Got the life shocked back into 'im, I guess. His short spurts chasin' things returned to his glory days of actually catching 'em again, so he was off on his own too. It was best as I needed the space, needed the quiet.

At night when I wasn't readin', which I did often, or sleepin' which I did rarely; I was in the field. I was unfoldin' those stalks, one of the many things I learned as of late. Standing 'em right back up, unharmed, still attached and all. Had to do it in those brief moments Elias thought he was sneakin' off.

It was like time was movin' fast and slow at the same time. Day to day I was doin' what I was 'posed to, goin' through the motions at least, 'cause I was really focused on makin' sense of it all. I knew there was something I was meant to put together, but it was like every time I opened a door there was another one there with a lock and I was findin' keys everywhere, though not the ones I needed.

I was thinkin' all the time and it wasn't until about six weeks in when I really started figurin' things out. I started marking the journals and gettin' them in some sort of order I could understand. At times it seemed like I was never gonna sort any of it out since none of it could've been real. I could've found myself reading and thinking my Pa was writin' tales if I ain't know no better.

Then I finally read something that changed everything for me. For a minute I forgot what I was lookin' for to begin with and was overtaken by it. There was something else there beneath all this that sent me on a downward spiral.

I'd been lookin' for answers to questions I didn't even know I had. I had put together the timeline, which wasn't quite finished, but I had enough to find out what I needed to know, and it turned my world upside down...

I discovered that Mama really loved me; she really did, much as she could, much as she was capable of. I was her baby boy and all, and there was never no doubt about that. Pa mentioned it time and time again, how much she loved me, the way she loved me, and how much I meant to her. I never thought it was 'cause she chose to.

I found out my real Ma had died in childbirth and although my Pa loved her with all his heart and soul; he was left there; a man who'd lost his wife, all by himself, with a newborn babe. That's when Mama came along. He met her and she stepped in from when I was months old. Doin' all the things that a mother does, no question, but for her own reasons.

Now I knew that she ain't really love me, not really. She was simply tryna win my Pa's heart so she could make a baby of her own. Pretendin' to love us so she could steal him. That was all I needed to read. I didn't need no order for that. That was simple and plain enough. My Pa had been naive, but not me.

Everything was different, I had a whole 'nother life I ain't even know about. Someone I looked like. I thought of every time Pa told me, "You look like your Ma." What had he really meant? Did I have her smile, her eyes? 'Cause I never did look nothin' like him the way Elias does.

I was outraged. That's not something you find out once you all the way grown and thinkin' you're all put together, only to find out you're still in pieces. My mind was flooded with all kinds of thoughts. Did I look like my mother... my *real* mother? What did she look like? Did I act like her? What did she act like? Why hadn't Pa ever told me about her? I ain't never seen so much as a picture of her. Where is she? Where can I pay my respects to the Ma I never got to meet?
I was mad. I started thinking about Pa, and how, when he was layin' there, he wanted to tell me something

about my Ma. It wasn't like him to keep something from me, 'specially something like this. I kept tryna think and figure out why he might lie to me about something so important as this. Even there on his deathbed, he made sense enough to tell me to watch out for my brother and how I might do so. But when it came to him speakin' about my Ma, he couldn't. Why? I wondered what he'd been tryna' tell me.

I started thinkin' of everything; all the parts of his journals I could make out, his warnings. It was slowly comin' together. Mama was not my Ma. She was a stranger and an imposter. This pretend human from who-knows-where who was fillin' in. He didn't want to break my heart, but he wanted me to protect my brother from makin' the same mistake he'd made.

I was revved up in a way I hadn't been in a while, and I wasn't sure if I was feelin' totally crazy or saner than ever before. I had to get my mind right. I hadn't felt this way since we lost Pa, but now I felt like I had lost him all over again. Finding out that I'd lost the only Mama I knew and yet discovering I had a Ma I ain't never even knew I had, was a lot to take in.

I was lookin' for something strong to make me forget how much hurt I was feelin' so I took to that moonshine like a bear to honey. And it sure had the effect I wanted it to. Made me stop hurtin', but it didn't make me less angry. I was pacin' and cussin' and throwin' things.

Mama was probably rollin' over in her grave... I started laughin' at the thought of it. She mighta been! It was funny that after everything I'd found out, that was my first thought. Hey, maybe they both was rollin' around in their graves, but I wouldn't know since I ain't know where my real Ma was...

I was thinkin' real clear on a night like this, belly full of dinner, followed by many swigs of moonshine. I knew what I needed to do. I was gonna tear that design right up now and fast. It was gonna be one less thing to worry about, and if Elias caught himself coming out here with that nonsense, he was gonna get it too. After all, this was for his best.

Maybe I wasn't nothing like my Pa. I wasn't stupid. I wasn't gonna let some woman step in and make a fool of me, not again. I already did that and that was time I wasn't never gettin' back. At least I wasn't dumb enough to make kids out of it and make them suffer and lie to them.

Whole time I was readin' those goddamn journals I was thinking I was gettin' to know my Pa when I was really gettin' to know a damn fool. I wasn't readin' and meetin' him for the first time 'cause I was now an adult---No, I never knew him at all 'cause he was a damn liar. Maybe Elias *was* his favorite, since he was so quick to forget my Ma the minute she died. Yeah, for all I knew, maybe he killed her. Yeah, that seemed 'bout right, couldn't make no sense of why he wouldn't tell me about her otherwise. Was either he was a lyin' murderer or that damn alien witch done cast a spell on him?

Now her and her crazy friends was 'bout to try and take the only thing I had left, my baby brother.
He was gettin' himself together. Bein' responsible, thinking 'bout the future 'steada daydreamin'.
First time I'd seen him happy since we put Pa to rest. He was walking 'round smilin' all the time and really gettin' involved in the farm again. They wasn't gonna take him from me, I'll be damned.

I was rippin' that design up. I didn't even care anymore if they stood straight up, but I had to be careful even in my stupor since if they wasn't standing straight up it would still be a clear signal. Not on my watch! My Pa done already made enough mistakes, and I was here to clean up his mess. That's why I was back.

I was out there in that cornfield, steadying myself out enough to be able to unfold the stalks. The more I stood up, the better I felt. Was like every time I came out here the damn design got bigger somehow, but it couldn't have been. I was out here almost every night pulling 'em up. It was like something I wasn't never going to get done.
I was thinkin' how I missed Bruno. Any other time I was out here, he would've been beside me.

Lately he was sleepin' all night after playin' all day, like Elias, when he wasn't sneakin' away. I was good and trapped in my own mind, sippin 'on my jar, when I thought I saw something. I did.

It was my moment. I called out without thinkin' about it and sent whatever it was in the opposite direction. I started chasin' after it when I saw these real funny sparkles. Got me thinkin' I was drinkin' more than I should've. Guess my tolerance wasn't as high as I thought.

For a minute it was like that creature had disappeared into thin air, but not really 'cause I could still see it somehow. I was runnin' but it seemed to be floatin' away...I was catchin' up, though, when my heel found one of Bruno's holes and my ankle rolled leavin' me in a pile of profanity. Layin' all sweaty and outta breath in the dirt, in pain and drunk, dozin' off in the moonlight.

I was lovin' making rounds again. Something 'bout this month and change made me fall in love with this place all over again. It was the way I remembered it as a kid: big and interestin' and new. Maybe since I was seeing it all through her eyes.

We would be out there as much of the day as we could. She was so darn sensitive that the sun always made her red. When it was us and she was her, I seen what it did to her. Her blue blendin' with the red was so beautiful to me. That's how she got her name here: Violet. It came from how much I loved those shades of purple.

It was me and Violet and we was livin' the farm life and it was perfect. She was a natural. She had a real way with the cattle and the horses, plus she had a green thumb. When I was tellin' her 'bout this place, I started rememberin' why I loved it so much. Made me feel smart. After all, this is what I knew best, and I was good at it. All this time I'd been looking for something else 'cause I forgot how good I had it. It was a beautiful place, and I was lucky I had so much. A place to call home with Evan to have my back, even if he was grumpy most of the time and Bruno, even if he had been actin' like a mischievous lil pup lately.
Showin' Violet around brought me back to the times when Pa would show me around and he seemed like he

had it all. He was the big man in charge of everything, dealin' with life and death and everything in between on this farm. I was so impressed and all I ever wanted to do was help, however I could, to be part of it.

I thought of how I used to come out with Mama cause she liked plantin'. She taught me no plant was ever really dead if you used it to start a new one. I liked seein' what they grew into.

Walkin' around with Violet was really makin' me feel like I never did need to go anywhere else. I loved where I was. Maybe all I was missin' was someone to love it with me. Wasn't hard to get a girl to notice me in town, but I never thought I was much to look at. I mean, I heard people say I was, but when I looked at myself in the mirror, I was a regular guy. Them girls in town, though, they musta been seein' someone else 'cause Evan would say they was throwin' themselves at me.

It seemed like every time we made it into town it had grown some. There was some new shops to buy stuff at and there was more girls. Some of them was great to look at and even great to be with at first, but they never ended up takin' much seriously.
I had a whole home life I had to take care of and I needed a girl who was willin' to come be a part of that with me.
Most them girls seemed to like what they saw more than anything else. They wasn't listenin' or carin' about me.

They wanted to play around for a bit and I ain't never really been like that. Even if I caught feelings for a rare one, I knew what it led to, so I always pulled back. Evan wasn't the same when he came back home, so I wasn't 'bout to go chasing after something that was gonna leave me worse off. If that was the case, I'd rather stay on the farm wonderin' what it might be like off of it, rather than travel off it and wishin' I was still home.

But with her here, I didn't have to worry 'bout none of that. I was here where I was happiest and she was remindin' me why, while givin' me another reason to be here. We was spendin' a lot of time me and her, with Evan off doin' whatever he'd been doin'.

Evan always seemed to be readin' something these days, but when I come 'round he act like I'm buggin' 'im so I try not to bother 'im much. I guess he did end up pickin' Pa's journals back up, so I figured it was that all over again, since he was acting real weird. He never was one to sleep too well, but now it seemed like he never did. He'd be messin' 'round in the field doin' who knows what. I was startin' to get a little worried 'bout him. At the same time, there wasn't much I could do to save him from himself.

For the first time, I was feelin' like I should enjoy myself a little, and I was. It was in the simple things... I never knew how much I could enjoy milkin' a cow or fetchin' eggs. And now that she was better, I never knew how much fun I could have chasin' through the fields after her like kids playin' hide and seek.

I was enjoying it all, and I was tryin' my best to keep a small eye on Evan, but I knew how he was when he got in those moods. He'd start pityin' himself and he didn't want no help with that. He was the type where you had to have the time to pry something out of him and I really ain't had time.

Only time I had lately was fallin' asleep at night so hard, hopin' it was morning so I could be with her again.
I had tried to aquaint 'em in passing, but Evan ain't seem to care and ain't do much more than nod and wave.
I didn't take it personal since I know how he gets and neither did Violet since she pretty much gets what I mean.

I must have been livin' the life that was meant for me because everything was fallin' into place. Things that was chores ain't seem like it with her beside me. Her being there let me know what I was capable of.
She couldn't stay out all day and on particularly hot ones she stayed inside. It was lucky for me I had a lot of chances to sneak her back in the house with Evan elsewhere. I knew he was never goin' into the room Violet was in. He'd bust into any other room without knockin', including my room and the bathroom, but not that one.

It was eight years after Mama passed that I finally convinced Pa to divvy up her stuff and take it outta his room. I ain't wanted nor expected him to get rid of it, I wanted him to take it out the room so he wasn't feelin' sad and stressed out every time he meant to relax.

I knew it was tough on him 'cause he ain't want no help and Pa was always demandin' help 'round here. He boxed it all up his self and put it up in what used to be our guest room. Then that place kinda became off-limits. Not 'cause anyone said so, but it felt that way. It was only me and Pa in the house at that point and we both missed Mama so much each in our own way, but we was gettin' to the point where we could deal with it. We thought that maybe not seein' her stuff everywhere might help us heal a bit better.

Was a few times I found myself moseyin' on in there thinkin' if I touched something of hers, I might go right back to a moment where I was with her, but Pa ain't seem to like that much. He seemed bothered by me bein' in there and I thought it best to leave it be, rather than upset him. I knew how hard it was dealin' with losing her.

Since Evan been back, he don't go down the hall that far no more. Ain't no real reason for him to have to since his room is down the other way, plus he has his own bathroom. I guess it's less that he doesn't do it and more like he can't. It's as if that part of the hallway don't exist to him no more nor the room that goes with it. He can't seem to pass a certain point down the hall without gettin' all choked up. Since he don't do so well with his feelings, he don't go nowhere near it.

That's why I was smart enough to never keep Violet in my room. I knew he'd come in and she could never keep her form in our intimate moments. We usually spent most our time outside, but since Evan had been spendin' so much time out in the field at night, we found ourselves spendin' more time in that room together. The more time I spent in there, the more tempted I was to go through them boxes that were as much mine as anyone's.

I remembered how much it meant to me when Evan gave me the journals that belonged to Pa. Hearin' him in my head as I read his words was good for me.
I thought anything Mama would have in these boxes would give me that same feeling. I'd been feelin' so carefree that I figured why not? Going through the boxes made my head was spin.

Violet told me it was too much too fast and, like always, she was right. I thought I'd start one box at a time. There was a lot of books in the first box, and I got the sense they was journals more than books. Wasn't easy to make out Mama's writing, and it seemed like they was all smudged up and dusty or something. Violet could make out more than I could.

Readin 'em kept us busy in those still moments we laid together. We was waitin' to see if we could go sit beneath our tree under the night sky or if Evan was still out there messing 'round. I missed it, but I was okay long as we could sit out there at sunset. We both loved that so.

Was 'bout six weeks in when I got up one morn to do rounds and figured it was worse than I thought.
Found Evan outside, obviously been drunk as a skunk the night before. He was layin' out in a pile of dirt. Must'a tripped from one of Bruno's holes. That was one of the new things that he'd been drivin' me crazy with lately. He'd been diggin' things up, leavin' carcasses all about, hunting after our own chickens; things he should have known better. I understood, though. He was adjustin' and all.

Evan was layin' there all sprawled out. I ain't really know if I should help him up or leave him there. Either way, he was gonna be mad. I thought it best to let Bruno do it then I couldn't be blamed for it, and I'd walk up like I ain't know.

That's what I did, and it worked out alright, but he was obviously still drunk, with all the nonsense he was talkin'. I walked 'im back to the house, helped 'im up the stairs, then laid 'im down. I took care of his leg, wrapped his ankle, which was swelled up, and I rested it up on some pillows.

He was actin' a real fool and his drunken, half-'sleep talk was really gettin' to me. It was crazy. I thought he had gotten himself in order. How was I 'posed to talk to him like this?

"Hush now, you fool," I muttered makin' him drink some water.

He was fallin' asleep mid sip, mid-sentence. I made him lay back down. He was gonna regret this when he sobered up.

I ain't know what to think. Readin' those journals had really got to him. He wasn't himself. He'd been sneakin' in and out of Pa's room and I wanted to say something 'bout it, but since I was sneakin' in and out of another room myself, I didn't really have a leg to stand on. It made more sense if I left him to do what he was doin' and I did what I was doin'. Finding him out there like that though made me think I might wanna start payin' more attention to him.

I left Violet to rest; she needed it. Plus, lately she wasn't so good at staying discreet, as she put it. I did what I could. Been a lot to take in that morning and my mind was foggy.

I wanted to be honest with Evan, but he was goin' through his own thing. I didn't want to put more on 'im. I didn't know what to do. I knew I wasn't gonna have real time with Violet for the next few days havin' so much farm work to do. Seemed to be Evan been slippin' on his half and I was in for a ton of catchin' up. I had to keep this farm thrivin' for my family....

I'd learned so much since we first touched.
I now saw things differently. It's amazing how much you can take in from an interaction with one individual. They don't teach you that, they can't. It was the most meaningful encounter I'd ever had, no words necessary. I thought that was something only we experienced.

If only it hadn't been interrupted by what I soon understood to be protection. I reacted defensively and rightfully so, as I was being torn into. My intention was not to cause harm, but survival is instinctive.

I was damaged and my best bet was to forcibly remove the bottom part of my lower limb. It would be susceptible to infection, and I didn't have the proper equipment to manage it. It was already shutting down. I felt the numbness take over and I almost couldn't tell what I was stepping on or if I was even stepping at all. I had to seek shelter, so I found a small place and took cover. I sat mustering up strength, and I twisted and pulled as hard as I could in one swift motion the way I'd been taught. It was as excruciating as I'd been told, but I remained silent. It was all I could do to heal in the proper manner.

I knew I was going to need some time to rest.

I tried to compose myself. I was shaken, both physically and mentally. I needed to plan my next move, and I didn't have much time. I heard voices which reminded me how little time I really had. They were yelling in distress, and I knew it was because of what I'd done. I was afraid they might see me in my condition.

There was a hole in the shelter, and I hid on the opposite side of it, still able to observe them. They seemed too distracted to notice I'd been there at all. I stood there because I didn't have anywhere else to go, but also because I wanted to know if everything would turn out okay.

I watched, though I risked being spotted, but the only one who seemed to notice my presence was Bruno. He was in dismay, and it only made me feel worse. I was going to have to stay. I watched them. They were so desperate. They loved him like he was one of them. I could see it and I could hear it by the way they talked to and about him. They tried their best to help him, although in the end all they could really do was make him comfortable.

I waited a long time after they left to be safe. Then I waited a little while after that before I dared approach him. He was laying there barely breathing, paying the price for his loyalty. It was hard enough for me to be anywhere near him. I stared at him, making an effort to view him the way they did, but I could not see what was so captivating about him. I was still contemplating whether or not I wanted to risk the same reaction he'd given me before, and then he looked up at me. He'd lived a whole lifetime and seen more than most.

My breathing was already starting to get caught inside me when I went for it, and then I did all I could. I touched him and reached deep down inside myself. I wasn't sure how it worked here, but I was hoping I might be able to do something to correct the error. As I expected, my breath was cut short and before I knew it, I fell to the ground.

I wasn't sure how much time had actually passed when I woke up still wheezing and trying to remember where I was. I wondered how long I'd been out there vulnerable like that. I was lucky this part of town was so empty, and that people were few and far between. I couldn't breathe and I wanted to flee. Not necessarily away from Bruno, as I think we had come to an understanding. I wanted to retreat because I wasn't quite sure what to expect anymore.

 I thought I'd come prepared, but perhaps I hadn't. This was nothing like anyone had told me it was going to be. I looked down at the hairy third member of their clan to see if I'd had any effect on him. I heard someone say something, so I started to leave. It was him—it was Elias.

I left quickly, as I was worried Elias might still be holding a grudge from what had occurred earlier. But he called out to me. "Wait." I heard, but I wasn't sure if I should stop. "Wait, please."

I let him catch up as I neared the opening. Elias looked at me and hesitated. I saw Bruno get up and leap onto him, which was a good sign. I was immediately relieved when I saw their happiness---an interesting emotion. Elias really did love that dog. Perhaps dogs weren't the lesser being as I'd previously thought.

Although Elias seemed to be enjoying their reunion, he kept an eye on me, looking at me strangely.

"He's going to be fine," I told him as I left to find an undisturbed shelter. He mumbled something I couldn't quite make out, while I stood still trying to determine my next move.

"Come 'ere. He's good, I swear," he reassured me.

I found that both the way he talked and his attempt to inform me of something I already knew was amusing. I stepped back in and called Bruno over. I knew that would cause me to have shallow breathing again. I had finally caught my breath, but I thought it important to demonstrate peace. I petted Bruno and he happened to be more charming than I once believed, despite the fact that I could feel my breath shortening.

"He meant no harm. He was doing what he felt he needed to. He had a good reason to do what he did."
I at least understood that.

Bruno was an interesting character; unattractive and salivating, but somehow pleasant nonetheless. I understood how they might've formed a bond with him. Elias was on the ground and still looking up at me in a peculiar fashion.
"He'll need rest."
Like me, Bruno really did need rest.

Elias was still looking at me in a way that made me feel uncomfortable. He laid Bruno down and I was glad I could help him, even if it cost me a lengthy recovery.

I had to go. It may not have been evident, but I was severely injured as well. I needed time. I left.
"Wait, please," he called out.
Should I wait? I asked myself. Instead, I said, "He'll need to rest," and I proceeded to walk away. I turned one last time to look at him. Although he couldn't get the words out, I knew he wanted the same thing I did: to sit a moment and regroup.

We walked over to the spot I'd laid in earlier, escaping the sun while the sky was as blue as his eyes. It was somehow familiar to me as we sat below it.
I was worn, but sitting here made sense to me.

"You was d... d... di... diff'rent when I f... fir... irst saw you," he stammered, but I knew what he meant. I thought he might have preferred this form, but then again, his initial reaction was so calm and unlike what I had expected, though I wasn't quite sure why. I slowly let my guard down again.

"I took on a form more familiar to you," I told him. "I thought it would help you feel at ease." The moment I went back to my natural form is when he stopped looking at me in that way I didn't like. I realized he liked the sight of me in my natural state and I was both intrigued and a little nervous about that. That's why he'd been glaring at me. Now that I was completely visible, he seemed so comfortable. Then he noticed my limb, which had now become evident to him.

"Your leg!" he exclaimed. He couldn't understand. It probably looked much more awful to him than it actually was. It wasn't good, but it could've been far worse. I was okay though. I was going to need rest, but I also had to finish my work. I needed more time. I was actually grateful for Elias' assistance. It really put me at ease. I found myself connecting with him. He didn't have to say much. I was used to that.

I was going to ask him for more help, but I still wasn't sure if I should. I needed shelter. It was urgent to get somewhere so I could begin to heal. I felt my body go limp, and I thought I might hit the ground again, when I found myself caught in a warm embrace. Elias picked me up in a way that lulled me enough that even in my impaired state, I was able to put my guard up so that Evan didn't ask things Elias couldn't explain. I let him take me, holding my guard up the whole time. I felt like forever had passed, but when I felt comfort, I let go. I knew I was going to be safe. I was barely conscious as he left.

I needed rest, but not as much as they did. Even in my fragile state, I needed a lot less hibernation, which was one difference between us. Also, I was more active when the sun wasn't beating down on me, and I often spent the night working while they slept. Time passed by really quickly, but I enjoyed it. I bought myself more time and was taking advantage of it. I was learning the lay of the land and how everything worked.

The way Elias spoke was different than the way I did, but I always knew what he wanted to get across. When it came to what he did, he knew everything there was to know about it. His knowledge of the farm impressed me, though he knew so little of what he could potentially do. He didn't quite understand things the way I did, at least not yet.

I'd shown him a softer, easier way to collect milk from cows. I thought it surprising that after all this time milking cows, he'd been doing it in a most difficult way. I wasn't necessarily good at everything, but I very much liked the horses. We had quite a rapport. I was also good with plants. Gardening was something I understood.

What I enjoyed most of all was spending time with Elias and exchanging information. He was learning what it was like being together. I knew what he was capable of, what we were capable of. He was something else. He put me on high alert because the inadequate part of me showed up and I often had to suppress glowing around him.

The farm was his area of expertise, but there was a lot that he didn't know about himself, so that's what I was showing him. Watching him hone his skills was enthralling.

Elias was learning to enjoy our productive time as much as I was, and I was learning to enjoy the frivolous times as much as he did. Now that I had healed, we wasted time running through the stalks. I hid as if he couldn't find me. Even in my best camouflage, it was pointless, yet endearing and completely absurd.

Time passed differently here. There were three parts to each day; one that I could only go out into in small increments and the other was the darkness that I knew very well. My favorite was the third part; the in between moments, a harmony of colors wrapped up in each other in magnificent patterns. It started blue and went into various hues of red and orange and of course, shades of purple. No matter how many times I witnessed it, it was alluring and magnificent.

It was around what they refer to as, "many weeks had passed," when things started to become worrisome. Everything between Elias and me was above satisfactory. We learned so much about each other in the short time we'd spent together. I gained more knowledge than I ever could've at home. I realized there'd been severe miscalculations by those who had been here before me, and I was now eager to discover more.

I spent minimal time during the daytime out there with him. The sun affected me differently, whereas it didn't take such a toll on him. I didn't have to stand underneath it long before it left me sore, drained, and purple. He seemed to think it was the cutest thing. His affections were different, but I liked the way he thought. I let him refer to me as something he could pronounce: He called me "Violet." I thought it suited me, especially once he explained why to me. Actually, it was less a description and more like bundled up words he stammered through, but I always knew what he meant.

He aimed to give me most of his time, but maintaining the land and Evan kept him preoccupied. The small one seemed more like those I had been taught about; erratic, emotionally unstable, weak. A ticking timebomb. He seemed to be acting suspect, but I trusted that Elias knew him best.

I was curious that he had yet to investigate me, being new and invested in his relative. He was less protective of Elias than Bruno. He didn't know me and didn't care enough to look up at me during introductions. According to Elias, he was rough around the edges, but that was out of character, even for him. It didn't matter to me. I had no intentions of bonding with the small one, or as Elias would correct me: "Evan."

I was going out in the night more often now that Evan was uprooting my signal in the field. He had become excessively inebriated and disoriented and started destroying my work. He had no idea what he was doing. So, every night I followed behind him and mended what he'd messed up.

Elias and I were getting less time together because he worried about me being seen. In my condition, I could hardly keep my form. I stayed inside more often, at least until the sun set and things were less obvious. The less I could hold form, the less I could be out, so I spent a lot of time in that room. In fact, I spent the majority of the day in there and now most of the night because our spot was constantly being compromised by Evan.
Being confined to those pale-yellow walls encouraged us to investigate the packages that took over much of the room. Elias was learning to handle a lot, but this was too

much. He couldn't take it. It was draining; I recommended that he take it slow. We started with the memoirs. I could read them, he was able to read some, but I helped him make out the rest. He needed time to process things.

With Evan damaged, Elias had to take on a much bigger load of the work. I couldn't assist him so I was often in the room alone. I found myself going through the boxes and discovered a most pleasant way to pass the time: research. Things were coming together, everything made sense now. Each day, I relayed the information I'd discovered to Elias, and we started coming to terms with it all.

Elias was acquiring a lot of knowledge and so was I. He was eager and obviously persuaded by his brotherly bond to share the information with Evan, but I thought it best for him not to—at least for the foreseeable future. He wasn't going to take the news in the same way Elias was.

Time passes by at such a different pace here that I can feel it in the air and see it in the sky. I wasn't quite sure how I would continue to change within myself, especially now, having been given more time. Here, a seed grows much faster, though it feels like it takes forever. All the waiting rendered me helpless.

I was grateful for the fact that Evan wasn't as mobile as he was before the accident and that I didn't have to go behind him in the field. I needed that signal intact.

It was harder these days, but any chance we got, we'd sneak out beneath the sunset. I loved Elias's eyes on me and when he referred to me as Violet, I became her. I was here. It was simply us, the three of us.

Though I wasn't seeing as much of Elias as I wanted, I understood he had to maintain our way of life now more than ever. Evan was never going to be of any assistance if he didn't stay still and get better. Our moments spent together were fewer and farther between, but powerful.

I often sat by the window to catch a glimpse of Elias. All I could do most of the time was wait, while I became acquainted with new emotions like impatience and desire.

I tried not to feel trapped because I knew it was for my own good. Perhaps it was my depleted state, but I understood the urge to protect and the need to be protected. I did my best not to focus on outside. I closed the window and laid down. I still needed so much rest.

I suddenly heard the doorknob jiggle. Any other time that had occurred, I felt a rush inside but not this time. Elias had gone into town, so I couldn't fathom who might be trying to come in the room.

I stood up as quickly as I could, which wasn't exactly fast, though I managed to bolt the lock in time. I was so nervous that I was glowing. I calmed myself for the two of us. There were a few thumps, but I disregarded them. Perhaps Bruno had gotten in again. He was drawn to this door.

I laid back down. I thought it was best if I recharged now. That way when Elias was done, we might sneak a moment out in the sunset. He reassured me he'd be back by then. It was one of the few things I could still do. He always insisted on carrying me back, no matter how heavy I'd become.

I tried to get comfortable, but a shooting pain made it impossible. I muffled a scream and breathed deeply. I was exhausted. I readjusted, closed my eyes, and began fading out. The doorknob jiggled again, but I didn't worry this time. If it was Bruno, he'd see himself out. After all, the only one with a key was Elias.

It had been weeks, and I was still tryna heal. I couldn't waste time layin' around when there was so much to do. I mighta been drinkin' some, but I know what I saw. Bruno's damn holes mighta laid me up, but I wasn't done. I felt like a prisoner with Warden Elias breathin' down my neck, but I was on a mission. I needed to find out so much more, plus I needed to stop communication and I couldn't do that while in bed.

I'd been figurin' a grand escape plan since none of my other ideas had worked. I always got caught in the hall, 'cause I was so damn slow. Then I got lectured and taken back to my room as if I was a child or something. I was havin' too much time on my hands, and I was never good when that happened. I was sick of being called crazy and referred to as a "balloon 'bout to burst." I was gonna' gather my evidence and prove to Elias I wasn't a nut needin' to be managed. I was also tired of the pain in my leg and my heart, and needed to get to things I knew Elias wouldn't give me. I had to get up.

It was one of those times that I saw Elias when he ain't know I was there: he was sneaking into the room. It hit me then; I had been limpin' around from time to time, unable to stay still. That's how I was and every time I went past the room, I seen the light was on. I could see the glowing 'neath the door. I thought it was sunlight at first, but then I seen it at night. I ain't know why he was in there, maybe lookin' through his donor's belongings. He wasn't going to find nothing 'cause what he ain't know was that all the stuff that mattered was up the staircase in Pa's room.

As I tried my best to hobble quietly down the stairs, I could tell he was still in there. I wanted to run down and confront him, but I could barely walk, and I figured it was not yet time. I needed to find what I was lookin' for first. I knew that if he was also lookin' for something he wasn't gonna find it in there, not when there was a whole secret closet leading to an attic full of clues.

I made it to my room, winded and in terrible pain, but it was worth it. I was really hating Bruno right then. I was crippled 'cause of him. He was extremely restless lately, so Elias was keeping him outside most of the time. Fine by me. He didn't make sneakin' around any easier. Here I was with four jars tryna sneak up the stairs on one leg and he takes to jumpin' on me. I didn't even know how he got in. I don't know how I made it up with the other three and hid the evidence of the broken fourth, but I made it back to my room unseen. I would've been pretty proud of myself if I wasn't hurtin' so bad. Instead, I was achin' and puttin' up my leg so the throbbing might stop.

I hate to admit it, but it ain't work the same when I tended to my leg as when Elias did it. He had a way of making it feel much better. In the meantime, a few swigs of the good stuff sure was refreshin' and necessary to clear my head. I had really started puttin' everything together. Time without my farm obligations had me seein' real clear. I had time to sleep a full night and really get a sense of all that was happenin'.

Watching Elias sneak around in those last couple weeks really let me know I had to keep a better eye on him. I was waitin' for him to go out so I could sneak back into Pa's room. I needed to go through that alien's belongings. There had to be something up there I was missing. With all that female stuff up there, I knew there was some clue that would tell me something.
Maybe she was the one who killed my Ma so she could replace her. I needed to get up there and I knew there would come a time when he would have to head into town.

I waited and waited, then I gave 'im a reason to leave. Once I heard Elias' footsteps, I gave myself a good whack on the ankle. After he heard me screamin' and moanin', he decided he had to go into town to get me something that would help my pain. It was a little later than our usual trips to town, but this was something that couldn't wait. Alcohol was a hell of a painkiller, but Elias ain't had to know about that. I needed him outta the house.

I heard the truck start. I did the math and when I figured he was 'bout halfway to town, I managed to get myself out of my room and make it to Pa's. It wasn't easy, though I was gettin' better, and by using the wall for support, I could even bring my jar with me. It was a long journey; between leanin', steppin', sippin' and draggin' myself to that room.

I was spent. I had to sit. I sat a minute in Pa's chair and thought about him sitting in it after a long day of writing. I smiled at the thought of it, then a swig brought me back to reality. I ain't had time for reminiscin' 'specially for someone who ain't deserve it.
I was runnin' out of time. Elias would be back soon enough, and I was movin' slow as it was.

I'd been goin' real crazy in my room tryna put the puzzle together without all the pieces. I knew I was doin' what I was meant to. There was something I needed to find out. I had to know why, I needed to know how, but mostly I needed to know where my Ma was, and most importantly, *who* she was.

Through it all, I was still aimin' to protect my brother from my Pa's mistakes. Not because he asked me to, but because someone had to. Between the two of us I was the one with the strongest mind and no one was gonna soften me up enough to be a sucka. Even laid up, I was unstoppable. Wasn't nothing gettin' past me!
I was gonna find it upstairs amongst all the stuff. Had to. I wasn't sure what "it" was exactly, but I'd know it when I found it. It'd point me in the right direction 'cause I

done read everything 20 times over and 20 times more after orderin' it all. It still ain't tell me what I needed it to.

I dragged myself over to the closet, and exposed the opening in the wall behind where the clothes hung. Then I dragged myself over and pushed the clothes to one side. I looked up from the bottom of the attic staircase. I took another swig for strength. The way I was feeling, I might as well be climbing a mountain.

I looked at what I once thought was a closet and almost started cryin' at the thought of the stairs. I think I actually did cry a bit. There was no way with this pain in my ankle and foot that I was going to make it up there. I felt useless. I could barely stand. I needed both hands, so I sipped on my jar, then put it on the step and braced myself to stand up. I was gonna get up there one way or another.

I heard a sound, and sat straight up. I was in Pa's room on the floor in front of the closet. Guess I ain't make it up there after all. I ain't even make it up off the floor. I had tried to stand but couldn't. I then scooched myself over to the nearest windowsill and pulled myself up. I didn't know how long I was out or how much time I had left 'til Elias would be back. I tried to tell time by the sky, but I was distracted by Bruno adding salt to the wound diggin' around out there. Man, I would've been done by now twice over if it wasn't for him.

86

My ankle was even more swollen. I wasn't gonna make it upstairs. I was barely gonna make it to my room.
I knew I better close that closet and get there 'fore the Warden returned. I'd have to think of another way to get 'im into town. I made it to the closet, leanin' against the wall the whole time, when all of a sudden, I heard a sound coming from down the hall. I turned in the direction of the noise, but it wasn't Bruno 'cause I could see him out the window and it wasn't Elias 'cause I couldn't see the truck.

I finished that jar in one big swallow and it charged me up enough to make it down the hall and right into that room to face whoever was there. Not that it mattered 'cause it was locked. But the light was on and I could hear something and then the light went out. I knew someone was in there, so I started pounding on the door. I forgot about my pain and remembered the keys in Pa's room. I headed there to get 'em.

Yeah, Elias had been actin' different. Forcin' me to take some time off. Maybe he knew 'bout my Ma. Maybe he thought I knew too much. Bet he thought I'd stay laid up and wouldn't go lookin'. He thought wrong. That was probably the plan all along, to keep me outta the picture. Maybe he was a fool like Pa, too dumb to see the truth. The aliens was after me like they had been after my Ma, and Elias was being pulled along as well. One thing for sure, they wasn't gettin' what they came for. I had to stop them.

87

I was makin' my way slowly but surely. I heard a terrible sound, so I moved faster. Crazy but in the moment I ain't even feel no pain. I grabbed Pa's keys and his gun, and I moved towards that room full speed. I unlocked the door. It swung open since I was basically using it to hold me up. I regained my balance, as fast as I could. Man, that pain came back full on and I was hurtin' for real.

I saw something that felt familiar, a glittery blur. To hell with my pain. I stood strong, steadied myself and aimed the gun. "I ain't scared of you!" I yelled, and I wasn't. The form became less blurry. Then suddenly, I saw a girl, a brunette. Elias' neighbor girl maybe?

There was this fuzziness like static on a bad channel, then a flash of everything Pa wrote about, standin' right there before me. Bright, so bright I could barely see.

I couldn't take any chances, so I pulled the trigger.

No traffic was a rarity, but I had been the only one on the road for miles now. I never thought I would adapt to city life, yet here I was. I no longer knew what to do with myself in the quiet. I could barely pick up any reception for a station, and everything looked the same. Nothing but green landscapes that I had lost appreciation for.

Silence gave me too much space to think. I was no good when I was inside my own head. I missed the noise: the yelling, the honking, the construction, the barking, the sirens. Growing up, I distracted myself by listening to the sounds of the city. That way, and with stuff constantly going on, I was always too distracted to focus on my own insecurities.

Having come from the country and being used to the stillness, I found a therapeutic rhythm in each city sound. It gave me something to grab hold of for stability. It allowed me to concentrate on something other than my thoughts. It was a coping mechanism I'd been taught. I practiced it in the back of my head during conversations when I felt nervous or shy. It helped me to stay in control.

Back out here in the country, there weren't any distracting sounds to focus on, and even the static on the radio cut in and out. I was getting overwhelmed. I could feel it. I hadn't had such a reaction in a long time. I came to a slow stop. I wasn't sure what I was doing back here, but my presence had been requested and I could never say no to him.

I can't imagine it had been easy for him. I gave him so much trouble when all he wanted to do was protect me. I knew he meant well, which is why I loved him. Perhaps it was his approach. I spent so long wondering what we were running from. I always felt protected though I was never sure from what.

His initial approach was to pretend that everything was completely normal, as if I hadn't recognized his high level of stress and strange behavior.

I parked my car and sat in a daze. It was 15 years ago that I had to be pulled away from this place kicking and screaming on the same day we buried my mother. I breathed in deep. It was so quiet, so very, very quiet.

I'm not sure how long I sat in the car trying to compose myself. I'd picked up my favorite book which was laying on the passenger seat and made it through the entire story of *The Cask of Amontillado* before I realized the sun was setting in the deep purple of the sky.

I got out of the car and slowly walked up to the house. I had a strange feeling, like I knew the place and then again, I felt like I didn't know it at all. I was experiencing lots of emotions at once and it was showing.

Before I could knock, the door swung open.

"Well, ooooh weee, if you don't look exactly like yer Ma!" He exclaimed, grabbing me and squeezing me tight. I'd missed him so much. He never was a fan of the city, so as soon as he thought I was grown enough to take care of myself, he left and went back home.

"Oh Ellie, you oughta get that under control," he teased, raising his bushy eyebrows.

I was glowing like a flashlight at that point, because I had missed him so much. "It's not the same out here. There's nothing to focus on," I shrugged.

He hugged me again and ruffled my hair, like when I was a kid, except now he had to reach up to do it. "That's not true. There's plenty to focus on, as you'll learn."

I believed him.

I hadn't been here in a very long time, but it was all slowly coming back to me. I stepped back to take it all in. It was exactly as I remembered. I grabbed the chair to steady myself.

"I could turn the lights out, it'll save me on the bill, if you wanna keep the place lit up for me," he joshed, snapping me out of my thoughts and giving me that devious smile of his. He put his hand on my shoulders and looked me in the eye like old times when he was trying to get me to calm down. I could see it in his eyes: focus.

"Focus on the sounds around us, the softer sounds, focus on the sound of the wind creekin' through the house. Focus on the chirpin' crickets and hootin' owls. Focus."

And I did. I focused, and I became calm. I hadn't done that in a long time. I had mixed emotions between how much I'd missed him, coupled with all the history that flooded back to me the moment I pulled up and looked at this place.

Since he had moved back, he visited me every three months, but the last two times, work had prevented it. He called me to get together, except this time he asked me to meet him here. The last time I was here, I buried my mother. Then my uncle had a mental breakdown, salted the land and burned strange patterns into it. Then, against my will and with no real explanation, I was ripped from everything I knew and loved and forced to live in a congested, smoggy, noisy city.

As an adult looking back, I now understand why he'd done it. As a child though, you start to lose your mind; when you have no idea why you're always so afraid. You don't understand why you can't go home, and why things can't be normal. Growing up, I unintentionally gave him a hard time, which he didn't fault me for. He knew I was mad at the world because I never got to meet my dad and at 10 I'd lost my mom, after she'd been sick for months. Then I had to leave the only home I'd ever known without explanation to spend years pretending to be normal when I was anything but.

I experienced a roller coaster of emotions; between me being uninformed and hopeful, and him informed yet hopeless. All I had were questions, and he was doing his best to give me any answers that he could. Once puberty hit, there was nothing he could do to hide the truth from me anymore. Though only one quarter human, my hormones hit me like any other adolescent. The only difference was that I wasn't losing control of my emotions or growing hair in new places. Instead, I was reading minds and waking up to find myself floating above my bed.

I was only 12 when one day, while sitting in my room, I discovered I was glowing. Not as an expression of flawless skin and not in the way that pregnant women do, but actually, literally glowing like a lit up candle. I reacted by screaming hysterically, which only made me glow brighter, and made me scream even more.

My uncle raced into the room and in a completely calm voice said, "We need to have a talk." Did he know about this phenomenon? Turns out he did. Why didn't I? How could I not have known?

He sat with me and finally explained that my mother made him promise her that I'd live a normal life. He had agreed against his better judgment. He made the mistake of not telling my father, and that regret stayed with him. Then again, this had been her final request, and he felt he owed her that much. He promised to keep things as normal as possible for me. He'd kept that promise for as long as he could.

Suddenly learning that things weren't as they seemed didn't shock me at all. Deep down, I always knew that something was different. But why couldn't I remember details?

It was that same night that my uncle gave me my very first journal which had been written by my grandmother. It is only then that I learned of my origins. I read more written by my grandfather and then some by my mother. Most special to me were the three journals written by my father. Each of them more than explained my uncle's secrecy and fears.

It had been traumatic for him when my mother inevitably gave in. She fought hard, but it was beyond her control. She lay there sick and withering longer than necessary because she was fighting her biological impulses to save me.

My father Elias, whom I was named after and whom I favor, was the first known specimen. I am told that he was a genuine and caring man and from what I've seen; he was handsome too.

The journals were my lifeline. They held the answers to the array of odd characteristics I'd been uncovering about myself. As I read them, I slowly recalled what I'd forgotten after I'd lost my mother and left the farm. I remembered her being blue in color and sometimes glimmering, especially whenever she spoke of my father. Until receiving and reading the journals, I didn't understand why the years before leaving the farm were absent from my recollection.

As I touched each journal, I felt intentions and feelings and something like memories, though they weren't my own. My grandmother's journals were written in code which I interpreted effortlessly. She wrote intelligently, philosophically. It was meant as a warning, as teachings to anyone who might follow behind her. My grandmother spoke of peace and unity, but she was also a realist who knew better. She too had been a casualty of her own genetic code.

I could actually see her as I read my father's description. She gleamed a bright blue that I somehow recognized. It wasn't a shade reflective of being overwhelmed by emotion, rather it was what happened when we separated from ourselves. She stood holding my father's hand. I knew it was him because of how he described it, but I couldn't see him because the glare was too bright. I was there too, standing in the field. As I turned the pages, I watched it as if I were standing within a movie clip.

The farmhouse was so new, so different.
I could see my grandfather running towards them, screaming as she held tight to my father. I wanted desperately to see him, but all I could see was the fact that she wasn't the only one shining. He was softly illuminated too and willingly walking beside her as she glided along. Her toes barely grazed the top of the grass. Her eyes were glazed over. It was eerie.

It was my grandmother's mission to return home with my father, whom they deemed, "the specimen." Although she didn't want to go, she continued to do so as she was no longer in control of herself. Luckily, she was aware of this enough to have a failsafe. She had warned my grandfather, made him promise against his wishes, to formulate a plan in case of an emergency.

It was a simple, discreet plan. Most importantly, it was painless. She knew that my grandfather would ultimately have to put her down, otherwise it would have been impossible to subdue her. Once fully engaged, the only way to stop her was death. My grandfather promised for her and for his son's sake, but he never believed it would actually come down to that.

But it did.

My grandparents' plan was to use my grandmother's allergy against her. She (like myself and my mother) was deathly allergic to dogs. My grandfather kept dogs, but because of Grandmother's allergies being so bad, they couldn't come in the house. During the day they roamed the farm and at night they were secured in a section of the barn he'd set aside for them.

He tried his best to scream and beg her in an effort to reach her. Then he came to the sad realization that she was not going to come to her senses. He had no choice. He had to follow through with his promise.

"Go to Mama," my grandfather commanded, looking broken and defeated. This was a command the dogs knew to respond to by being playful and affectionate. They would jump up on her, lick her, stay with her, thus slowing her breath. It would be a peaceful death like passing while sleeping. It could not have been easy for my grandfather to make that call. That's when my uncle lost it. He had been convinced that my mother would be strong enough to break through the programming. When my grandmother came out here, she'd looked for a mate to make a specimen with to bring back with her. She'd found my grandfather grieving his first love and raising my uncle Evan, who was only an infant at the time. Even in the midst of suffering, he was kind and sweet and offered her shelter and anything else she needed. He was nothing like what she'd expected, nothing close to what she'd been taught. In fact, she wrote that she felt everything she'd been taught about this planet was riddled with propaganda and misinformation.

She easily let go of her preconceived notions and fell in love. She wrote how she first fell in love with my infant uncle, how he'd weakened her with his cry. That she became dependent on his scent and on the way it felt when she held him and he looked up at her.

"Ethan is a beautiful man who is easy to love, but I first knew real love when I looked into Evan's eyes. Soft honey eyes I knew he'd gotten from his mother. He looked at me and cared nothing of who I was, where I was from or why I was here. He cared only that I loved him, and he loved me back as a result."

Loving Evan taught her about motherhood, but he would never do as a specimen. A full human would never work, so my grandmother moved forward with the plan. She made a specimen, and even though she was doing what she was supposed to, she already knew there was no way she was going to be able to follow orders.

Once she'd held my father, it confirmed that she would no longer remain a mindless slave to the nonsense she'd been fed. She would not allow the breaking up of her family, nor could she willingly hand over her child to be experimented on or controlled for the purpose of studying the human race.

Her programming, so to speak, was biological in the same way you'd imagine a computer program or a virus. It was an involuntary reaction, with her brain as the mainframe, which had been hacked into, sending her home with my father, Elias, when he turned 10 years old.

My grandmother knew the plan but refused to comply. She warned my grandfather of the imminent danger in the same way my mother had warned my uncle. But my uncle, optimist that he is, thought she'd be the exception to the rule.

After my father passed, my uncle let go of all his bad habits and was front-and-center, making sure my mom had everything she needed to take care of me.
There were some things she couldn't do, and he eagerly filled in, completely devoted. He was the link to my human side and the closest thing I had to a dad.

I didn't remember the unearthly things about my mother, and I later found out why. A signal had been sent out to me the moment she was disrupted. It was meant to protect our species. The matron would have to die to be stopped and would return to human form after dying on Earth. If a human managed to get ahold of the child, the signal sent out reprogrammed said child. At which point, their unearthly DNA went dormant, and their human biology became dominant.

When my uncle gave me my grandmother's journals, her essence spread all over those pages, slowly restoring my memories, every word revealed who I really was.

My uncle wanted to tell me, but his promise was to let me become fully human in order to protect me. He hadn't had a mental breakdown after all. Instead, he used what my mother had taught him in order to put up a signal to ward off others. He figured it would keep them away (in fact my mother guaranteed it), but as a safety precaution we moved to the city anyway until he knew for sure. He hated the city with all his heart, but what better place to hide than lost in a sea of people where no one gets to know you because no one cares? Fact is, my uncle did not take my home away. Instead, I was given a new one. Now, here I stood inside the old one wondering, "why? "

Of course, my uncle was making coffee, his only vice. I stood there recovering memories of everything when I suddenly started choking. Then without warning I was on the ground. My uncle dropped his mug and leapt over the table.

"I'm okay, I'm okay, " I tried to say, but I couldn't stop laughing.

"Bruno no, down, down! How'd you get in?" My uncle scolded in his gentle way.

"I'm okay," I reminded him as always.

He was traumatized after what had happened to my mother, so of course this was his natural reaction.

Unlike my ancestors, I had an advantage. I had regained my knowledge and understood how I'd forgotten it. I'd learned to make parts of my unearthly DNA go dormant. The first skill I'd honed was making the parts of me that were allergic to dogs turn inactive. I did it so Uncle Evan could get Bruno, who'd been living in a neighbor's care. He was there instantly to retrieve Bruno. He then found us a place with a yard for him, which was an expensive rarity for the city, but it was worth it. I worked on making my allergies lie beneath the surface. I had to focus, and it wasn't foolproof at first, but after years of practice, I became an expert. My Uncle still panics though, because if I'm caught off guard I may not react fast enough. I was fine however, and had to say hello to Bruno 'cause I'd missed him too.

I helped my uncle clean up the mess. Then we sat and drank coffee, and I made the part of me who hates it go dormant because I knew how much he loved his fancy coffee beans. We spoke for hours. He explained why I was finally allowed back here. The allotted time of threat had passed, and I now knew the way to prevent it in the future.

The salted ground was finally growing back and I could fold it in the way I was meant to. I could care for the farm better than anyone.

"No way, I'm a city girl now and it's all your fault," I laughed, but meant it.

"It's engraved in you. I ain't worried 'bout that. Put that city girl side of you down for a nap and focus on the bigger picture."

"Keep the pattern burned in there, which will work fine," I contested. I couldn't pick up and move. He must have asked me here because he was lonely.

"Someone's gotta take care of Bruno," he chuckled.

"That's what you're here for," I retorted.

"But in case I wasn't here," he replied in a tone slightly above a whisper.

Then it made sense why he'd avoided eye contact with me until then. When he finally did look at me, I knew exactly why. I remained quiet, but I lit up and tears fell one after the other.

"See, you never could mind your business," he chuckled. I couldn't help laughing too, not because it was funny, but because, as always, his jokes were poorly timed. "I ain't have you come out here to make you cry." Then he wiped my tears and I stopped gleaming.

He had something for me, something Bruno had dug up. He knew it was for me when he saw the design. It was in the shape of a small black oval, like a smooth skipping stone. Although the symbols looked familiar, I was unable to read them. He then handed the stone to me and the very moment it was placed in my palm, it turned red and flipped open, exposing a button.

Violet kept sayin' things like, "You'll eventually see what you're capable of." I thought it was simply a phrase 'til things started happenin'. I could see and do things that others could not. Guess all my knowledge had been locked up after everything that happened with Mama. It been slowly comin' back to me ever since I touched Violet, but it was when I opened the boxes full of Mama's journals that it really hit me.

At first, I got a rush that made my head spin. I wasn't just reading 'em, I was seein' it all clear as day, like I was there. It was all smudged up kinda and I couldn't make it all out or so it seemed, but the more I touched 'em, the more I read 'em, they was clearer. I needed to tell Evan, but he hadn't been himself lately and it was a whole lot to take in.

Now I understood why I didn't remember: my memories left when Mama left. My Pa never told me 'cause he thought it was the best way to protect me. I guess, 'cause I had that thing where I was always lookin' for something more. He thought it mighta sent me lookin' for something I shouldn't find.

I wondered why Evan didn't remember? I kept reading. I saw Mama standing in Evan's childhood room. She was lovely. She was standin' over Evan when my Pa walked in. He looked so young.

"He's my boy," Mama almost cried, "my first baby. I don't want him to forget me."
I'd forgotten what she sounded like. She was all teared up.

"I wouldn't let 'im forget you," Pa reassured.

"You're right," she agreed. "I worry too much. We'll be fine, we'll be fine."

Why was she so sad? Pa walked out the room and she put her hand on Evan's head. I could see her hand glowing. It was right after that where he could only remember her in human form. Any other abnormal memory would have been too blurry to take seriously. I had learned the power of a glowing hand. Violet was right. I was learnin' what I was capable of.

It wasn't easy, and it was better when we did things together. We could actually lay our hands on the ground, take an old plant and make it bud again. Wasn't something I'd do all willy-nilly since it tired me out, but I wanted to jump start some of the parts on the farm I'd been having trouble with. I was tryna' prep this farm for a family.

I had my hands full with Evan laid up and me makin' up for his lack of work. With Violet inside so much more durin' the day, I used a shortcut here and there to finish things so I could spend more time with her and our growin' babe to be.

It helped my plants stay alive and green, even when I wasn't payin' as much attention to 'em as I should've been. It was hard to handle it all alone, on top of keeping Violet happy and chasing behind Evan. He, with his hurt ankle and all, still managed to somehow get a hold of and drink a bunch of alcohol. It wasn't helpin' make nothin' better. I sure was hopin' he didn't think he was keepin' his drinkin' a secret cause he smelled like he'd been bathing in moonshine. I'd smell it on him whenever I'd come in to help him out.

He'd moved around on his ankle too much. He wasn't never gonna heal, and he was constantly in pain. I'd have him lay down and get him talkin' 'bout something so when he wasn't so focused on me, I'd help him with the pain in a new way I'd learned. It would calm him, though I couldn't do much more and completely heal it without facing a lot of questions, plus I hadn't the energy.

One day, though, he was hollerin' out in pain real bad. Because I'd been tendin' to the farm way too much, I didn't have the energy left to help him that way. I tried, but I was better off simply driving into town to get 'im something to help him sleep or else it was gonna be a long night.

I made sure Violet was okay 'fore I left. If I went now and quick, I would make it back in time to sit under our sunset. It felt like a longer drive in the later hours, bein' we usually always went to town earlier in the day.
I could see the sky starting to turn colors as I pulled back up to the house. I was already sprintin' towards it 'cause I knew how slow she moved now and how much she looked forward to comin' out, bein' she was cooped up all day. My sprint turned into a run when I heard a loud bang coming from inside the house.

There stood Evan mumblin', a gun in his hand. "She killed my Ma, they killed her... your mother killed my mother!" I grabbed the gun from him. He was drunker than I'd ever seen 'im. "Evan, what are you...?" But before I could finish asking, I knew what had happened. I screamed, pushing past him.

I couldn't form words. She was gaspin' for air, and I fell to my knees beside her. I looked in her eyes. I couldn't lose her. I couldn't lose them. I laid my hands on her. "You can't," her eyes screamed.

I can and I was. I could feel it workin'. I knew 'cause I was feelin' weaker and weaker, and she was gettin' that twinkle back. 'Fore I knew it, she was standing over me, looking at me. So was Evan, who'd suddenly sobered up.

I was sooo tired.

I looked at Evan square in the eyes and he nodded. He hugged me tighter than he ever had.
"I'll take care of your family," he promised.
Violet sat next to me. I kissed her and put my hand on her stomach. I felt my eyes getting heavy. So heavy that I had to close them.

IN THE WAKE OF
THINKTECH

Technology offers endless opportunities and possibilities. There is always something else it can do. Some other way it can serve us, accommodate us, or make things accessible to us. We're inspired by it, enamored with it and on a constant mission to improve it. We've grown dependent on it, so much so that it seems as if we control it less and less, while it controls us more and more.

As technology advanced, and did more for us, we did less for ourselves. We even allowed it to think for us, as it was programmed to know all the answers, which we never questioned. People soon stopped asking, "how?" and "why?" and became more concerned with "when?" When is the newest update coming out and what will it be able to do? Every device and appliance was controlled by remote or voice activation until simple things like physically switching on a light or unlocking a door became things of the past.

In 2073, *ThinkTech* released a groundbreaking product that could've easily been ripped from the pages of a science fiction book. This invention not only changed technology it completely changed the ways of the world.

ThinkTech:
You Think it, We Make it Happen!

ThinkTech had developed an incredibly tiny microchip, no bigger than a pea, and loaded it with an array of capabilities. The chip was then implanted into a human's cerebrum, the part of the brain that controls reasoning and movement. Although it seems as if something of this magnitude would require major surgery, it was designed to be a remarkably simple procedure. It was quick and painless and took no more than two hours to complete. In fact, the actual implantation only took about 15 minutes. The rest of the time consisted of observation and synchronizing the newly implanted chip to the system. The only side effects were four stitches and a slight ringing in the ears, which usually lasted no more than a few days.

Because of the ThinkTech chip; remotes, buttons, switches, and even doorknobs became obsolete. Now, if you wanted something done, you simply thought it and the corresponding ThinkTech technology would respond; from the simple action of opening a window to the more impressive task of controlling a vehicle. ThinkTech evolved in such a fashion that within no time it made all other technologies seem primitive.

People lined up outside for days in any temperature to be the first in line to get the implant. Even those with less available income managed to acquire one thanks to convenient payment plans. Chip installment appointments were scheduled months in advance and if you did not have one, you were soon in the minority.

Within no time, businesses switched over to the ThinkTech system, requiring a chip simply to enter certain establishments or to continue their employment. Soon, the chip became obligatory as everything was quickly becoming synched to ThinkTech technology. Without a chip, you were rendered helpless, unable to activate or access much of anything.

There remained a small group of skeptics who had opted out of getting a chip. They stood by warily, watching as ThinkTech monopolized the industry. These skeptics had been silenced by the hype, though we would soon find out that it would've been in everyone's best interest to heed their warnings.

We soon became victims of our circumstances, confirming that their suspicions had been warranted. As with any technology, there is room for malfunction or malware, and like anything computerized, it can be hacked. That being said, we learned the hard way that ThinkTech technology was no different.

It began so subtly that no one batted an eye. Murder, even mass murders, were a common occurrence in the news. As unfortunate and heartbreaking as it was, it had become the norm. The news was filled with reports of chaos and destruction. We continued our lives like we always had; if you were directly affected you did your best to heal and move on. If you were not, you paid your condolences and were grateful that it hadn't happened to you.

Over time, claims surfaced that some people had done things they couldn't remember doing, and hadn't meant to do, such as transferring funds or unwittingly turning off their home security systems. They blamed the chip claiming it must be defective. These complaints were promptly squashed and ThinkTech representatives released a statement categorically denying any responsibility. They blamed people for misuse of their product, re-emphasizing the quality of their business and the trust they had gained.

These allegations and events were merely the tip of the iceberg. In the months that followed, while that same small group of skeptics watched from the sidelines in dismay, their suspicions were confirmed. It was one thing to suspect problems, but quite another to watch them manifest.

MARCH
A rash of unlikely people, without any prior record or involvement in criminal activity, suddenly began committing crimes. It wasn't strange because it was so out of character for the perpetrators, it was strange because of the sophisticated, well-thought-out manner in which the offenses were made. It was as if these former law-abiding citizens had been secretly

masterminding criminal plans, which they then executed with ease, in flawless, *meticulous* detail.

These were everyday people; a friendly mail carrier, an amateur photographer, a volunteer firefighter with four kids, a retired cat enthusiast, and a recent high school graduate who was working at a local store. Even more peculiar, they'd only been caught because they'd turned themselves in. They'd walked right into a police station after realizing they'd somehow committed a crime. In fact, they claimed that although they had taken some items and money, they had no control over their actions and no recollection of what they had done with the items. People chalked it up to people doing weird things; another story on the news, another article in the paper, and everyone continued living their lives without giving these events a second thought.

APRIL
Two politicians were found guilty of leaking classified information to a known threat. They too, made claims of not being able to recall their actions. No one believed them. After all, most politicians are notoriously corrupt.

MAY
A platoon of soldiers on a mission to extract a hostage lost contact with the command center for several hours. Nineteen out of the 20 soldiers along with the hostage were found miles away, travelling in the opposite direction from their post, without their equipment,

clothes, or any memory of what had occurred. It was theorized that the one missing soldier had been taken because he was the only one without a ThinkTech chip. However, since he was never recovered, that was never confirmed. Only ThinkTech knew for sure but refused to deny or confirm whether the missing soldier had a chip or not. They claimed it was irrelevant and against company policy to violate the privacy of their valued customers. Instead, ThinkTech offered their sincerest condolences for the unfortunate event. As a grand gesture in support of the military, they then donated a considerable sum to help fund a search mission. ThinkTech didn't stop there, they also donated money and a gift basket full of ThinkTech products to the missing soldier's family, which they signed:

"We are with you. Complements of ThinkTech. "

Reports flooded the news proclaiming how family-friendly ThinkTech is, and how they'd stepped up to support the troops in a crisis.

JUNE
A major infectious disease research lab went into lockdown after the chief scientist was found dead. It was reported that a co-worker found her unresponsive, lying on the floor of her laboratory. Security cameras showed her lab assistant strangling her before he stepped out of view of the camera.

The assistant was found two days later. He was arrested while casually stepping out of his vehicle as he arrived home, acting as if nothing happened. The bizarre nature of this crime became a major piece of gossip as people claimed it was the case of a lover scorned. It was quickly deemed a scandal and all anyone talked about. Rumor had it that a successful, married scientist at the height of her career had an affair in her government-funded lab, with her young research assistant. The news reports told of their many late nights conducting "intense research," which included studying each other's bodies. Some reports explaining the murder, indicated that the two of them had been caught having an affair only days before the murder. They reasoned that after being caught in the act, the lead scientist had immediately ended it. Then, her young lover, feeling used and betrayed, murdered her.

The prosecution ran with the story, describing it as the case of an assistant working across from his former lover. Humiliated and rejected, knowing that this was the closest he'd ever get to her again, "He lost it." They claimed that his emotions had gotten the best of him, and that the scientist had paid with her life.

The assistant however, plead not guilty. According to him, there wasn't any malice between them. The end of the affair had been mutual he explained, as they knew they both had to do what was best for their careers. Not only did he deny wanting her dead, he denied killing her altogether. The lab assistant swore that all he could remember was driving home after he'd gotten off work. No one believed him and with the video footage showing him assaulting her, it was an open and shut case. The jury quickly agreed on a verdict without much deliberation. He was found guilty!

Everyone had something to say about the case, everyone had an opinion. Some said it was one more terrible thing that happened to a woman who had everything going for her but had made a bad choice. Others said it was karma. Some were broken up about it, even if they hadn't known her directly. People claimed the allegations were false and that there hadn't been an affair at all. They said the situation had been severely misinterpreted, and that conclusions had been drawn before the trial. Her husband refused to acknowledge that there was any adultery and only spoke once, describing their marriage as strong and loving. He believed the whole tragic situation had caused a media frenzy, by spreading false rumors and slandering his late wife.

The husband wasn't far off. His wife's murder dominated the news. Debates ensued on the topic of; sexism, having an affair with a younger man, gender roles, societal double-standards, and workplace affairs. Special news reports filled primetime hours, featuring those closest to the victim, each speculating on the reasons behind the "affair."

Those closest to the suspect appeared dumbfounded as the press described someone completely different from the person they knew. Anyone who had regular contact with the victim and/or killer, or anyone who had even seen them in a room together, was interviewed. Then, as time went on, as with everything else, the story slowly faded into the background. Then, a co-worker unexpectedly came forward to tell her side of the story...

Millions watched as she appeared during a special report on live TV and declared: "Guilt has eaten me alive, and there's no amount of money worth me not being able to live with myself." The coworker confessed that she had lied. She then alleged that she'd been paid off by someone she refused to name. She said that she'd been the one to find the doctor on the floor. The doctor had no vital signs and that she was the one who'd called for an ambulance. She alleged that someone, had essentially paid her not to tell anyone what had really happened.

As it turns out, that same coworker had walked into the lab that morning and found the doctor slumped over a countertop, her white lab coat splashed with various shades of red, indicative of both wet and dry blood splatter. Horrible, deep wounds were gouged into her head and neck area, and a pair of scissors (which appeared to be the true murder weapon), lay close by. The otherwise spotless, sterile laboratory was covered in in bloody fingerprints.

The coworker then called for an ambulance, though she knew it was too late. Within minutes, three men in green jumpsuits arrived, confirming the doctor was indeed deceased. They then removed her body and cleaned up the mess. Then, a fourth man in a business suit, pulled the coworker aside and offered her a check, casually adding more zeros to the number with each protest.

All the man in the suit wanted in return, was for her to corroborate his version of what had happened. The coworker agreed but insisted that she'd only do so for the benefit of the victim's family. She wanted to spare them the horror of the gory scene that would now haunt her. At the time, she believed she'd done the right thing, but now realized the family deserved to know the truth.

Everyone was in an uproar once again as the coworker's confession elevated the scandal to a completely different level. The murder was no longer considered the result of a shameful affair and crime of passion, it was now thought to be entangled in some sort of cover-up. The attorney general called for a re-opening of the investigation and that every part of the case be doubled-checked even going so far as requiring that all witnesses be thoroughly interviewed again.

The conversation suddenly shifted as people wondered: If there was in fact a cover-up, and if so, who was behind it and why? Anyone not paying attention to the case before, was definitely paying attention to it now. The public was on edge, wondering what might be divulged next.

Then, KBBR news announced they were going to host a national news Special Report. They would be airing an exclusive live interview with the medical examiner who'd performed the deceased doctor's autopsy. A short yet alluring snippet of the interview ran during every news break, showing enough to pique interest and remind us to tune in...

A woman's voice off camera asks, "We were told that the cause of death was due to strangulation. Are you saying it was not?"

The medical examiner sits, fidgeting under a spotlight. "Asphyxiation was indeed the cause of death, but we now know that a stabbing occurred postmortem."

"Stabbing? There was nothing indicating a stabbing in any of the paperwork completed at the scene nor by you, the medical examiner," said the off-camera reporter matter-of-factly.

The fidgety examiner, wiping large beads of sweat from his brow, replies: "Yes, yes, I know. I was asked not to record it." He then swallows hard as if he'd taken a huge gulp of water. He continues, "they literally paid me for my silence, but I really believe the truth must come out."

The trailer ended with a fade-to-black, complete with dramatic music and details of the date and time the interview would air. Everyone waited in suspense as they watched the commercial for the millionth time, wondering who had paid the examiner for his silence. And what was it he was now so adamant about disclosing?

By 8:00 pm the following Thursday, most people had completely cleared their schedules in order to catch the much-anticipated broadcast. By 7:30 pm, most people were already planted in front of their televisions or watching their phone screens, ready and eagerly awaiting the answer to the question they'd heard loop that entire week.

Then, 8 o'clock came... and went. Disappointment is an inadequate term to describe what people felt when at precisely 8 pm, all TV screens tuned to Channel KBBR suddenly went blank. Disappointment soon turned to frustration then irritation. When 8:30 rolled around and still nothing, everyone sat in the desolate glow of disbelief. Some switched to other stations to make sure it wasn't their connection that was faulty.
It wasn't the connection.
It was indeed Channel KBBR. All other channels were airing as usual.

An hour later, while still commanding the highest viewership in the country, millions held out hope for the

promised broadcast. As they watched their screens,
large letters suddenly appeared across the blank screen:

*KBBR TELEVISION WOULD LIKE TO APOLOGIZE
AS WE ARE CURRENTLY EXPERIENCING
TECHNICAL DIFFICULTIES*

The message outraged millions as it went on to indicate
that KBBR techs were, "currently handling the critical
situation," and that the previously scheduled broadcast
would air the next day. That night many fell asleep right
there in front of their TV screens, holding out hope that
the difficulties would be repaired sooner than estimated.
They weren't.

The apologetic message scrolled on a loop until the
following morning. By then, the majority of the
population was already engaged in the new day's
activities. Only a few noticed the channel reactivating at
10 am. A new message appeared briefly stating:

*WE ARE HAPPY TO ANNOUNCE THAT THINKTECH
HAS ACQUIRED EXCLUSIVE RIGHTS
TO OWN AND OPERATE CHANNEL KBBR*

The official announcement stated: *ThinkTech graciously
bought Channel KBBR to prevent any more technical
issues. ThinkTech believes that people deserve access to
reliable information. ThinkTech makes it their mission to*

provide people with the best of everything, in the same
way they have always done with all their products.

That day, the newly acquired Channel KBBR followed up
on the highly anticipated report. However, the "Special
Report" ended up going in a vastly different direction
than the previews had suggested.

KBBR anchors explained: being that technical difficulties
delayed the anticipated special's original air date and
time, there had been room for further investigation. Of
course, no one mentioned that Channel KBBR had been
mysteriously acquired by ThinkTech prior to the
originally scheduled broadcast, thus making them
complicit in regards to the "blackout/technical
difficulties." Further reports suggested that ThinkTech
hired a private investigator. Motivated and funded by
ThinkTech money, the investigator had thankfully
uncovered a devious scheme in the works.

The investigation revealed, reported the TV anchor, that
the co-worker and medical examiner were a couple and
that they were complicitly working together to draft a
book about the events that had occurred at the research
lab. After all, the heinous workplace murder and scandal
had rendered the lab inoperative and compromised
precious time designated for important research.
Funding had come to a complete halt and employees
were being deemed "unnecessary for operations." Both
the co-worker and the examiner feared their careers

would be tainted by association. They needed another way to secure their financial future—a tell-all account of the whole situation—and for the story to become lucrative, they needed *publicity*. That was the sole reason the co-worker confessed when and how she did. That's why, when the attention died down, the medical examiner came forward to drum up more. The investigator declared, "It had simply been a Public Relations stunt on the pair's behalf."

The story wasn't quite what everyone had expected. The medical examiner had seemed so sincere about revealing some great message to the people. Hadn't he genuinely wanted to unearth a hidden agenda? Or was his pending "revelation" really a con?

People demanded answers. Other news stations assured the public their reporters were conducting their own investigation and interviews and that they were fact-checking what ThinkTech's KBBR television network had brought to light. Other channels raced to gather more information, trying to outdo each other with endless rounds of "evidence" and "exclusives." With so much free publicity, ThinkTech's first acquired channel became an instant success.

It was the beginning of a new era of television programming. ThinkTech began acquiring additional networks. Soon, some genius in the marketing department came up with a points program that tracked screeners' watch time, rewarding them with exclusive deals and discounted prices. It was easy to enroll in the program and all a viewer needed to do was upgrade their personal chip, then link their account exclusively to local ThinkTech channels. Then interactive channels were added to the points program, revolutionizing screening.

It was a perfect marketing plan and a win-win for the consumer. Everyone knew ThinkTech was all about innovation and customer satisfaction. What could be more satisfying than getting paid to do something you love? The points program validated each hour a person spent immersed in ThinkTech technology. Soon, channels and shows that did not award points became virtually extinct. ThinkTech was the most fun way to screen, and also the most rewarding. It was an offer impossible to pass up.

AUGUST
A global pandemic blanketed the planet. People got sick in record numbers, terrifying communities and baffling doctors and scientists alike. The rapidly spreading virus was unlike anything they'd seen before. The CDC moved quickly, searching through old files and documenting cases that might reveal something they may have missed.

New strains of illness are not uncommon. They can be prepared for, though some lives may be lost in the process. Sickness is a situation we were familiar with. We often heard on the news that a certain number of people had died due to a new strain of flu or the latest disease carried into our region from afar. We were used to reports of deaths due to a new virus or to contaminated food. With a population of billions, a few million lives lost hardly made a dent.

Still, diseases have a way of evolving, no matter how we study and analyze them. At first, the CDC recommended vaccinations, and reiterated common sense actions like washing hands and avoiding contact with the afflicted. We had cured diseases before. We had developed complex vaccines and eliminated life-altering ailments out of existence. We knew that eventually, this latest virus, like so many before it, would pass.

It didn't.

Unlike most situations in life, illness does not discriminate. Sickness affects the young and the elderly alike. It does not consider gender, culture, economic status or religion. It simply targets biological cells. The pandemic quickly spread like wildfire. The government began imposing quarantines and restricting travel to gain some form of control over the spread. Diseases long dormant seemed to explode to life before our eyes. Smallpox. Yellow fever. Polio.
Outbreaks like these had been virtually eradicated, even in developing nations. Yet here we were suddenly faced

with devastating illnesses. People were dropping like flies. Gloves and face masks became the latest fashion trend. Physical contact of any kind was a risk no one could afford to take. People weren't only calling in sick, they were calling in to avoid getting sick, and consequently, businesses took major losses. We were floored, confused and concerned for our future.

No one could quite pinpoint what was going on. News reports were vague, and the information provided to us was minimal. The public was scared and preoccupied, and the CDC claimed to be uninformed too. The ailment was a nightmare cocktail of the worst illnesses to have ever devastated the population. The pandemic seemed like a form of biological warfare. It attacked the cells in a way never before seen. It grew, changed and exhibited unusual characteristics in everyone it affected. There was no pattern. No two cases were alike. It was as if the disease was intelligent, and had already cultivated immunities to our antibodies only to resurface in another place with a stronger attack strategy.

We watched in horror as the virus was soon described as the "super plague." It took our loved ones from us in record numbers through a combination of aching, fever, paralysis, and the inability to eat. Organs shut down one by one, and people suffered until their very last breath.

Outside the city limits lived that same small group of skeptics. They hadn't labeled themselves though city people referred to them as, "Opt-Outs," because they'd all opted out of getting a ThinkTech chip implanted. Though they lived without the most recent technological updates, technology was not totally absent from their lives.

Ours was a throwaway culture, and the Opt-Outs took full advantage of that. They were not linked to ThinkTech products like most people were, so older devices were perfectly acceptable to them. They surrounded themselves with discarded devices. They had a lot more time on their hands and possessed natural abilities. Some had engineering backgrounds cultivated when they lived and functioned within the city limits. They repurposed parts and devices to make living on the outskirts most comfortable.

Most Opt-Outs were well off. Their off-the-grid lifestyle encouraged them to be self-reliant and inventive. They produced their own energy through solar power and generators made from scraps. Fortunately for them, what others considered junk, became valuable in supporting their anti-ThinkTech lifestyle. Many of them had been farmers who planted crops and owned livestock. The Opt-Outs had learned to be self-sufficient.

While they weren't above going to the city when they needed something, it had become difficult to access certain places. Recent trips to the city had highlighted limited access to people without an updated ThinkTech chip. The Opt-Outs were not tempted. They'd rather make what they needed or go without, rather than risk getting the chip.

While city-dwellers feared contamination and those in charge sought to eradicate the virus, the Opt-Outs continued to build their community. They built strong foundations and used every bit of technology they could repurpose. Without the chip, they managed to obtain amenities associated with luxury, without the danger of contagion. Despite a few cases of the common cold and a case or two of the flu, the Opt-Outs hadn't experienced any of what the main population had.

The "super plague" racked up an incredibly significant death toll in the short time it had been present, yet the Opt-Outs were somehow immune. How had they remained untouched by the virus or mass death in their small community? It was an enigma. They had on occasion, been in contact with the mainstream population, but still managed to escape infection. How? Everyone wanted to know.

As the surrounding population disintegrated like sugar in water, the truth began to surface. None of the events that had transpired over the past few months had been isolated incidents. Someone had been hacking us. They had been slowly playing with the chip, learning its capabilities, deciphering its codes, and inputting their own.

The mass murders had been a well-placed distraction. Each time, the public was stricken by the cruel behavior of a depraved murderer. We mourned the losses and empathized with the bereaved. Each event became the object of our focus, taking over the newscasts, blogs, talk shows, and radio. Everything else was placed on the back burner.

We frequently held moments of silence to unite as a nation. As a people, we simply stopped questioning, asking or investigating the harder questions.

As time passed, we became clearer-headed and started to question our governments' actions once again. We began to pay more attention to what was happening abroad and began to debate and pick things apart. Every time, as if by some grand coincidence, another mass murder would occur to distract us. Countless innocent deaths, all diverting us from what was before our very eyes—or to be literal, what was behind the murders.

It was the chip.

The chip had been hot-wired to be a distraction while, ThinkTech studied what more it might be capable of. Every time we grew suspicious of something, or started to seek the truth, another mass murder would occur. Each one worse than the previous, having the most injuries and the highest mortality rate.

All of this had been purposefully orchestrated. It had to be more drastic than anything that had taken place before in order to guarantee our immediate attention, reactions and responses, and most importantly, to cause us to lose focus.

We hadn't realized that the chip was capable of so much more than its ability to work electronics. Its technology went far beyond providing us with a more leisurely life. In fact, the chip could be reversed in our direction and in the same way we used it to control objects and machinery, it could be reprogramed to control us.

The emergence of mass murders was only the beginning. It only required the emission of a tiny signal to prompt selected individuals to cause mayhem. Each terrifying event needed to be more tragic than the one before. That way, the public became side-tracked deterring them from natural curiosity. After all, an appalling act deserved our attention as we became caught up in how important it was to reach out with our deepest condolences. As a show of respect, our focus became directed toward our peers and fellow community members. Every time we did so, ThinkTech got back to work, unnoticed.

March rolled around, and the people we least expected, appeared to be executing covert missions better suited to a spy movie. "Stranger things have happened," Is all they said when something couldn't be explained. That's exactly what they told us about the recent slew of strange incidents...

Four completely normal people with no history of training or knowledge of computer programming had actually hacked into the system. They cracked open safes and obtained secured property with ease, bypassing first alarms as well as back-up alarms without effort. No one would've discovered what had happened if they hadn't eventually confessed.

Stranger things have indeed happened. We weren't paying as much attention as we should have been. Instead of truly investigating the depth of what had really occurred, people shrugged it off as an odd series of occurrences. The general consensus was that, "criminals can emerge from unlikely places." Of course, the underlying stimulus ran much deeper than we were even aware of. We knew these acts of violence and theft were well out of character for the perpetrators particularly because of their lack of past criminal behavior. We'd heard that, "a bit of money and a few secured items had been stolen." A vague statement circulating which made the events seem less significant than they were.

We were purposefully given a fraction of the story. The government didn't want us to know the details and it quickly became obvious that they did not take kindly to follow-up questions. They claimed that the public couldn't be trusted with sensitive information without inciting panic. So, our government decided it best to leave out important details in press releases. They assumed that if we knew what had been stolen, we'd have concerns and questions officials weren't ready to answer.

The missing items had been thoroughly investigated, far more intensely than the public knew. The government put the four so-called "criminals" through the ringer in hopes of recovering the missing goods. They gave each a lie-detector test and interrogated them in ways only money can silence. None of them could remember a thing about stolen goods, nor about what they had done with them. The officials didn't care. Instead, they ransacked their homes, businesses, and vehicles in an attempt to find the "stolen goods." Every device they owned was inspected for any clues that might link them to the crime and to where the items were hidden. It was one dead end after another, and despite a rigorous investigation, they failed to find what they were looking for.

When the public started pressing officials for more answers about what had been stolen, another mass murder took place, conveniently diverting our attention once again. After all, some measly stolen items weren't nearly as important nor as interesting as live coverage on the tragic loss of life? Everything paled in comparison, which is exactly the reaction officials had hoped for.

Mission accomplished: we'd stopped asking what had gone missing, otherwise, the government would've been forced to tell us about the medical records, the footage of ThinkTech product testing, and the stolen data related to chip installation fails. Instead, they continued to hide the fact that they'd lost the chip prototypes and detailed lists of projects in the works. Additionally, though less significant, millions of dollars had also been taken.

It's no surprise that in April, when two politicians were found guilty of leaking information, we didn't think twice? We'd become so used to corruption in government. Nothing about crooked politicians surprised us anymore. We continued on with our lives, and didn't even ask what had been leaked. We were satisfied by the fact that some were finally being held responsible for their scheming and dishonesty. All we wanted was for them to serve time like common criminals, instead of receiving the usual slap on the wrist. We felt a sense of satisfaction seeing politicians punished in the same way the rest of us were. After all, they were not above the law and our sense of vindication outweighed our curiosity regarding the sensitive information they had brought forth.
We should have asked more questions. Instead, we were completely focused on their convictions and on the fact that they had committed a crime. They needed to pay their dues. Because of that, we never truly looked into what sort of files had been given away, nor to whom

they'd been given, or for what purpose. Not that the government would've told us about their top-secret contract with ThinkTech related to chip studies and military operations.

Perhaps the contract, otherwise known as *Operation: Good Soldier,* seemed like a good idea at the time. They'd reportedly been conducting studies using the chip and quietly working on a way to cure PTSD. They'd had the best intentions... but we all know that the best intentions pave the road to hell.

It didn't take long for researchers to realize the true potential of the chip. Initially, they claimed to have resolve PTSD by programming the chip to make soldiers forget traumatizing events they'd witnessed in the field. Unfortunately, the chip was the very reason a platoon of soldiers had led such a strange mission in May. They'd rescued a hostage but lost everything else, including a fellow soldier and any memory of the mission. Still, we didn't ask a lot of questions. We all knew that soldiers sometimes conduct missions where they incur casualties or end up with some missing in action. It was sad, but it was a reality. Soldiers knew the dangers when they signed up, and their families knew too. While everyone hopes for the best outcome, it isn't a surprise when we lose a soldier. It's an unfortunate casualty of war. People grieve and then they move on the best they can.

No one bothered to ask how in the world a soldier had suddenly gone missing outside the combat zone. Nor had anyone asked how 19 people could be redirected, while not a single one of them remembered anything about the events that occurred. This is partly why experimental chip research and the top-secret contract between ThinkTech and the United States military, remained a secret.

ThinkTech had worked hard to maintain their trusted reputation. They could not afford to be associated with controversy that might draw negative publicity. They had to bury the situation and the soldier as soon and as deeply as possible.

Money has a way of producing vague details. Even morally sound people quiet down for the right price. In a Public Relations move, ThinkTech reportedly donated funds to aid in the search for the missing soldier. They made sure the public knew how sympathetic they were to his grieving family. Behind closed doors however, they were much less personable, letting their lawyers and finances do the talking. The public was never told they'd found the missing soldier's body. Instead, ThinkTech paid off those in the know, in exchange for keeping the secret. Whenever anyone asked questions, they were answered in the form of a generous banknote.

Perhaps the family was not so easy to convince but the ThinkTech gift basket and free chip upgrades were a great start. They gladly accepted, and afterward were much easier to persuade. Maybe they, as with the soldiers, had been programmed to misplace certain memories and information.

Everything was lining up with one newsworthy event leading into the other. In March, the four newest offenders obtained government information and embezzled money to fund research. In April, two politicians leaked information about a top-secret contract between the US military and ThinkTech Industries. This led to May's loss of a soldier and his chip. Then came the month of June.

The researcher's murder had been portrayed as a lover's quarrel and a heat-of-the-moment murder. But it was so much more. Before we became distracted by the ultimate screening innovation, we had been in awe of the initial story. We thought we had been given all the facts. We knew of the alleged affair and we believed that the cause of death was strangulation. We had been convinced that the information brought forward by the dead woman's co-worker and the medical examiner was motivated by financial gain. We had specifics about the adulterous relationship and had heard the opinions of those closest to the victim. These things kept us pre-occupied so we wouldn't notice the other very significant things that were happening.

We really didn't know much. We were clueless about the details of the murder and the conditions in which the doctor had really been found. We didn't know the actual condition of the lab nor had we been privy to the results of the autopsy.

Our government clearly did not want us common folk to know the extent of the brutality or reasoning behind it all. The deceased scientist's coworker hadn't lied. She had indeed found the doctor slumped over a countertop in the laboratory. As she'd previously indicated, the doctor had been repeatedly stabbed in the neck and head area without any obvious explanation. As the medical examiner tried to tell us later on, the stabbing occurred postmortem with the sole purpose of removing her chip. The coworker had called an ambulance, but the ambulance had not come. A cleanup crew arrived instead, erasing the victim's presence and minimizing the violence of the situation by cleaning up the lab and paying off the only two witnesses—the coworker and the medical examiner.

We thought we had seen the entire crime on video, but they hadn't showed us all the footage. We also assumed the whole video had been shown at the trial. After all, we'd seen the lab assistant assault the unsuspecting doctor as she cleaned the countertop. He'd firmly grabbed her around the neck and though she fought back, he easily got the upper hand. Then he stepped out of the camera's sight, dragging her with him.

What we did not see, was the way the lab assistant stabbed her with surgical precision. He searched for her chip beneath blood and tissue, opening the wound enough to pull it out with his fingers. He then slipped the chip into a small case. Then the lab assistant—a man who swore continuously that he had no recollection of his crime—callously wipes his bloodied hands on the counter and on his pants, then casually walks out.

We should have noticed that memory loss was a common factor in each case. Maybe some of us did, especially the soldiers, the four criminals, and the lab assistant who all swore they couldn't recall anything that had happened. Even after being relentlessly interrogated and put through a series of investigative tactics, they had come up with absolutely nothing. All signs pointed to a form of amnesia. Then there was the missing researcher's chip. It had to be of significant value given the chip had been stolen, then mysteriously "misplaced."

Looking back, it's obvious that this was a conspiracy theorist's wet dream. A series of elaborate cover-ups hiding something unbelievable, yet terrifyingly true. The Opt-Outs had been labeled "crazy" which was an effective tactic in discrediting them. They must have found it bittersweet, when their fears were validated and their worst nightmares came true.

Hush money closes mouths and prevents thorough investigations, but it can't stop the inevitable. Everything done in darkness eventually comes to light and it was finally becoming obvious that ThinkTech was behind it all. They'd concealed theft and murder, but despite their best efforts, they could not hide what happened in August.

The stature and severity of the "super plague" brought everything into the light. Life quickly lost its day-to-day pleasures and excitement. Instead, it became about surviving, or hoping to survive, while watching everyone around you suffer and die. The super plague was beyond any disease we'd ever known. Public health leaders and laboratories pushed research to figure out a viable cure (or at least something to alleviate the erratic symptoms), until they'd exhausted all possibilities. Many became self-motivated to find a cure. They pulled out all the stops to save those closest to them and prevent the world from crumbling at their feet. Despite vigilant attempts and sincere efforts, it was to no avail.

At first, ThinkTech remained one step ahead with damage control. In fact, the pandemic had barely begun when ThinkTech suddenly rolled out vaccination trials, opening clinics and offering home visits to customers immobilized by the illness. Yet, ThinkTech's bottomless pockets and ability to make facts disappear began losing power. People were beginning to realize what was really going on and that ThinkTech was behind all of it.

We soon discovered that the super plague was no germ. The contagion—the hack, really was a virus, a literal virus, translated to our body via the very chip we'd allowed them to implant into us. It programmed our bodies and our brains to believe that we were too sick to be cured. We finally realized that we'd lost control of our thoughts and impulses. We had been allowing the chip to do most of our thinking, and now we knew we were no longer in control of ourselves, and it terrified us.

The super plague was essentially internal biological warfare, which we had facilitated. We were the ones who lined up for ThinkTech and their products. We had practically volunteered to be pawns for those who had hacked ThinkTech's chips. We were happy to have a chip that promised to make our lives easier. All it had to do was read our brain waves as code and respond accordingly, then send a message to the corresponding equipment. Making the chip work for us did not require much effort. It took about as much thought as any other involuntary action; like breathing or sneezing, and the more one performed an action, the easier it became. The chip learned our mannerisms, habits and schedules. It stored our preferences and learned everything about each host so it could suggest things it knew we'd respond to. We lived in unison with it, happy when the chip predicted our next thought before we even thought it.

Unfortunately, it turned out that hacking the chips was relatively easy. Tech savvy nerds had hacked into them many times before, though never to this extent. The hackers had somehow programmed our own cells to attack us and become unresponsive to the vaccinations. The chip controlled our bodies, while the program compromised our immunities. We became susceptible to anything and everything. Even simple seasonal allergies became fatal. We were at a loss. What could we do? The attack was coming from within.

It became a crisis far beyond what ThinkTech's hush money could cover. It quickly became clear that finding a cure was in ThinkTech's best interests, and their self-motivated "charity" became their lifeline. ThinkTech's owners and employees may have lived in the lap of luxury, but they were as susceptible to the super plague as everyone else. ThinkTech could not sell products or provide services to a non-existent population. They couldn't profit from corpses or bribe people that did not exist. If we were dying, and ThinkTech was left lording its power over a shrinking population, it would be nothing more than a hollow victory.

SEPTEMBER
ThinkTech announced a plan to remove malfunctioning hardware free of charge. To make the process easier, they created a lottery to determine who would get their chip removed first. It was to be a random draw, and everyone eagerly waited to hear their name called.

It was a lovely, inviting day. The warm sun shone vibrantly from above. Shade was scarce, but the heat was mild and there was a refreshing breeze. Even the birds were singing a rare tune, though no one noticed. The people who were left sat inside, wide-eyed and desperate in front of their screens as they waited for the announcement. Who would be among the first 50 to be called?

In any other context, 50 would have seemed like an insignificant number, but with so few people and only five official cities left, 50 appeared to be a fair start. With rapidly declining populations of under 500 people per city, the chance of your name being called seemed possible.

People had forgotten what it was like to be hopeful. The lottery filled that hollowness with something to look forward to—a chance. The battle against the super plague had been grim. ThinkTech engineers had written a counter program that slowed the deathly illness caused by the hacked chips, but slowing the process was hardly the same as a cure. It was not good news; it was simply less-bad news. But now there was a plan to use the counter program to hold the virus at bay, until ThinkTech removed the faulty chips. That was good news, and the public welcomed it. We needed it.

Those of us in the last existing communities hoped this was the answer to getting everything back to normal. The lottery was random, so it was fair. It did not depend on how far along you were in your sickness. If you had a chip, you were eligible.

And so, the first 50 names—10 names in each city—were called out on the last live news streams. Shortly after the broadcast, those randomly selected people received a call with details about when ThinkTech would pick them up, and what they should bring with them etc. A few people in that first 50 were so debilitated by sickness that their loved ones had to prepare them for the journey.

The chosen 50 were then brought to their local ThinkTech compound. Every one of them underwent the "corrective removal procedure" by official, accredited ThinkTech surgeons. The procedure was a delicate, month-long process involving precise surgery, recovery, observation, and rehabilitation.

As soon as the chip was removed, everyone in that first group, including those seemingly on their deathbed, seemed to be recuperating well. It was as if they had gotten over nothing more than a simple flu bug. Although there remained some physical damage, it didn't seem likely to be for the long term. With the chip gone, people needed to retrain their brains to be the primary source of thought and relearn the simple actions the chip had taken over. It wasn't that people had lost their physical ability to perform actions such as turning a doorknob or twisting on a faucet but rather, they had to relearn how to connect their thoughts to their bodies. With the help of the chip, people had gotten into the habit of simply thinking about doing things, but not actually doing them. Whereas their pre-chip brain could send a message and have their body respond in less than a second, it took up to a half hour for their bodies to relearn to do so after the chip was removed. Even when it did respond, it now took much more effort and concentration to perform the simplest of tasks.

The human brain is not a muscle, but it does behave like one. Each of the 50 went through weeks of physical and mental rehabilitation to reclaim their brains. There was a rumor that people were actually able to smile again, showing teeth and all. Once ThinkTech's therapists and researchers were confident their patients were doing well, they publicly confirmed that we were headed in the right direction. We had fought this literal virus issue and we were winning.

We truly needed that victory. It had been so long since people had hope and the will to move forward. They had lost all motivation. The virus claimed so many lives, leaving those behind to drudge along from one moment to the next, wondering when their own chip might malfunction. Most of us were not really living anymore; we were simply waiting for our number to be up. Now, we were waiting for our number to be up in a whole different way. We could be fixed. We could still have a future.

So, we enthusiastically awaited the next lottery.

The second set of 50 were chosen using the same framework; the drawing, the announcement of names, the follow-up informational phone call, the pickups, followed by an all-expense-paid month-long stay at the local ThinkTech compound.

This time however, two lives were lost during surgery, but we thought nothing of it. We knew they had gone in very sickly and weak. It was unfortunate they had been incapable of handling the stress of surgery, but with the massive number of lives lost during the year, two lost was nothing to dwell on. The other 48 went through procedural rehabilitation then were sent home. ThinkTech announced their progress, along with the date of the next lottery.

It was time for the third group of 50 to be drawn when, to everyone's shock and dismay, people from the second group began to show a resurgence of super plague symptoms. ThinkTech postponed the lottery and launched an investigation into how it was possible for people to still be affected once the chip was removed. They asked us to be patient.

But we had changed. We were no longer solemn, numb, melancholy drones awaiting the inevitable. No sir. We had regained a sense of hope. We had been shown it was possible for things to return to some sense of normalcy. To have that taken away from us now, was driving even the sanest of us out of our minds. People were becoming hysterical and panicky. There was a spike in the number of suicides, and several accidental deaths from people attempting their own chip removals. You can imagine how an untrained hand removing an implant from the brain caused havoc. People spilled their own blood and the death toll rose.

ThinkTech tried desperately to reassure us we were still headed in the direction of progress. With their sketchy past of cover-ups and half-truths, it was hard for people to take comfort in their words. It was not long before the riots began, emphasizing public distrust in the ThinkTech brand. Desperate, ThinkTech ignored good taste and good sense, and continued with the drawing, even as the number of survivors from the second group shrunk to only six.

Of course, ThinkTech's spokespersons couldn't tell us that their "at bay" program was failing. The virus was becoming stronger and had somehow learned to download the sickness into our DNA so that we would still suffer even after the chip was removed. With everyone panicking, ThinkTech clamped down on that piece of terrifying information, and moved forward with the next lottery, all the while reassuring people that they were making progress.

The riots stopped as soon as the next group of 50 was drawn. In the background, ThinkTech diligently worked to slow, if not stop, the chips' malware from being downloaded into the hosts' DNA. Their efforts seemed to pay off. The third group of 50 was a success. The new program had stopped the download, so there weren't any cases of sickness after the operation. The fourth group was as successful.

Everyone was in high spirits again, something so rare in those days. After the success of the third and fourth groups, it was all anyone could do to wait for their chance. We'd seen that, no matter how far the sickness had gone, you would be fine once the chip was removed. Morale was a thing again. Everyone was optimistic and everyone was ready.

The fifth group of 50 was drawn, gathered, and brought to the laboratories. Success had changed the atmosphere. Everyone was less somber and less cynical. ThinkTech's malware protection had been quite successful in inhibiting the download of the sickness into the DNA before the chip was removed. People were encouraged that normalcy seemed like a possibility again.

Then, like rain on a festive parade, the doctors began the fifth round of surgeries and made a gut-wrenching discovery. The chip had somehow been updated. Instead of downloading sickness, the chip was now programmed to burrow itself deeper into the brain making the removal fatal.

This changed everything. We'd lost what little time we'd had on our side. Things needed to be accelerated. Those who were not so far along in their super plague symptoms had to be x-rayed immediately to see if their chip was even accessible anymore. Removal surgeries were no longer precise, time-consuming processes with recovery and rehabilitation. The process turned into an assembly line of desperate hack jobs. Four cities soon became three, and those with burrowed chips turned to suicide instead of painful suffering.

Through it all, the Opt-Outs remained healthy and productive. They could have never predicted that their wariness towards the implant would turn into their best defense for survival. Most were not conspiracy theorists who had planned to live off the grid, they were simply a small group of people with shared ideas on invasive technology and biological upgrades. Their isolation had been more of an accident and happy coincidence.

Soon, and thankfully for us, they began taking in those whose chips had been successfully removed.

I continued reading, not realizing how invested I was. I hadn't noticed my grandmother enter the room, much less sneak up on me until she ripped the book from my hands. Her face said it all, but she continued anyway,

"Do you realize how serious this is? You do know that your sister could lose her rank if she gets caught sharing something from the Level 3 library with you, right? Do you realize how much trouble *I* could be in, finding you with a Level 3 book and not reporting you? Lenore Rose, you cannot continue to put me in these situations!"

It was her use of my full name that drove me nuts. "Nor, Grandma, just Nor," I grudgingly corrected for the millionth time.

"Well, *Lenore Rose*, I will refer to you by the name my daughter gave you, thank you very much."

All I could do was sigh as she used that line every time, and every time it worked. It remains that she had caught me red-handed. Unfortunately, I knew my sister was going to be next to let me have it since she hadn't exactly loaned me the book.

Obviously, I never intended to get anyone in trouble, however, I was not the best at expressing myself, so instead, I stomped my foot and whined. "But they're not

books, they're journals! They are your journals which makes them mine too! Why can't I read them?"
I followed it up with another stomp and then I crossed my arms over my chest. I realized how I ridiculous I looked, but I was that frustrated. I bit my lip to keep the words, "it's not fair," from escaping, making myself look worse.

My grandmother's bushy eyebrows were furrowed, so I already knew what was coming next. "Do I really need to explain protocol to you again Level 1?" She scolded me, then immediately assumed *the* stance, which I instinctively followed. "Because I can assign points for you having this," she pointed towards the journal still tightly in her grip, "but I thought that after your recent demotion you wouldn't want that... "

"No, assigning points will not be necessary Madam Elder Level 4. My apologies," I interrupted the lecture that I knew by heart and saved myself from an hour at least.
I broke my stance. "I hadn't realized we were ranking at home," I mostly mumbled under my breath.

"Oh, Lenore Rose," she chuckled, "it's always been this way. You the granddaughter, me the grandmother. I've always outranked you, even, no especially at home," then gave me that smile causing me to forgive her instantly.

I only had myself to blame for my current demotion in rank, until the probationary period was up. My grandmother always said I was so busy trying to be Level 4 that I was missing the significance of the first three, whatever that meant. It didn't really matter since I hadn't made it past Level 2 yet. I wished that I could age out and learn everything, but that wasn't how it worked. It wasn't about age, it was about "effort". It was an entire system set up against me and any question I had.

"Protocol." Protocol, that word had been used so many times it had lost all meaning for me. It was the answer to everything and yet it answered absolutely nothing. Protocol meant you weren't getting a real answer and you had to accept it for what it was. What was wrong with asking "why?" It seemed to be a worse word than a dirty one. Most levels never cared enough to assign points for language but ask why and you were given double.

I was ready for my Rite of Passage, even if no one thought so. Okay, so I hadn't exactly proved it with model behavior, but I meant well. Falling in line without question wasn't exactly my style. I have an inquiring mind, what can I say? But I had intended on maybe watching my point intake and staying on track for the time being because getting demoted to Level 1 at my age was really embarrassing. The demotion was temporary, but it felt overwhelmingly permanent and binding especially when I was being given points by Level 2's, who were years my junior.

My grandmother must have sensed me pouting because she handed me the broom then touched my arm in that knowingly way. I watched her as she cleaned an already clean house and I humored her as I went through the motions myself, sweeping a spotless floor. I knew why she was really upset with me, even if she was making it about the book.

She vigorously and pointlessly scrubbed the stainless countertops. My grandmother was the epitome of size not determining strength. She claimed to be five feet tall and although we gave her credit for all sixty of those inches, we knew she fell a few inches shy. She was solid though, muscular, and very fit. She was an overachiever like my sister Annabel Lee. And like my sister they were similar in that they didn't only do what was asked of them, they went above and beyond. They didn't learn, they memorized. The ancient term "teacher's pet" suited them perfectly.

It was as if their training never ended. Even at home they had exercise routines and strict schedules. As an Elder grandma hadn't slowed down and though she was no longer in her glory days, her years of relentless work did her justice in her old age.

I pretended to sweep as she was yet again taking out her disappointment in me on household chores. I very well may have been the sole reason for our home's constant state of perfect cleanliness.

As she reorganized rations her long silver hair fell to the side revealing the scar behind her ear. Seeing it was so rare that my eyes were glued to it, examining it as much as I could while it was exposed. She detested it and did her best to make sure it was always hidden beneath hair, a hat or a scarf even while she was home so I almost never saw it.

She wasn't an original opt-out, she was part of the preceding group after chips had been removed.

Her scar embarrassed her, but having the chip was not a choice she'd made. It was her parents, my great grandparents, who gifted her with the chip and the scar was a constant reminder of everything from a former life.

I followed the shockingly fresh-looking pink zig-zag-like pattern with my eyes. The scar was about the length of her ear. The raised pale pink skin made it look new. It must've looked way worse fresh; and it must've been so painful.

Hers looked different from others because her chip hadn't been removed in the draw. She was one of many who risked their lives in back-alley surgeries during the frantic wait. Only she'd survived it. The rugged scar was evidence of that.

Her parents chose to chip her, but it was her who had it removed. I thought of how scary that must've been, especially where she must have had to go to get it done. I wondered if she had gone alone.

I was deep in my thoughts when she snapped around and shot me an ice-cold look as if she could feel me staring at it. She quickly tied a scarf around her head and went back to cleaning.

I couldn't blame her for wanting to disassociate from the past, we studied what she went through. It was sheer mayhem when ThinkTech chips began decoding into human DNA. It had been in response to successful removals.

The chips basically tunneled into the brain to avoid being removed. It was as though they had a mind of their own. No one knew what to do nor what to expect. It was crazy and what made it worse is that they couldn't be removed without the person dying. All anyone could do was wait to see what would happen next and what happened next was instant and all at once.

The chips simultaneously installed a program into the DNA. Those who still had chips essentially became robots. They became the shell of a person, the face of someone you knew, but not the mind or memories. They were no longer their former self. They no longer ate or slept. They didn't need to because they had been rewritten. I shuddered at the idea, especially when I thought of it from my grandmother's perspective.

We heard about what was happening, and though it was sad and all, it never really affected me on account of not knowing anyone out there. But she did. Plenty of Elder Level 4's did. I didn't envy them one bit. It must've been devastating to see people you knew and loved walking around aimlessly, a mere shell of their former selves.

They were referred to as, "P.O.D." Programmed Organic Droids. PODS, but we called them "the cleaners," because that's exactly what they did. In fact, that's really all they did. They cleaned, literally cleaning up the mess caused by thousands of years of pollution and waste from overpopulation. Day and night, one small area at a time, the PODS went through dumps and landfills, sorting, breaking things down, grouping them into reusables, recyclables and biodegradables.

Some PODS cleaned old, abandoned neighborhoods starting with the exterior then moving on to each individual house. When the cleaning was complete, they planted trees, bushes and flowers. It was a slow process, but PODS worked continuously without human limitations to slow them down.

They were correcting humanity's errors which seemed like a wonderful thing, except it included humanity itself. They cleaned everything, and that meant humanity's very existence.

Before people turned into PODS everyone still lived in their homes with family or friends, some of whom had chips and some without. When the program kicked in, it was a huge problem because those who were chipped began attacking and trying to kill anyone who wasn't. It didn't matter who you were or how old you were, anyone who'd had their chip removed was a target.

The PODS instantly turned from regular harmless cleaning folks to hunters whenever they caught sight or sound of an unchipped person. Once someone was on their radar, they wouldn't stop hunting them until they were dead.

For obvious reasons, it sent people into hiding, hence our heavily protected underground community. We were not to jeopardize our position in any way, which had everything to do with my recent demotion. I had been caught up on the surface, but luckily Annabel was the one who found me. How far I'd gotten had been left out of the report. When she turned me in, she downplayed the charges to: "attempting to go out." She was not about to lose her rank because of me, so there was no way I could get away with it completely. One thing for sure, I'd been given a lesser punishment thanks to details she'd held back.

Though I may not have been punished publicly to the extent I should've been, I was definitely enduring consequences to the full extent at home. Annabel made me earn her silence for sure by passing on to me any home task that would've been hers. She made sure I was at her beck and call. When she finally decided to relax each evening, she wouldn't get up for any reason. After all, that wasn't a problem since I could do or get anything she needed me to.

It often felt as though she'd purposely wait for me to be in the middle of something, to ask me to do something for her. She even had the nerve to give me that same smile grandma did to make me forget I was mad. There really was no reason to be mad since she was the one who'd saved me from further discipline. Plus, I couldn't exactly protest or make my punishment obvious when she pulled that card in front of my grandmother, which she did often. My grandma would have lost her mind if she'd known what I'd really done, which is probably the real reason Annabel left out the details.

Being her errand girl was nothing compared to the real hurdles in my way. Fetching warm socks and washing uniforms was the least of my concerns. I was more worried about getting back out on the surface. Getting caught meant I would be watched more closely, which made an already difficult task nearly impossible.

I may have let my sister and everyone else think it was my first time out there, but I'd been out one time before. Thankfully, I had a knack for going unnoticed, which apparently applied even when I stepped outside the community in which I lived. One had to be at least a Level 4 before qualifying for surface certification. I was so great at being invisible that they could've learned a thing or two from me. No one was allowed out alone or without proper clearance, but no one ever noticed me, unless I asked a question that offended protocol.

Only small groups of surface-certified Level 4's were allowed to do survivor sweeps which they did every 30 days. They used to do it more frequently, but things were riskier these days, and they often came back empty handed. I was never quite sure why since the details were never discussed with lower levels. We didn't need specifics however, to know how dangerous it was out there. Whenever a community member didn't make it back, that was confirmation in and of itself.

Time and time again, I watched Grandma wear out the floor by pacing when Annabel was out on survivor sweeps. I knew it must've been harder for her because she couldn't help but fixate on the fact that Granddad never came back from a sweep.

Though Grandma never talked about it, protocol and all, I had recently discovered a lot about him and my mother in a series of journals, notes and documents I'd found hidden amongst my grandmother's things. As strict as Grandma was, as strong as she stood behind principle, her keeping these journals demonstrated there was still a side of her that could and would break rules. Getting caught with evidence such as that would immediately strip her of her rank and tarnish everything she and my sister had worked for. She kept the journals anyway and the more I read, the more I understood why.

My recent demotion and suspension left me with a lot of free time which was never a good thing where I was concerned. Whenever I got bored, I generally got into trouble. I couldn't help myself from wanting to know the answers to the questions no one seemed to be asking.

Here I was stuck at home as part of my sentence, while my grandmother took on more elder responsibilities and Annabel doing the most by pulling rank. Home became so empty it felt as though it was mocking me. To stay sane, I set out to discover as much information as I could. After all, it was much more interesting to snoop without anyone home to hinder me.

I was bored senseless and finishing yet another one of Annabel's "you owe me" tasks, when right there like buried treasure was the answer to every question I'd had, plus answers to questions I'd never known to ask.

Getting caught reading a forbidden book would mean another scolding from my grandmother. She'd go on about me knowing I should've never had a Level 3 book in the first place, but getting caught with her most personal and private journals was different. I was afraid to even consider her wrath. I had found them nonetheless and was obsessed with them. Every spare moment I got; I snuck in every page I could.

Over the next few days, I desperately waited for the house to be empty so I could return to my secret treasure. My tell-all history lesson, without any regard whatsoever for protocol. I knew there had to be a reason why my grandmother kept something like this. Maybe it was the sentimentality of it all, or it could have been for much deeper reasons.

So, every chance I got I read and learned.

I laughed to myself thinking that if I'd applied this kind of determination to my studies, I'd have reached Level 4 a long time ago. This was different though. It was personal, and I felt a great need to redeem my mother...

It appears that my mother, Virginia, had been an unexpected and accidental success until the very end. Her unintentional genius got her through every level with ease. Of all the things said about her, no one ever called her dumb. Not a single version of her story refuted the fact that she was a mad genius and know-it-all.

She reportedly died on the surface at the hands of a cleaner, but not heroically during a survivor sweep the way my grandad had. Instead, she had gone against protocol, uncertified and in violation. It was a disgrace.

My grandmother was everything our community stood for, and my granddad was a hero, a legend. It was believed that my mom had come along and blemished their record and good-standing. Although my grandmother never actually said it aloud, I knew by the way she talked about my mom these days and by the way she was so patient with me, it was her way of relieving her own guilt. Like me, my mom always wanted to know the truth but knew no one would give it to her. She and my grandmother constantly butted heads because of it.

Mom was part of the first generation of non-Opt-Outs born in our community. Unlike me, she was a little more subtle in her rebellious ways and was able to play both sides by being a good student who rose through the ranks with ease. All the while secretly breaking protocol while she worked on my granddad's plan. She truly was the perfect combination of my sister and me.

Right before she lost her father, my mother had begun discovering more and more hidden truths. It was round about the same age I am now that her father died. It happened around the same time her questions were beginning to be answered. I imagined my mother in the exact same position as me when he passed; sad, missing him, looking for ways to somehow feel close to him, and wishing for one more chance to prove her worthiness. In the end, she chose to honor him by continuing his life's work.

She wrote,
Something broke in Mom when they handed her what was left of my dad: his identification band. At that moment, something connected within me. I suddenly understood what he had been trying to tell me and I knew exactly what I was supposed to do.

I knew what she was feeling when she wrote those words. Exactly the way I did whenever I read her words. It was like she was here, like she was talking to me. She kept telling me it was my turn to finish what they had started.

I read some of her entries two or three times. There was such beauty in her unedited thoughts, and I was impressed by her research and theories. She was funny too; her observation notes had a sassiness to them that reminded me of that side of Annabel only I get to see. The more I read, the more I felt like we could have been friends, best friends even. She sounded like someone I'd get along with and someone I could risk breaking protocol to by whispering forbidden ideas. I wished that to be true because honestly, I hardly remembered her, certainly not the way Annabel did. I had a few blurry memories, but I was only three when my grandmother came back with her identification band. All I could think of was, why wasn't it on my mother's wrist?

My mother was smart and knew how to fall in line. She committed herself to the system especially hard after losing her father and shortly after, she jumped up two levels, ranking out to a Level 4 at age 15. She'd set a new standard, a new goal.

Whenever I asked Grandma about Mom, she'd say she was "troublesome smart," which is the same thing she said about me. As smart as she was and as great a student she proved to be, she never cleared for surface certification. She spent years trying, but for one reason or another failed or was denied.

It was after her third denial that she gave up on going about it the official way and that is where things began to fall apart for her. Getting caught out there without permission or training was considered treason. Such behavior put everyone in danger and therefore was not taken lightly.

She was given many chances to correct her behavior due to her stellar past, her parents and her charm, but she was on a mission. She tried to explain it, but to others she sounded insane. Everyone was shocked and blamed it on a breakdown set off by her father's death. Over time though, the community lost patience and felt less sympathetic to a mourning daughter and more fed up with her as a protocol-breaker.

She continued the pattern of sneaking out and getting caught, though not every time, but once was enough. Despite my grandmother's warnings, demotions, probation, and holding, she escaped to the surface every opportunity she got. It was precisely one of those secret surface visits that cost her, her life.

My mother had been on the surface and was found by a cleaner. After that, it was like anything good she'd done before, no longer counted. Her reputation was smeared with rumors of everything from her trying to run away to working for cleaners and intentionally giving our position away.

There was even a rumor circulating that she'd fallen in love with a cleaner and spent time on the surface with it. Some said my sister and I were spawns of PODS which was why Annabel was machine perfect at whatever she did, whereas I had malfunctioned.

All of it was stupid and annoying, but nothing could be confirmed because no one really knew what happened. Tech was down that day so there wasn't any camera footage or live stream. A fellow Level 4 found her, and as with my granddad's passing, simply handed my grandmother my mother's remains: her identification band.

I barely had any memories of her passing, though I do remember how people seemed less affected by her death than when we lost others. I don't remember anyone except Annabel crying.

It was my mother who was gone, but the community focused on my granddad's legacy and his legendary sacrifices instead. My mother's end was nothing to dwell on, because of the way they thought she had endangered us. In fact, they were upset with her for betraying them. They'd once looked up to her, as a Level 4 leader, and as an example. She was a friend and role model turned careless, thoughtless, disappointing. Those who knew what the surface was like, held the strongest grudge. They knew what was up there and felt like she had selfishly risked everyone's life.

Over time my mother began to fade into nothing more than whispers and tales. She became that person you don't mention, which is what hurt me the most.
They all thought of her as the enemy, when in fact she had been loyal and devoted like her mother had been and definitely as honorable as her father. They didn't understand.

It seemed that genetics were strong and blatant in our family from our looks to our need to go on secret missions. What was now becoming my mission, was once my mom's, which had started with my granddad.

Montresor was a scrawny little nerdy kid directly at the heart of it all. He was related to the leadership in the ThinkTech industry. He'd been taught by the fanciest tutors and trained in tech and coding as soon as he was old enough to read, which he did early. He was privileged, so his chip had been removed the minute there was cause for concern.

As part of the Think Tech elite, he nor his parents, who were my great-grandparents, had to wait for the draw. However, they lived in a house of chipped staff, so their safety was not guaranteed by simply removing their own chips, which they hadn't realized.

When the program went out to those with remaining chips, Montresor managed to escape. Along the way he bumped into a group of survivors which included my grandmother. That's how my grandparents met: two terrified, traumatized, confused preteen kids leaving everything they knew behind. They were finally on the same social status; both simply survivors taken in by the infamous Opt-Outs and hoping for the best.

It was easy to be humble in the middle of a human droid apocalypse which is what forged my grandparents' relationship. They may not have had similar upbringings and beginnings but in the end, they were more alike than ever, scared and alone with nothing or no one they knew. They were both so desperate to leave the past behind that they had not realized how vastly different they really were.

My granddad's life was steeped in technology, though that wasn't his true nature. He had acquired knowledge the average person doesn't have. It came from years of being in the room while important meetings were taking place and from mandatory lessons about the family business.

He was young but gifted, and although the Opt-Outs had lesser technology it was technology nonetheless. It gave him enough of what he thought he needed in order to change everything. Although the Opt-Outs had established restrictions for surface access, he had his own plans. It was not to oppose them, but to protect them, and to correct things.

No one, including me, really knew his origins, until recently. He didn't want anyone to know that he was ThinkTech royalty. He was ashamed the world had fallen apart at the hands of his family. He was too young to have orchestrated any of it, but felt guilty nonetheless. What he'd witnessed before the ThinkTech debacle stayed with him and it moved him.

He discovered a way that not only gave him access to continue his work, but also the ability to save more people. It was my grandfather, who continued to rise in the ranks, who began the survivor sweeps. Every seven days they went out onto the surface to search for anyone who might still be out there.

It was a successful mission because they needed numbers. They needed children to build the future, and people with specialized trades and other talents. They praised Montresor and although he was happy with each rescue, his focus remained on the research.

They called him brave and daring, but really, he was a scientist testing a theory and observing POD behavior in order to perfect his program. He worked in secret, but not so secretly that my grandmother and mother hadn't caught on.
He sometimes wrote about interference and arguments with my grandmother. She wanted nothing to do with the surface except ushering in more survivors. She hated that survivor sweeps meant endangering our community, but she remembered what a relief it was to feel safe and felt that anyone still out there deserved that.

Though she understood why my grandfather led the missions, she despised his ideas and his theories. The mere thought of him coming within range of a cleaner and risking his life to test an alternative program he'd written infuriated her. He tried to explain, but she couldn't hear him past her concerns.

His plan was to write a reversal code, essentially an antivirus to the chip. He was gifted with computer programming and with technology in general. He had years of experience and was naturally bright, which made coding a breeze for him.

My grandmother never knew what he knew nor how much he knew. She was right to be scared. The PODS were not to be taken lightly. Once they went into hunting mode, they were very efficient. The best defense was to avoid setting them off in the first place, so they'd remain calm and continue with whatever they were doing.

I knew cleaners were dangerous, but you're not given full details until Levels 3 and 4, because it's against protocol to talk about them. People didn't return and tell us all about survivor sweeps, especially to lower levels like me. When survivors were found and taken in, they were sworn to follow the community's rules which meant not discussing surface world details. Instead, they were expected to level up and become productive members of our secret society.

The surface had merely become a historical concept to me. We had a few rooms that simulated it, plants even, but we had nothing to really compare it to. Prior to going out, those rooms were my favorite places to sit, but now they seemed lackluster and boring compared to the real thing. At least it was safe; disappointing but safe from cleaners.

We were taught that PODS were on a mission to destroy the human race. This was bad enough, but what I didn't know was the extent of which, plus the true horror of how, they were going about it.

As I read on in horror and disbelief, I pitied Level 4's for having to witness such atrocities, though I couldn't help but consider them brave. No wonder Grandma paced the floor when Annabel was out. I knew that in the future, I would be pacing right alongside her.

I thought about the many times I hated the use of the word "protocol" as the end-all-be-all answer to a lot of my questions. However, I now understood why no one should have to be aware of this disturbing knowledge until absolutely necessary.

I thought of my sister and wondered what she'd seen. We hadn't lost anyone since she'd been certified but that didn't mean she hadn't lost a survivor along the way. I literally would have no way of knowing. I knew my mother was killed by a cleaner, but how had never been disclosed to me.

I almost wished I hadn't read some of my granddad's graphic entries. My head was swimming and tears streamed down my face as I pictured the girl, the one writing to me hoping to become my best friend, getting ripped apart and torn to pieces. It now made sense that an identification band was all that remained once a person ran into a cleaner.

When we learned about them in history class, there were no pictures, simply a description of people who'd had their chips overrun. So naturally I pictured people without thinking of the consequences of not eating or sleeping. They may not have needed to, but it definitely affected them physically. I never thought of the toll it would take on the body, nor how worn out and beat down they would look. *These were not the people I once knew; they hardly resembled themselves anymore. They were emaciated even if they didn't necessarily require food. Their eyes were sunken in with dark circles around them and their thin dry yellowed skin was stretched across their protruding bones. Overworked hands that felt no pain sorted glass and metal scraps without caution. The countless hours and lack of self-preservation left their hands mangled in such a way that it was hard to believe they were functional.*

I hadn't realized I was still crying until a tear hit the page and the ink began to run. I immediately gathered myself, not wanting to cause damage to the journal. What a terrifying realization. This was nothing like I'd pictured. Cleaners weren't a robotic version of their previous selves; they were a monstrous, animated corpse-like version hunting you down. If they caught you, they shredded you apart with their broken twisted hands and exposed bones. They chased you down until they caught you, then ripped you limb from limb with their bare hands. Then they scattered you like fertilizer and scraps for whatever beast ran around on the surface.

I thought of my mother experiencing that sort of pain, then torn to pieces and discarded. It weighed on me knowing that she died trying to save us and release us, though she'd never get credit for that. She was worth more than a rumor mill for idiots. She couldn't explain everything without causing panic and what she tried to explain only led them to believe that she'd lost her mind.

So, she became more reclusive and more determined to work on the code. She was focused on perfecting it. They kept mentioning the code and referencing it, but I hadn't found any. I rifled through everything and still found nothing. What was I missing? I read theories on how to deliver it, but not what to deliver. I was frustrated and fixated.

When I was alone, I absorbed it all and when I wasn't, I couldn't stay out of my own thoughts. My grandmother kept asking me if I was feeling okay because I was constantly in my own head trying to solve a puzzle which made me uncharacteristically still and quiet.

I used to be so eager to go to the surface to find out what made my mother risk leaving us behind. I didn't know why she was out there, only that she was, and I wanted to understand why. Now that I did, I was not the slightest bit eager to go back up there or to ever see one of those things.

The only thing that motivated me was the vindication I knew my mom deserved. Not only would people respect her again, but they would honor her and be ashamed of themselves for ever having doubted her intentions.

My granddad had been close, but my mother perfected it or at least she thought she did. She went on about adding onto the code, but never the specifics of what she added or where it was. I had lost myself in trying to find it. Was there something I was missing? I tried to think like the girl I had gotten to know over the last week, how she thought, and how she and I thought so much alike.

I read things that seemed like I'd written them myself, looked like my handwriting even. I wanted to tap into her mindset. If she had only mentioned the code, but not what the code was, there was a reason. I knew it must be hidden, but I knew it wasn't embedded in what I had read over and over again.

I thought about my mother, first generation born, what did she have or own to hide something in?
I thought of my granddad, he was the first to hide the code, but he'd obviously hidden it somewhere he'd meant her to find. I beat myself constantly with the possibilities. I searched every inch of our home backwards and forward.

What did he have that my mom would have had access to? He arrived from the outside world with two items besides the clothes on his back, and none of them intimated *ThinkTech code.* The first was a ring. Shockingly humble for his background, but if his goal was trying to fit in like a common person he had succeeded. My grandmother still wore it. The second thing he'd arrived with was a book which now sat on a shelf. I'd read through it; a collection of old stories and insanely long poetry. I didn't care for it much, but he must have. He must have loved it to keep ahold of it through everything he'd been through while trying to get to safety. He'd held onto it through countless near-death experiences.

Then it hit me: the code was right there hiding in plain sight. Right there in that book was the code which could be pieced together in relation to our namesakes.

I was overjoyed by a victory I wasn't at liberty to share so I had to stifle my celebratory screams. I'd finally found what I had been so desperately looking for. They were speaking to me; it was a message for me.

I sat with the book in my lap. I was extremely proud of myself and now had an entirely different appreciation for the mad ramblings of a heartbroken man.

I did not let my sister walking into the room interrupt my self-congratulatory moment. She walked right past me, while I continued to pat myself on the back. I flipped between the pages overwhelmed and excited, while strategizing my next move. My sister walked past me again but this time she laughed out loud.
"Finally!" She exclaimed.
"Wha?" I asked snapping out of my own world and looking up at her. She was grinning from ear to ear.
"I mean, it took you long enough, but hey, what can you really expect from a Level 1 anyway?" She was clearly amused and laughed on as if it were the best joke ever.

I mocked her laughter then abruptly stopped, emphasizing that I was not amused.

"What are you talking about?" I asked, suddenly realizing what she meant as the words left my mouth. She gave me that notorious smile, then said, "We need to talk, Nor."

CHAPTER II   UNDERSTANDING EVERYTHING
                            I DID NOT KNOW I DID NOT KNOW

We sat across from each other at the table.
I was awestruck and overwhelmed all at once. I felt like
I'd passed a test I didn't even know I was taking.
The best part was that I wasn't celebrating a victory I
had to keep to myself, I could now share it with Annabel
and we could compare thoughts. I generally told my
sister everything, but lately I'd been keeping so much
from her and it had been eating me up inside. It was
such a relief to discover that she knew. Wait a minute,
she knew?

"Wait a minute, you knew?" my words tumbled out of
my mouth. "You did know!" I said in an accusatory tone
as if she had denied it, which she hadn't. "If you knew,
why didn't you tell me instead of having me sneak
around?"

Annabel burst out laughing. She laughed like a mad
woman, exaggerating and throwing her head back while
tapping the table.

"What's so funny?" Clearly, I'd missed the joke. I sat still
and stared at her blankly. "What?" I asked, slightly
irritated that I wasn't in on the joke.

"It's so funny to me. What you call sneaking around,"
she shook her head, "tsk, tsk, I could've caught you a
million times," she said acting like she needed to catch
her breath after her exaggeratedly hysterical laughter.
"Then to make it worse when you put the journals back,

you never put them back how you found them, and you *know* how Grandma is." She wiped imaginary tears from her eyes. "If it weren't for me, you would've been caught several times over. So, you're welcome," she said, raising her eyebrows dramatically. She stood up and leaned in close to me and whispered, "small details, kid." She then tapped me on the forehead and added sternly: "focus."

I didn't move or react, I sat still and stared at her blankly again.

"So, is that what we have to talk about? Not putting things back where they belong? Who are you? Grandma?"

The smile disappeared from her face and reappeared on mine. I usually took that jab when I wanted to casually remind her that she was my sister and not my mother. My sister was my best friend and we got along more often than not, but sometimes she forgot that she was my sibling and not my parent. It was my own fault for always putting myself in positions she had to bail me out of. Deep down I knew she was entitled to feel like she could tell me what to do, she really did take care of me and protect me, she had earned that right. Even now with her telling me to focus, I knew she meant it in the best way no matter how condescending and annoying it was to be scolded by her.

"Lenore, I'm serious," she said in that tone I hated. She looked like she was about to take stance and pull rank. I straightened up.

Although I hated to admit it, she was right. She usually was. I must be more careful and pay more attention. I don't think I even stopped to think about putting the journals back precisely how I'd found them. There was a lesson in that, and I felt foolish. That's one detail that would've never gotten by Annabel. She was deliberate that way, and always aware of her surroundings. I admired her because of it and relied on her for it. I was scatter-brained, yet somehow managed to hold myself together. I couldn't be upset with her for calling me out.

I was all tensed up as she lectured me for a bit. I let her because I knew I deserved it. She let me have it about the risks of being out on the surface, especially without the proper training. It was thoughtless and selfish of me. It was unfair to the community, and "what was I thinking?" She went on for what seemed like an eternity.

Then, she went in a direction that had nothing to do with me. For a moment I thought she was talking less to me and more to the absence of our mother. Annabel was always so collected but I let her have her moment and sat through part of a speech that wasn't meant for me. She exhaled hard, composing herself by literally shaking it off. Then she looked me right in the eye and said:

"Don't you think Grandma's been through enough?" She flicked my identification band then tapped my forehead again. The sound echoed through my brain. I hated that she still did that to me, no matter how used to it I had become.
"Plus, I might miss you too," she whispered.

177

There was that smile again.

I couldn't help but roll my eyes. I looked down, grabbed my identification band and thought about it for the first time ever with detailed facts. It sent chills down my spine. It was a reality check. I did not want my identification band to be the only thing left of me. I swallowed hard and tried to keep from picturing my mother's gory end. It played on a loop in my mind and I had no tears left.

I focused instead on Annabel. She switched between empathizing with my curiosity of the outside world and condemning me for my careless actions that could've cost us everything. She purposely took all the right steps to reach her rank and all the proper procedures to be surface certified and she was right where she needed to be. She could not be wasting her time worrying about me getting myself killed nor risking her rank by protecting me.

I watched my sister as she continued on about "being cautious and treading lightly." She was off duty, but still so well postured and authoritative. I hated when she brought her authority home with her, though she did so often. Sometimes she was "on" without even meaning to be.

She paced the floor filling in details as if protocol was no longer a thing. I was on the edge of my seat, hanging on to every single word. I never thought of my sister as a rebel before, yet there she was, completely disregarding rank and levels and it was awesome.

To her it was less about breaking protocol and more that she needed me to understand that what I read was not a fairytale. It was real and terrifying. She lived it and it was something you couldn't unsee.

She was rigid and although she was not dressed in uniform, everything about her body language said she was still on duty. Except her hair, which was loose. She only wore it down at home and I loved it like that. It was so alive and bounced with each stiff step. She had a head full of spiral curls. They looked deceivingly short, but stretched straight to the middle of her back until they would slip through your fingers and twist back into tiny little soft brown ringlets that sat back on her shoulders. Her hair had always been beautiful, but since she had become surface-certified, it had subtle highlights caused by the sun, which made it so lovely. Unlike mine which was dark brown and wasn't curly nor totally straight. Instead, it fell in an awkward semi-waviness that went in every direction. Even right after being brushed it looked messy.

I may have appeared spaced out, but I was paying attention, so when I saw her forehead tap coming, I dodged it this time.

"I am focused," I said.

She smiled and relaxed a little, pulling a chair close to me and sat down. Finally, she was officially off duty. Although a second ago she was telling me things she never could have on duty (or ever), it was how she spoke, the tone, her cadence. It was like she was giving a lesson to a subordinate and it always created a distance between us when she did that. She now sat there beside me not as in levels, but as an equal. I could actually talk to my sister now.

We went back and forth in a Q & A session that threw protocol and caution to the wind. I had to stop and take a breath. All my life I had been reprimanded for asking too many questions and now I had actually run out of questions to ask. I was on information overload and suddenly in my anxiety I could see how steps, levels and protocol made sense. It was a deliberate process that eased you in because too much might not be the best way to learn. Not everyone could handle it. I barely could.

It wasn't that a certain feeling of comfort and safety had left me, but I now feared things I'd never heard of before. It hit me hard. Problems I never worried about flooded my mind. I suddenly couldn't breathe. Gasping for breath, I leaned forward, and put my head between my knees.

"It's a lot. You don't need to know everything right this second. Breathe, Nor, breathe," Annabel reassured me as she rubbed my back.

Only a week ago I was totally uninformed and risking everything to catch a glimpse of something in order to answer questions that made no sense. What was so great about up there? What was so tempting that it was worth abandoning me for? It was becoming clear that it was not what happened. There was a much bigger picture and reason why she was up there and it definitely wasn't because she liked it better than being with us.

For the first time I let go of my anger and the misinformation I'd held onto for so long. I released my childish perspective, believing that if I understood what was up there then I would understand her and why she'd left us. I now saw it for what it was. She was fixing something that was bigger than us, bigger than her. I understood that now. I knew why my sister needed me to know. What I thought had been my mission was actually our mission. Where my granddad and mom had failed was that they were alone in their pursuit, but we had each other.

One thing about my sister and I is that we differed in many ways, most ways in fact, but it wasn't a bad thing. I was always best at things that required her more effort and vice versa. This is what made us the best team. Being opposites made whatever we did together successful because we had two separate ways of seeing things. She knew that and planned accordingly with her to-do lists which led me to come across the journals. She could've come out and told me, but she wanted to see how long it would take before I found where the code was hidden. That part really was a test, she was curious about how long it would take me to come to the realization. Although she teased me as if it had taken me forever, it had taken her far longer to make the connection. She reluctantly admitted that she was impressed by me.

When she finally discovered the book containing the code, she couldn't read it nor understand it in the same effortless way I could. Annabel had many strengths, but code wasn't one of them. I'm the one who got her through that class. It was my thing, not willingly but it happened to be a consequence of too many points. Taking on code shifts was an easy way to reduce points.

Writing programs is where they wanted me because it would force me to be still and stay out of trouble. Plus, I am actually really good at it. Once, I even developed a program that wrote programs for me, but apparently that meant I wasn't taking my work seriously.

I did not want to level out at a 3 in coding, but I think that's what my grandma was setting me up for. She made me practice every chance she got. When something bugged in the system, she never hesitated to volunteer me for a shift. Lately there were many opportunities for extra shifts because of all the coding errors. So, prior to my suspension, that was how I spent most of my time.

Annabel needed me because of the effortless way I "got it." We needed to try and understand what mom thought she had perfected and also how and where it was hidden. Annabel needed me for once and for a moment I felt worthy. I wanted to sit there and absorb all her accidental compliments.

I'd always needed her to cover for me, to bail me out, to stand up for me, to make me breakfast, to tell her about my day. For once, she needed me. She needed my skills and strengths to do something she couldn't. I was feeling rather good about myself, and I soaked it all in.

She hadn't wanted to tell me this information yet. She wanted to wait and do it right. Let me rise in ranks first and allow me to gather the information slowly, but I had not made it easy. My recent attempt at an escape and subsequent demotion made her realize it needed to be done now.

She'd set me up then watch me until I got in trouble, which was only a matter of time. Then she'd use it against me and give me one of her famous; "you owe me" to-do lists that caused me to cross paths with the journals. Otherwise, I would never have gone through Grandma's old things.

Knowing me as well as she did, Annabel knew she needed me to find the journals on my own and be intrigued. If she handed them to me and told me to read them, I would've treated them like an assignment and probably never gotten around to reading them. I laughed at how well she really knew me. She let me have a little fun and adventure the way she had when she'd found them. Then as always, she cleaned up my mess behind me. Meanwhile she watched, waiting for me to connect the dots.

"You were built for this kid," she said, as if it were a fact.

Another compliment that added to my confidence and my nerves. My heart was racing from both pride and pressure, but this was my job. I was built for this. Annabel had taken on so much over the years and this was something I knew I could do. This was something I probably could do. I hoped I could do it.

I grabbed us a few snacks then we sat there picking each other's brains for a moment. We threw ideas and thoughts back and forth trying to make sense of it all. I glanced at the book up on the shelf again. It had been there for as long as I could remember, but I looked at it differently now. All these years it sat there untouched; except the few times I'd picked it up out of shear boredom. I never thought it would be at the center of everything as well as the answer.

Until earlier today I'd been going crazy trying to figure out where the code was hidden. In the past few days, I had three recurring thoughts. One: don't get caught, two: my mom's gruesome death, and three: where is the code hidden? When I finally had the revelation and discovered where, I was interrupted. I hadn't actually been able to do anything with what I'd found because so much happened immediately afterwards. There hadn't been any time to take it all in, much less figure any of it out.

I took the book off the shelf once again and brought it over to the table. Annabel sat in anticipation as if something amazing was going to happen the moment I flipped between the pages. For a moment I thought I might have to find every delicately marked letter and word and rearrange them. As Annabel watched me closely, she saw my wheels turning. It was obvious she hadn't figured out what came next, and she was eager to find out. Her leg was shaking the way it always did when she had too much nervous energy. I tried to not let her excitement distract me.

One thing my mother and grandfather had in common was how vague they could be. They had a tricky way of saying things without actually saying them, as if to keep anyone else from catching on. I wondered: did anyone include my grandmother? I highly doubt she knew anything more than it being an old, tattered book. After all, she hid everything she found threatening. Why would she leave this out in plain sight if she knew it was something that would encourage us to take the same risks our mom had taken? The closest she ever got to it was when she dusted it. Neither of us had ever seen her go through the pages. If she had, would she even have understood what it contained?

I felt like I was under a spotlight while Annabel watched me so intently, while slowly moving closer and closer to me. Her enthusiasm made it hard to sort through my thoughts. I began to sweat, which I felt beading on my nose. I wanted to do my part, but not like this. I was getting edgy and the way she stared at me wasn't helping.

I pushed every thought aside and tried to focus on the book. "Small details, focus," Annabel had told me earlier. I closed the book and sighed. My sister was still watching me closely.

What did I actually know about Grandad Montresor? He was no ordinary man, from no ordinary background. He was smart and discreet. My sister had to have learned this too because throughout the journals, his innermost thoughts sounded like riddles. Getting to know him over the last week had been a mysterious journey which still contained a lot of gaps. It made me wonder what he had been hiding from. Even here in our own home, not only did he have something to hide, he had to hide it within the very hiding of it.

Despite how deeply it was hidden the message had been clear to my mom. So why not to my grandmother? Had she really been so oblivious that she really thought him mad? Did she believe my mother had simply broken down after his death? Did she not know the depths of it all? Or had she suppressed it because it was too much for her to deal with?

Focus. It wasn't about what Grandma *didn't* know, but more about what Granddad *did* know. He left a message for his daughter, and she knew how to find it because she loved him and knew him. I never knew my mother and hadn't known much about her either. It was only recently I'd come to know and understand her.

I still needed to figure out what she had been attempting to tell us. As many times as my grandmother reminded me of my full name, I knew the namesakes in the book were no coincidence. Like I said, Granddad was far from obvious and simple. He'd left a message for my mother, and she'd left us one as well.

I breathed deeply, still sitting with the book closed in front of me on the table. I tried to soothe my increasing anxiety as my sister awaited my next move. There was an order of operations I still needed to solve that began with the four pieces of writing plus each important word, phrase or mark. I turned between the pages so Annabel would think I was doing something, but really; I was lost.

It was not alphabetical; we both knew better.
It had to be something more complicated than our
timeline. It would be too basic to go from oldest to
youngest. Although my sister suggested it and I
appeased her to prove what I already knew to be true.
It was some other puzzle, a different riddle. I thought I
might explode.

I finally slammed the book closed and let my head fall
onto the table. It felt like it weighed a thousand pounds,
which I could no longer support. It was filled with far too
much information and theories. I wanted to serve a
purpose, but I wasn't sure I could.

My sister looked at me disappointed as if she
understood my defeat. I wanted her to look at me
differently for once. Annabel finally broke the deafening
silence. "I couldn't figure it out myself either," she said
softly, "but it's not like you have to figure it out right this
second, maybe after... " At that moment, I sprung up,
cutting her off and I opened the book again. She was
right again! "I couldn't figure it out myself," she said. My
granddad couldn't figure it out himself either nor could
my mother, but we had each other.

My mother knew she might not make it back to us and
that we were going to need each other. I motioned for
my sister to come closer, which she did without
hesitation "You couldn't have done it by yourself," I told
her. "I now understand that you needed me, and I
needed you in order to get it." I suddenly realized that
she needed to touch different points on the pages at the
same time I did, for us to understand the code together.

Her eyes lit up when she realized I was onto something. We were focused and silent, but this silence was different. It wasn't the result of defeat; it was anticipation. We slid our fingers over the last word and the book magically snapped closed. It lay cover side down. A panel on the back cover moved, exposing something. We both jumped and gasped at the same time.

I knew then that it was more than a book. It took me a second to feel a sense of pride. Granddad was the Prince of ThinkTech. It made no sense him carrying around a basic book. Annabel and I stood there gazing at the book as if it were magical or possessed.
"It's a keyhole," I exclaimed, surprised I could still form words.

"I don't know Nor," Annabel spoke past her shock. " I've never seen a key shaped like that."

She was right, plus after all, wouldn't a simple key have been too easy to solve? I looked more closely at the open panel and the supposed keyhole. It was nothing but a dull metal plate with a missing piece. Something small, round, and circular would fill it perfectly. Something ring-shaped perhaps.

"Grandma's ring!" I accidentally shouted coming to the realization out loud. Annabel's eyes widened as she repeated my words, "Grandma's ring!"
She hugged me, then we jumped up and down to relieve some of the excitement we could no longer contain.

It was now so obvious to us that the dull metal contained a ring-shaped hole. It was made of the exact same dull metal as Grandma's ring, which she wore on her finger. Granddad had arrived with those two things, the book and the ring. Now it all made sense.
"Grandma's ring," we exclaimed one more time, though this time the energy was different, like we were deflated. We must have had the exact same thought. We'd never even seen her take it off so there's no way we could've gotten a hold of it.

It was my second day back after suspension and I knew
it was going to be a blur much like the day before. I was
only there physically, but mentally I was far, far away. All
I did was obsess over one thing; Grandma's ring.
Annabel and I spent days suggesting then rejecting each
other's strategies for getting a hold of it. We had
explored every scenario from being completely honest
and telling her why we needed it, to slipping it off her
finger when she was sleeping. It was our new banter,
one of us putting forth an idea and the other listing all
the things that were wrong with it.

I was doing everything in my power to be on my best
behavior which meant trying not to seem as distracted
as I really was. I wanted people to think I'd made a full
turn around and was invested like never before. I
needed everyone to see me trying. I was working on
giving the impression that I was sorry and had learned
my lesson. As long as I came across as such, I could
continue exploring scenarios in my mind; *switch it with
another ring? No, how? Using something else with a similar
shape wouldn't work, would it? No, of course not.*

Even at lunch time my brain was still working. I
desperately tried to come up with a list of options while
hoping Annabel was having better luck. *Asking Grandma
if I could try her ring on? No, cause if she agreed, she'd
want it back immediately.* I sat there quietly and still,
which always gained me lots of attention. I assured

those who asked, that I was fine and continued thinking.

I had no interest in catching up with anyone at the moment. It was fair to think I would be excited to not be stuck at home, but all I wanted right now was to be there. I wanted to go where I could focus without people adding to my workload. *Could we get Grandma to do something she'd need to take the ring off for? She did everything with it on. What would I say?*
"Quiet and still huh?" a voice ripped me from my thoughts. I knew who it was before I looked up. "I knew your sister would whip you into shape, I never doubted her."

Though I was locked and loaded with a barrage of insults, when I looked up at him something clicked into place. I stood up and took stance even though he wasn't in one. It was obvious he appreciated that gesture and was surprised because it was so unlike me to do something like that.

Stance was a position one took that represented respect for command. When a higher level took stance, the lesser level was expected to respond, but to initiate stance as the lesser level was a way of demonstrating the highest form of respect. I generally found this behavior to be degrading, but I had recently learned the benefits of playing by the rules.

As I stood in stance I added, "Yes Level 4 Royalty Andrews, I'm ready to fall in line, sir."
"Sit Level 1," as he casually motioned me to rest. I sat down trying to hide the fact that I was annoyed.

As if I needed his permission to sit. I bit my tongue. "Royalty Andrews," really??? My eyes couldn't roll back far enough in my head whenever he came around. He took his name far too literally. Conceited and annoying, then sprinkle in a little misogyny and a big ego with Level 4 access and there you have it: the power went straight to his head.

His family was held in high regard because men were growing scarce in our community and his mother had six boys. They all happened to be considered cute, and 'Royalty Andrews' was the cream of the crop. He was the oldest and ranked highest. He was surface certified and part of the Select. Only a year older than Annabel, his experience outweighed hers.

He had quite a reputation and fan base since he was the last to lead a successful rescue mission on a survivor sweep and his training stats were flawless. He had justifiable confidence. He had every reason to be proud, but it was how he went about it that got under my skin. He had this undeniable sense of entitlement as if his name alone meant we were to bow before him. It didn't help much that most people did. Everyone swooned over him, excluding my sister and I. We never did understand his allure. Yes, he was well-trained, but that's about the extent of which either of us gave him any credit.

He had a thing for Annabel for some reason. I think he liked that she didn't turn to jelly in his presence. In fact, he wasn't even on her radar. This was not the first time he'd tried to talk to me about her. He was always attempting to work his way to her through me because

Annabel barely gave him the time of day. After all, she was very busy, and didn't have any time to spare during the workday. But here I was; accessible, easy to approach and could be directed to respond to him. Normally by now I would've been given points for being rude or dismissive, but today Royalty was exactly who I needed him to be.

He stood there talking to me with one leg up on a chair. His body facing the cafeteria as if he needed to always be on display. He held his hat in his hand, which technically should've been on his head, but this way, he could run his hands through his silky black hair while he spoke.

I looked up at him pretending to be interested. He batted those big, dopey puppy eyes that made everyone gaga. Though he was talking to me, he spoke facing the other direction and projecting his voice as if he was putting on a performance. He acted as though he was doing everyone a favor by making them part of his conversation.

I listened at his attempt to humbly brag; which included his stats, recent promotion, and some outdated tales of heroism. This was obviously an effort to remind me what a great catch he was. Presumably, he hoped I'd pass this info on to my sister. The same sister who was going to kill me for what I was thinking.

I braced myself for Annabel's wrath then took the leap. I laid it on thick, while I assumed stance again trying not to gag. "Level 4 if I may..." I purposely paused acting as if I shouldn't say what I was about to say. I looked down at my feet and moved them around pretending to be shy and all that. "Continue Level 1," he commanded, as his curiosity was piqued, the way I'd intended it to be. He generally hung onto my every word in case it involved my sister, though it never did. Instead, it was usually some finely timed dig that went right over his head or that he let slide because of her. This time, it very much involved her.

"I don't want to get any points added, after all, we're on duty. I wouldn't want to stir the pot but..." I paused, looked around, then said: "but Annabel..." I trailed off.

"At ease, Nor," he stated firmly, he'd never called me that before.

How quickly things had gotten personal! This was going to be easier than I thought. He sat down with lightning speed as if no one was in the room but us. He leaned in close and said,

"You may speak freely," he said in such a humble yet eager way that I hardly recognized him.

Being at ease while on duty was rare, but to speak freely was even more so. How I'd wished for this opportunity many times before so I could say exactly what I thought about him. I denied my impulse to do so and instead I willingly had a conversation with him. My plan was in motion. My grandmother walked by like clockwork, though I pretended not to notice. She saw me speaking with Royalty and by him sitting there with me, she determined it must be of a personal nature. All I could think about however, was that Annabel was going to kill me!

Over the next week or so I made it a point to be seen with Royalty during my break, at ease in the cafeteria, always staying long enough for my grandmother to see us together. Now even between lessons, whenever he saw me, he acknowledged me and not with stance, but with a simple nod or wave.

I kept putting off telling my sister about my plan while I secretly kept working on it, but it wasn't long before she caught on. She came home one evening and got right up in my face.

"What are you up to?" she demanded, narrowing her eyes so much that they were almost closed. "Since when are you and *Royalty Andrews* friends?" she asked suspiciously. She always caught on pretty fast, so I had to tell her about my plan. She listened quietly but reacted with deep breaths and dumbfounded facial expressions. She finally agreed to collude with me though she was not thrilled in the least. We simply did not have any other options.

"You're going to have to at least be kind of nice to him," I laughed while flinching fully expecting her to hit me. "This better work," she said, admitting defeat.
She was dreading the plan even more knowing they had a survivor sweep coming up which would give them a lot of unfortunate one on one time.

She agreed to go along with the plan. My idea was a good one and she knew it. Besides it was already in motion. I knew that if Annabel noticed Royalty and I together and thought something of it, my grandmother must have as well. They were similar that way. Things were falling into place.

I woke up earlier than usual after a mostly sleepless night. I hated the mornings of survivor sweeps. Grandma always made a big breakfast which only made it seem like a last meal. The tension was very high as no one wanted to say what they were really thinking; that Annabel might not come home.

I choked back tears when saying goodbye, which was harder than ever, given the facts I'd recently learned. When Grandma got up from the table to have a moment alone to hide her tears, Annabel and I sat for a moment in total silence. We forced ourselves to eat what could potentially be our last breakfast together. Despite my best-efforts, tears trickled down my cheeks.

"Stop it," she said sternly, "I'll be fine, like always."

"I just..." I trailed off because I really didn't know what to say then wiped my face on my sleeve.

"Don't worry about me, Nor, focus on what you need to do while I'm gone. You have a job to do, and I expect you to get it done. I'll be back to help with the rest of it."

I breathed that way you do when you're trying to hold back tears.

"You know that right?" she asked.

I nodded. "Yes, I know I have a job to do," I said through my tears.

"No, I mean, that I'll be back. You know that right? That I'll be back?" she asked again. I didn't know if she was trying to reassure me or herself.

"Yes," I said shakily, then cleared my throat and said it again more firmly; "yes, of course I do."
She looked at me relieved as if that was all she needed to hear.

"Plus, thanks to you I'll have The Mighty Royalty to protect me," she looked at me half smiling.
We both burst into uncontrollable laughter. It wasn't that it was necessarily funny, as much as it was better to laugh hysterically than to cry.

Grandma walked in surprised by the unusual, good mood rarely seen on such somber mornings. She had obviously finished secretly crying herself and came out expecting us to have done the same. Instead, we were crying from laughing so hard, holding our sides, and trying to catch our breath. She stared at us as if we were insane. Her confusion was all over her face, and then, as if it were contagious, she joined in with that chuckle of hers that we rarely heard.

We hugged Annabel tight, without tears as we had been taught to do for a proper sendoff. We had to share her now because it was time for community sendoff. Community sendoff was a small tribute for our Surface Certified Level 4's trained in survivor sweeps also known as: "the Select."

Everyone took turns showing their love and appreciation to those who were about to risk their lives. They were showered with gifts and compliments and well wishes. The tradition was anything but tears. Each of the eight from the Select had a designated area for gifts to be placed. The point was to pile them up as a thank you, but they were only to be opened upon their return. I guess it was meant to be an extra incentive.

We shouldn't have been surprised that amongst the well-wishers and gift-givers was Royalty's mother, Regina Andrews. She usually was, but this time the incredible size of her gift said more than simply good luck.

There are eight in the Select who usually break into four groups of two. Normally Annabel pairs with Carson James, but this time she had a role to play. It wasn't like it was a demotion to be paired with Royalty; he was elite in defense. Though I didn't like Royalty as a person, as a Select he was my top choice to be Annabel's partner. He and I had worked that out in the last week or so.
I had endured my lunches being bombarded with long, boring stories starring none other than himself. I smiled and nodded. I was never good at small talk, especially with so much on my mind, but he had no problem doing all the talking and filling every silent moment with updates on his most effective exercise routines. The only time he ever grew quiet was when I mentioned my sister. He always looked right at me and absorbed every word; I could see him taking mental notes.

Sometimes I'd go on about her to avoid hearing his same old stories and to stop him from flexing his biceps causing everyone to look in our direction. I told him all about her likes and dislikes and in return, he gave me names of those I should be nicest to for easy point deductions. It had become a useful relationship, which I needed to continue for the sake of the plan.

The Select stood up in front of everyone as family and friends stood smiling through their worries. I watched all eight of them rigid in stance holding it together. They stood staring into the distance at no one in particular, in order to keep their emotions in check.

Royalty stood beside my sister. As Elder Level 4, Lisa Carson, James Carson's mother, spoke of traditions and bravery, he slowly moved closer to Annabel, then slipped his hand in hers. Her eyes widened and I knew she was fighting her instinct to snatch her hand back. She looked right at me maybe because only I knew what she was feeling or maybe to confirm that this was part of the plan. It was, so I gave her a small nod. She squeezed his hand then returned hers to her side. Annabel's face turned several shades of red and Royalty's pupils may have literally formed heart shapes. My grandmother had missed it, but the gesture hadn't gone unnoticed, which, was all I needed. We then shared one last hug and as tradition would have it, they headed out in silence as the whole community took stance in respect.

Only an hour had passed, though it felt like forever. I was glad we didn't have lessons on survivor sweep days because I couldn't think about anything else.
A sweep took longer these days because they had to go out further or take different routes that no longer lined

up with the maps or led to dead ends. I hadn't known that before, I'm not supposed to know it now, but I do, and it's hard to pretend I don't. I knew Annabel wouldn't be gone longer than three days though. Everyone knew that.

"No need to worry about Annabel Lee," my grandmother said walking into the room. "She's well trained and smart."

"I know," I said, then stood still. I hadn't even realized I was pacing.

My grandmother heated water for tea and when it was ready, she placed two cups on the table. She knew I didn't drink tea, but I sat in front of the cup anyway. *This was my moment; I had a job to do.*

"Grandma?" I began, needing to choose my words wisely, my grandmother knew me well and this had to work.

She sipped her tea and waited, and I went for it.

"Grandma, I've been talking to Royalty Andrews a lot lately," I paused, trying to find the best way to say it.

She looked up over her steaming cup.

"I've noticed! And what exactly is that all about?"

"It's about Annabel, Grandma. Royalty has been talking about," I stopped when she started chuckling.

"Annabel Lee and Royalty? I highly doubt it, " she said shaking her head, still chuckling.

"But Grandma it's true, he came to me at lunch to ask about her being the one," which wasn't entirely a lie. He really did have it bad for my sister.

My grandmother shook her head.

"I'd know," she said. "It's an honor truly and if I made the choice, but," she stopped.

"I know, I thought that too. Annabel and *Royalty Andrews*? No way. But he said, they are, well she is really private about it. You know because they want to set things up before making an announcement. In the meantime, they don't want people thinking any promotions Annabel earns is because of him. You know how she is about rank."

I let that sink in for a moment and offered her more tea which she gladly accepted. She encouraged me to drink mine as she blew on her fresh steaming cup.
She was quiet and I knew it was because she was thinking about everything I'd said.

I took a small sip of my tea and leaned in close. "Yeah, that's why he's been taking up my lunch," I acted bothered. My grandmother listened, nodding.

"I didn't believe him, not really, but then today at community sendoff you saw it right?" I asked knowing she had not.

She had not noticed because she always holds her head high during send offs. She doesn't look down at their hands. Instead, she looks up, up towards, but not at Annabel. She looks right past her in order to hold herself together. I knew who had seen it though and it was only a matter of time before everyone else knew about it.

"Saw what Lenore Rose?" she asked proving she was eager for me to tell her. I had her right where I wanted her. I was worried at first when she laughed at me, but now she was interested.

My grandmother stood in suspense wanting to know what she'd missed. She sipped her tea motioning for me to go on. "They held hands, it was really quick, but I saw it. I guess it could've been a good luck thing, but none of the other Selects did that and oh, that present from the Andrews family?" I exhaled hard as if it was a lot to take in and took another small sip of my room temperature tea.

My grandmother was putting the pieces together. "Well, I thought the present from the Andrews was due to the partner change. They've always given well to any of Royalty's partners." She was thinking out loud more so than speaking to me.

Perfect, my plan was starting to take effect and sink in. I had one job I needed to have completed by the time Annabel got back, *if* Annabel got back. No, *when* she did. I pushed any negative thoughts aside and added to my grandmother's thoughts…

"A partner change now of all times? It's because he wants to protect her," I continued, which wasn't entirely false. I may have slyly hinted towards the partner swap, but when he took it on as his own idea one of the main reasons was to protect her with his impeccable skills he'd boldly and frequently proclaimed.

"He really likes her," that part was true, "and after today I think she really likes him too." That part was a lie, but it was the last thing I had to say because the seed had already been planted.

She was in awe as she got up from the table. Thinking aloud at some points and to herself at others until she was out of sight. Tea time had been a success, now I needed to wait for her to do some investigating. As I expected; shortly after she left to "tend to something," and though she didn't say what it was, I already knew.

I glared at the book harmlessly sitting on the shelf, but I knew better. It was taunting me; we were so close. Simply thinking about it was tiring me out. I needed a nap; a few restless hours of sleep had suddenly caught up to me. I laid down in Annabel's bed.

Everything was still a blur when I awoke, but I could hear Grandma going on and on as I stretched from my nap. She sounded excited. As I walked towards her, she was going on about how she couldn't believe this was happening. She never imagined the Andrews and the Wests would unite. Grandma was quickly gathering all the necessary ingredients for making bread, which meant she was about to make a *grateful loaf.*

It was obvious she had been talking to Madam Elder Level 4, MaryAnne Suthers. She had a hobby of noticing things and making sure everyone else "noticed" them too, which is what I had relied on. She didn't let me down either. Poor Annabel, soon everyone would know about her make-believe relationship.

Grandma had a new bounce in her step that morning and was going on about how; when we hope hard enough it works and then something about the brother my age.
What had I done?

I wanted to terminate the mission immediately, but it was the perfect time to take it to the next step. Meanwhile, I helped Grandma in the kitchen and agreed with her in terms of how surprising it was. After she'd done her fair share of gushing and planning for an imaginary future, I interrupted her.

"That's what I wanted to talk to you about earlier." I swallowed hard, "Royalty has been talking to me at lunch and he..." I was trying to hold myself together. I knew she was going to be excited, but not this excited. A part of me felt guilty, but I went on, "He wants to have a ring for her, and the youngest Andrews brother works metal. He said he'd make one, but I have no way of knowing her ring size. I'm supposed to figure it out, but I don't know how. I can't ask anyone because Royalty wants to keep the engagement private. I've even ruined the surprise by telling you."
I tried to appear sad which wasn't hard because lying to my grandma like this really was making me upset. "I don't want to let Annabel down," I added, tearing up

204

from a mixture of not wanting to let my sister down, wanting her to come back right now, and for lying to my grandmother's face.

I sat in the kitchen and put my head down on the table. A whimper escaped while every emotion hit me all at once. Then, I felt something in my hand.
"Take this," said my grandmother while rubbing my back.

The ring was in my hand...

I turned towards her. She stood rubbing the spot where the ring had been as if she had removed a piece of herself. "You tell him it should be a bit bigger, but this should do for size," she said softly.
My plan had worked, which made all the deception worth it.

"Don't you lose that; you hear me?" she asked sternly. "In fact, I'll go with you now so that I can tell him how important it is and that he should be careful," she said flatly walking toward the door as if she was going right that moment.

"Grandma, you can't. You're not supposed to know, no one is. Only me, Royalty and his little brother."

She froze in her tracks and looked at me.
"You need to tell him to be careful then," she said. I could tell she was nervous about giving the ring to me. "Put it on so you don't lose it."

"Of course," I said, then nodded making eye contact so she knew I understood. "I promise," I added and that was the truth.

I put it on and looked down at my hand. It fit my middle finger not my ring finger, but it was still the first piece of jewelry I'd ever worn aside from my identification band. I spread my fingers and admired it, even though it was made of a dull metal and shined less than my band, I liked the look of it. I never thought I had nice hands until now, what a difference it made. It was nice to wear something that not everyone else had or was forced to wear.

"I was only a little older than you when your grandfather gave it to me. It was the first time I felt like I was home since, well, you know. It's simple, but it's what it meant," she said smiling, while gazing into nothingness.

"Well, I like it," I said, and I did. I liked how it looked and I liked what it meant. I liked that I had it.

I finally had the ring; I couldn't wait to tell Annabel!

It was worth it.
"We'll have to size down for you if you don't fill out a little more," I heard her say.

"Wha?" I said looking up from my hand still on display.

"You know when you need to be sized, perhaps for an Andrews as well," she said hopefully.

I gagged; it was *almost* worth it.

"Go on," she directed. "Go and hand it off to L1 Renegade Andrews before your sister gets back. You know how observant she is; she will be suspicious if she sees that on your finger."

She said it as if Annabel would be back any second and although I wished it were so, I knew better.

So, I got prepared to go off, I wasn't exactly going to give it to Renegade, but I needed to act like I was. I needed to do anything that would keep me from focusing on how many minutes had passed since Annabel had left.
I needed a distraction.

Something heavy pushing down on top of me pulled me right out of my sleep. I woke up, pinned down.

"Wow, my bed sure is extra comfortable tonight," said Annabel laughing while laying on top of me dead weight.

Although she was crushing me and practically squeezing the life out of me, I'd never been happier to see her. I hugged her and pushed her off, then hugged her again. I'd made a habit of sleeping in her bed when she left for survivor sweeps, it made me feel closer to her.

"You see Grandma already?" I asked, knowing that my grandmother would not sleep until she knew Annabel had returned safely. Annabel nodded, still laying on top of my legs.

I wondered how long I'd been asleep; it didn't feel like long.

As if she read my mind, she answered my question and said, "It's still the middle of the night. We didn't get very far so we headed back when we found a survivor."

"Wha?" I asked, half asleep and making sure I heard her correctly. I rubbed the sleep from my eyes and tried to sit up. It was dark, but I could still make out the smile of satisfaction she was wearing.

"Yeah, and we're whole," she said with raised eyebrows as she finally got off of my legs which had turned completely numb.

She washed up then crawled into bed next to me. We had always been close, but even more so lately. I was so relieved to see her, I didn't even mind laying on the edge of her small bed with whatever amount of covers she spared.

I asked her about all the things I shouldn't know about, and she told me everything. I think it was a relief for her not to have to hide that part of herself anymore.

It was good for us because I could really get what she was going through. I now understood why she sometimes came home upset or needing space. Before I thought she was being mean or selfish or even cutting me out due to my demotion and it was causing a rift between us. I often felt like she brought her rank home and I felt beneath her by lack of knowledge and understanding and it was taking a toll on our relationship.

But now we lay there in the dark and it was as if she was telling me a bedtime story about a big green place under a brightening sky. A place that was once a bustling city with rows and rows of buildings, now a shell of its former self.

Whatever remained, the hollowed-out structures and remnants of homes were now covered in tangled greenery. Signs of civilization slowly fading into the background of what now belonged to wildlife and of course; the PODS.

Although the mood on the surface was desolate, knowing they were risking their lives, almost as if they were trespassing, there was still an odd beauty about it.

She described the way the earth had sprung to life, reclaiming the land where it had basically been stripped down to nothing. It grew untamed, engulfing parts of walls and of structures that could no longer be broken down. They withstood the devastation, but now as a support to nature. A place that once created pollution and waste was now a safe haven for nature, offering shade and gathering pools of water when it rained.

It was serene, but deadly.

PODS weren't the only dangers on the surface; so were the animals that now roamed freely in great numbers. Some species we were familiar with. Level 4 surface certified hunters brought some back for rationing or as pets. The other ones they avoided, many of which were dangerous and considered *us* to be *their* rations.

It was rare, but some buildings still held on to all four walls of a room and that is where the lost hid, not just from the PODS, but from the weather and the creatures.

Those rooms sometimes housed the ones who got away. If someone was lucky, they might find a safe place despite the devastation. It was in one such room that they found her...

Janie, a small defenseless 11-year-old girl curled up in a ball, alone, hungry, dehydrated, and too traumatized to speak. She was so malnourished and exhausted that Royalty had carried her all the way back.

I could almost hear him go on about it as my sister described him rushing in and slinging the girl over his shoulder, keeping hold of her with ease in one arm while using the other to yield a machete to chop down the greenery blocking their path as he led the way home.

On the way there they had a close call with a POD, but on the way back, it had been easy to take cover in the overgrowth.

Annabel talked until her eyes were too heavy to stay open and she fell asleep mid-sentence.

I laid there a while staring into nothingness and thinking about everything I had learned. It was impressive that Annabel was part of a successful rescue mission, and I was excited to have a new community member. She may not have been a peer, but it had been so long since we had a newbie that wasn't born in. I was glad to see a new person that could hold up its own head. I wondered what she might be like and although I knew she could not talk about her surface experience with me, I thought that it might still be interesting to talk to her.

I thought about the surface world and visualized the eight of them tiptoeing between bushels and vines and ducking in and out of crumbling buildings.

I imagined the marvel of it all in that moment when my sister found a survivor and a child at that. Children hadn't been found in quite some time. We thought them to be scarce up there, and easily caught by PODS due to noisiness or aloofness.

I thought of how Royalty had now earned years of bragging rights for taking this poor child into his arms and leading everyone to safety.

I thought of how I'd have to sit through his retelling of it on my break. Most likely with less details about what happened and more about what he did and felt and which of his many workout routines had prepared him for it. I was already preparing to deal with it and then it hit me: I no longer needed to listen to nor waste anymore breaks with him. He had served his purpose.

I didn't have to pretend to laugh or actually laugh more at him than anything else.

I was almost sad for a brief moment until I thought of the bigger picture, Royalty had played his role in getting us what we needed. *The ring*, oh yeah, the ring, I sprung up and shook my sister awake.

How could I have forgotten, but then again so had she. In the hype of her surface rescue, we hadn't even thought about it.

"Annabel!" I whispered loudly, trying not to let my excitement get the best of me.

She groaned and rolled over and I gave her a good shake.

"I have the ring," I said clearly, and she snapped right out of her sleep.

"It worked?" she asked, sitting up, eyes widening.

It worked as I knew it would. I knew the only way to get the ring off of my grandmother's finger was to lower her guard with exactly what she wanted. The ultimate distraction was Annabel being ready for coupling and with Royalty, my grandmother's top candidate.

For me it was simple enough, he was an easy mark, he liked my sister, and he wasn't exactly a thinker.

I made it a point to be seen together as often as possible and every time we talked; I held his attention as long as I could. I made a few mild suggestions in regard to approaching my sister. I fed him a few of her likes and dislikes and forced Annabel to reciprocate which was the hardest part, but for her even a little was more than enough.

The partner change was a subtle nod and then there was the public display of affection. It was a very simple hand grasp, a squeeze, but that within itself was everything to those who knew my sister as the ice queen.

Quite frankly it was an ingenious plan, and it went smoothly, I was quite pleased with myself.

"You underestimate me," I said.

She shook her head. "I never doubted you or else I wouldn't have played along," then she let out a deep sigh.

I leaned my head on her shoulder. "What do you think it will do?' I asked her knowing she had no idea.

"Your guess is as good as mine," she said.

"Do you think something will open? Or something will come out of it? Do you think there is more code? Or what if..."

"Nor," she said softly interrupting my ramblings.

"Yeah?" I responded as I looked at her.

"Go to sleep," she tapped me on the forehead and laid down.

I laughed, but she was right, so I laid back down too.

We fell back to sleep because we knew we couldn't do anything until Grandma was out of range. We couldn't risk getting caught. Luckily there is always a dinner the eve of return and successful missions warranted the best dinners. They were bigger celebrations with no stops and that meant there was a lot of elder responsibility that would keep Grandma busy that day.

I rolled over to an empty bed as the smell of breakfast drifted towards me.

I hadn't had an appetite the day before as worrying about Annabel had made me sick to my stomach. However, now that I knew she was safe, I was overpowered by hunger and the scent led me and my growling stomach straight to the kitchen.

I sat at the table with my grandmother and sister, and it was a nice moment. I couldn't even think of it any other way. Yesterday, various scenarios of Annabel not returning haunted me, mocked me, temporarily drained me of hope.

I was so scared I may never have these moments again, so I soaked up every bit and especially the rare mood Grandma was in. Annabel's success made us all look good and with the expected proposal, my grandmother wore a very rare smile and laughed heartily at nearly everything. I hardly recognized her, but I loved it. Even when I goofily spilled my untouched tea she didn't lecture, she simply cleaned it up and called me silly.

Although we were eager to get to the book to solve this riddle, we didn't rush her out. We wanted to absorb every part of her positivity, her jokes, and her lightheartedness because we didn't know how long it would last, once she knew the proposal would not be accepted.

After dragging out the morning with her for as long as possible she gathered her things and left. We waited a bit to let her get some distance and when Annabel gave me the go ahead, I grabbed the ring, she grabbed the book, and we ran to her room.

We sat on the bed staring at the ring and the book on the bed in front of us. This is what we'd been wanting. This is what we had worked for these last few weeks by putting things in place to get the key so we could finally open the lock.

We sat there anxious yet hesitant because we were unsure, and because we were nervous.

Annabel took a deep breath then picked up the book and placed it in her lap. I scooted closer to her, and we followed the pattern the same way we had the first time. As soon as we finished, the book took over. It went from this old raggedy thing to an odd mechanical self-activating device. As we finished, it snapped, closed cover side down. That small thin panel slid aside revealing a mostly whole metal plate except for one missing piece.

We looked at each other again. This was the moment of truth.

"Do it," Annabel encouraged as we sat there gazing at the ring in front of us on the bed.

"No, you do it," I said awestruck.

She picked up the ring and stared at it. She then held it so that it aligned with the gap in the metal which was the exact same size. Then she stopped and looked at me, I put my hand on hers and we pushed it into place together.

We waited. The ring fit perfectly into the gap, filling it and making it one flat, solid, dull plate of metal.

Suddenly there was a soft clicking sound.

The ring spun in place slowly, then sped up. It turned to the right, then to the left followed by an odd pattern in small clicks and partial turns in each direction until the clicking slowed down, then stopped. Annabel put the book back on the bed and we both stepped back cautiously.

A soft humming began, and the spine of the book swung open. We didn't say a word, but looked at each other, then down at the book. I was frozen in place, so Annabel knelt down to see what had been presented to us.

Because I was dumbfounded and stuck in place, she tugged me down to join her by the bed. Still silent, we stared at the opening in the book.

There was a small black metallic cube lodged inside the spine.

I had a million questions, but all I could do was blink.

Annabel delicately grabbed hold of it and pulled it gently from its resting place. A sound of air being released followed the instant it was removed, and it became a book again. It flipped cover side up, spitting out the ring. Then the spine closed up seamlessly. There was no evidence of it being anything other than a regular old book.

I swallowed hard, impressed and curious. We sat on the floor looking at what appeared to be a grayish black cube. It was smooth, plain, and small enough to fit in the palm of her hand. She could almost close her fist around it.

"What is it?" I asked knowing she had no idea.

She held the cube in both hands, between both her forefingers and thumbs and twisted it as if she knew what she was doing.

Did she know what she was doing?

I watched her move it in ways that seemed calculated and purposeful, and even though I wanted answers, I still couldn't find words to ask what I wanted to know, nor did I know what to ask. So, I watched Annabel instead.

She twisted the plain looking little cube in what appeared to be a series of patterns though there didn't seem to be any buttons or dials. When she was done, she pressed each side and placed it in the palm of her hand.

The cube moved, unfolding itself as if it were paper laying thinly in a semi see-through shimmery sheet in her hand. It now took up her entire palm, flat and barely visible.

I moved behind her to look over her shoulder as she held it out.

She *did* know what she was doing.

"What the…?" I began.

I'd never seen anything like this, but apparently, she had, because her expression was very matter of fact versus my own. I couldn't see anything, but it felt like my eyes were super wide. My jaw dropped.

"It's a map," she said nonchalantly.

A map? I couldn't see a map in her hand, only a thin blurry sheet. I grabbed it from her hand to get a better look and was suddenly holding the cube.

Annabel laughed. "I knew you were going to do that" she said, "you'll have to open it yourself."

She walked me through it explaining how they use these for surface mapping especially now that the roads and ways have changed, and more roads had become dangerous dead ends.

I followed her instructions and it opened flat in my hand, but I still couldn't see a map. It was a shimmer with two dots: a steady green one and a blinking purple one off in the distance.

She took it from my hand, but this time it didn't fold up.

Before I could ask why not, she explained it was because we had both already programmed ourselves in.

I was very rarely this quiet, but I was so amazed.

She held the map and pointed out that the green dot was us and that the purple dot was a marked destination. The slower it blinked, the further it was, and it had only blinked once maybe twice since we'd opened it.

There was no marked path or way of getting there, it was like no map I'd ever seen.

Blank maps are not programmed, or they were deprogrammed either by being disabled or because the lay of the land changes so drastically that it has to be recalibrated or remapped. The way you did that was to go out with the cube to survey the surroundings. The more it gathered, the more it revealed as you followed the blinking light.

But this one was empty which meant we basically held a map that told us nothing more than where we were and that there was something somewhere else.

She closed her other hand over the map then slid it across it and the so-called map returned to its cube form.

All the words I couldn't form came out all at once, "What is it a map of? What's the destination? How could a map not tell you where to go or how to get there? How do you even program it? Do we need to go up there in order to…"?

"We?" she interrupted. "We are not going anywhere. I will see if I can sync it to something updated and if that doesn't work maybe I will go out for a training session and see if I can set it up," she said firmly.

"Yeah, but," I could not believe she would exclude me from the most important part. I started to protest, but before I could, I was interrupted. This time not by her, but by my grandmother coming in and calling her name.

She quickly handed me the cube and told me to put it somewhere safe. I scooped up Grandma's ring, threw the covers over the book and followed behind my sister. I chased behind her to find Royalty standing right there in our kitchen.

He assumed stance the moment he saw her and she returned the gesture.

"We are requested for a meeting," he said to her in the softest tone I'd ever heard him speak in. "You can have ten to suit up."

"I only need five," she said in that tone I hated.

"Five it is," he said rigid with lowered eyebrows.

She smiled that infamous half smile of hers then left the room.

I was in stance myself, without even realizing it.

"At ease, Nor," he said kind of chuckling and taking off his hat to run his hand through his hair.

I broke stance knowing full well what these next five minutes would entail; him retelling his heroic journey. I could do without it but had to tread lightly with my grandmother in earshot.

"You should be proud," he began, looking at the ground and smiling.

Yeah, I'm so proud of you I thought waiting for him to go on boasting.

"Your sister is a real hero," he paused a minute, "she deserves all the credit," he said putting his hat back on. He straightened up and cleared his throat as Annabel walked in long before the five-minute limit.

"Is that so?" she asked only this time the smile was a whole one.

"Something like that," he said blushing. She reached up to tap him on the forehead and he caught her hand. "I was trying to give the kid someone to look up to, you know besides me," he said, trying to hide his own smile as he opened the door for her.

She stepped out and he followed her closing the door behind him.

I stood there a moment wondering what could be so important that they needed to meet so urgently until I realized I still had the cube. I ran off to stash it and returned to find my grandmother serving me more tea. I sat down in front of it and blew on it pointlessly because more than likely I wouldn't even pretend to drink it until it was room temperature.

Grandma sat down across from me, and I handed her the ring. Her face lit up as she put it on. She clasped her hands and let out a sigh of relief.
"I take it everything went well?" she asked, still holding her hands together. She rubbed the ring as if it had been gone for years, when it had hardly been a day.
"It's in the works," I lied, hating myself for it. I sipped the hot tea. I didn't know what else to do with myself. As I put the cup down, my grandmother grabbed my attention and my hand. I looked at her and she smiled.

"Lenore Rose, I have something for you." She pulled a blue folded-up handkerchief out of her pocket and put it on the table. She unfolded it. There, against the deep blue of the handkerchief, sat a dull metal ring, exactly like hers. Grandma picked it up and put it on my pinky. It fit perfectly.

"I knew it," she thought aloud, holding my hand. "I saw you when you put mine on. It looked like it belonged to you and I thought this one might fit your finger. "She paused, rubbing my hand as she sipped her tea. Then she continued, "This was your grandfather's when he first came to live here, but as he grew, it stopped fitting. Your mother wore it until it was too small, first on her thumb and then on her pinky. Now it's yours and It looks lovely."

I looked at my hand in hers, and there were no words for everything I was feeling. I hated having this moment with her under the weight of my deceit. I wanted to confess everything.

"Grandma," I began as she sipped her tea. She looked me right in my eyes, and I lost my nerve. "I... um... thank you. This means a lot," I managed to say shakily. My eyes were watery. I tried not to let them overflow, but they did, tears dripping into my cup. I sipped my salty tea and tried to keep myself together.

Grandma and I sat there a long while, with only the soft sounds of us sipping tea. Then she got up from the table, and I remembered she still had a lot of work to do. With the dinner tonight, I was surprised she'd been able to spare me even this moment.

After Grandma left, I returned Granddad's book to its rightful place on the shelf. I started getting ready for the day. I was relieved that my temporary demotion was finally over and I was again closer to being a Level 3. In the meantime, I had to help with the dinner.

Being upper Level 2 meant I didn't have the worst job for dinner prep, but I did not have the easiest job either. Serving was not fun. The only upside was those stolen moments in the back when the other servers and I snuck bites of everything before it went out onto the tables. I cleaned myself up and went to put on my uniform. Then I stopped in surprise.

There, on my bed, lay a gown, bright pink and frilly. The thought of that *thing* being on my body nearly made me gag. It couldn't possibly be for me. But there, atop that monstrosity of sparkle and shine, lay a note:

> *Thanks Nor. Nothing would have been possible without you. Tonight, you dine with us. (My mother thought you may want to wear something that suited the occasion.)*
>
> *Royalty*

Dine with the Andrews, dressed in *THIS!*? Serving was a better option. I honestly considered hiding the dress and sticking to serving, so I wouldn't have to figure out which end of the ruffles to crawl into. Then again, I could only imagine what my grandma would say to me if she knew I'd been so rude. I reluctantly picked up the dress.

I was stuck halfway into that nightmare of frills and lace when I heard a knock. Yanking my head free, I went to open the door. Mrs. Andrews stood before me.
For a moment I stood dazed, then, with one arm still trapped inside the dress, I attempted to assume stance. Mrs. Andrews smiled.
"Please, Nor. At ease." She walked in casually, pulling the dress off over my head and smoothing it onto a chair. "I'm glad to see you got the dress. Royalty will be giving your sister hers."

This was the most Mrs. Andrews had ever said to me, and I had no idea what she was doing here. I stood in the doorway, baffled and trying not to laugh at the thought of my sister wearing something as ridiculous as that pink fluffy mess draped over the chair.

Mrs. Andrews didn't seem to notice. "Your grandmother said you'd need help getting ready. With the boys being so easygoing, and me taking no time at all myself... well, I said I'd help. Besides, I've always wanted a daughter," she continued, pointing me toward the chair. "Now I'll have two."

Bewildered, I sat down as Mrs. Andrews put her hands in my hair. She moved it around from side to side, placing it on top of my head while making sounds of vague disapproval until she was satisfied. "Oh yes," she said, letting my hair fall. "That's it... that's what we'll do." Then she tapped me on the shoulder. "Go on." She motioned me toward my room.

I sat there, still confused.

"You need to put something proper on to wear under your dress," she explained, smiling as I sat there like I was stuck-on stupid.

Yay, I thought as I changed into underclothes that would fit beneath the bright madness she was now referring to as her "labor of love." Once I was done, Mrs. Andrews sat me down and started painting my face, complimenting it the whole time she was changing it with colors and removing its hair. When she was done with my face, she pulled and tugged on my hair. She called it "gorgeous and full," when we both knew it was really tangled and rough.

After what seemed like forever, she was finished. My head hurt from whatever she had done to it in the process, and I wondered how mad Grandma would be if I went into the bathroom and undid everything Mrs. Andrews had completed.

Then Mrs. Andrews looked at me. "Do you want to see it?"

I was wary. The grin on Mrs. Andrews' face was growing bigger with every step I took towards the mirror. Then I saw myself, and I was stunned. I hardly knew the girl who stood across from me. What had she done?

"Oh, you like it!" Mrs. Andrews put her hands on my shoulders. I hadn't realized I was smiling. I wasn't a fan of the colors or the bigness of the hair and the dress, but I saw a good-looking person staring back at me from the mirror. I had never seen myself that way before. "Go on," Mrs. Andrews' laugh was kind of contagious as she spun her finger. "Give it a twirl."

I did. I threw my hands out and spun around. The dress took to the wind, flaring out and looking even fuller than it had before. I stopped for a moment and looked at myself again. My reflection smiled back at me.

"You look absolutely stunning, Nor," Mrs. Andrews fawned, and I couldn't help but agree. I felt beautiful. "Tonight is going to be so special." She gave me a teary-eyed smile, and I let her hug me tight.

The front door slammed open, catching our attention. Mrs. Andrews and I ran towards the sound, only to find Annabel rushing in.

"I'll meet you there." Royalty's voice echoed from the hall as he took off in the other direction, not realizing his mother was at our place. Mrs. Andrews followed behind him.

Annabel rushed into her room. I followed her, lifting the dress so I wouldn't trip over it. Annabel was madly going through her things.

"Are you getting dressed for dinner?" I asked.
She ignored my question. "Have you seen Grandma?"
"What? No, not for a little while." Why was she being so weird? "She left not too long after you."
Annabel continued to shuffle through her things, putting some of them in a bag. I had a really bad feeling. "What are you doing? What's wrong?" I asked.

Finally, my sister stopped and looked at me. I don't think she'd even noticed what I was wearing until that very moment. A grin took over her solemn expression. "Whoa," she said. "This must be the Lenore Rose they all talk about."

I felt my cheeks get hot. "You've got a dress to wear too," I retorted. Annabel shook her head. "Not tonight." She put her stuff down; she sounded defeated. Annabel sat on her bed, and tapped the spot next to her. I sat down, feeling inches taller seated on top of all the fabric.

"There's been an emergency meeting," she told me. Janie had finally spoken. There was a group, she said, of men and women and even a few other children. It was the group she had been separated from. They had lost each other running from an alerted POD. Based on mapping, the Select were able to estimate more or less where they could find them, but they had to go now, before the group got too far or lost too many.

"But you just got back," I protested. I couldn't take her leaving again. Not when we were so close to figuring out our own thing.

"I have to," Annabel replied. "There are people out there who need a safe place to be. Janie's sister is out there— her *baby* sister." She spoke softly as she took my hand. "I know I'd want someone to save you, Nor."

There was nothing I could say. She was right. It didn't stop me from crying though. Annabel hugged me tightly. "Stop it," she said. "You'll ruin your pretty little outfit, and you'll need to put it back on in a few days when I come back."

I groaned. Annabel could have punched me in the stomach, and it would have hurt less than this. I threw myself back on her bed as she finished grabbing her things. When she was done, she leaned over and tapped me on the forehead. "When I come back, we'll figure everything out, okay?"

I didn't respond, so she asked again. "Okay?"

I couldn't speak, so I nodded through all my anger and frustration, and hugged her with all my might.

"Are you going to find Grandma?" I managed to ask.

Annabel nodded. "You want to come with?"

I laughed, though it sounded more like a sob. "Like this?" I pointed to my dress. My face was red and smeared. We both laughed. Then I paused. "Are you really leaving right now?" I asked, though I already knew the answer. Annabel nodded. "Yeah, but I'll be back in no time. Just imagine me in something like this to get you through." She poked the ruffles and frills that were consuming me and we laughed and hugged, again.

Annabel left, wet from my tears. I stayed in her empty bed. I was a pile of sadness, red faced and breathless with runny face paint on my arms and hands, all wrapped up in a big pink bow.

It was the longest day and a half of my life, and I was going crazy. My sister left, saying she would be back in a few days. I assumed that meant the normal three, at max. Shortly after she left, I found out that this specific rescue could take double that time. The Select were not even due to return until day seven.

Annabel knew that when she said goodbye to me but didn't tell me. I was upset with her, even if I knew she did it because she could hardly tear me away from her as it was. The mix of worry, panic, and anger, and the general uneasiness of having so much weighing on me, made it hard to eat or sleep. I couldn't even think clearly.

The entire community was buzzing with excitement about the outcome of this rescue mission. It was much easier to be excited when it wasn't your big sister sacrificing herself out there for the cause. The community was looking forward to added numbers, new children, and people with new skillsets. All that mattered to me was Annabel coming home safe.

I wished there was something I could do. I felt helpless, and I hated that feeling. Lessons were always cancelled during sweeps, and I could only pace the same floors for so long. I needed something to keep me busy and out of my own thoughts.

Grandma kept herself occupied by planning a wedding that I knew was never actually going to happen. Although it pained me that her efforts were in vain, I preferred her being occupied. Overthinking, with idle time and solitude, was a recipe for disaster.

I was home alone with the cube beckoning to me. It called out to me, hidden among my underwear as it encouraged me to give it what it needed—details. "Configure me," it seemed to call. "Annabel will thank you later." Lying cube. But what else could I do?

Annabel was out there, risking her own life to rescue strangers and better our community. I was home in my pajamas, hair undone and chewing my fingernails as if they were breakfast, while I walked pointlessly back and forth. I was starting to lose it; I needed a purpose, and getting the details for the cube was the least I could do. Annabel would forgive me. It was similar to her mission—a necessary evil. Besides, I desperately needed the distraction.

I pulled myself together as I plotted. First, I had to do some recon. Who was on panel? What would shifts look like later this evening? I focused on this, a new mission to keep me from going insane. I headed out and walked around.

Without lessons, there was not much going on. People were gathered in groups here and there, around the community. It was all social and at ease—no uniforms, no stances. I listened to them chatter about who the Select might save and what that meant for the rest of us.

As I passed through the groups, I considered the little tidbits Royalty had told me about some of our fellow community members. Perhaps Royalty had been useful for more than getting Annabel and me the ring. He really had taught me a lot about how to buy favors or, as he put it, "be charming."

For the first time, I realized that Royalty might actually be clever. He was never blatantly so, but had a way of collecting useful knowledge about people and what they liked, such as the things I'd told him about Annabel— useful insight and small ways to get her attention.

Royalty taught me that although rank may be about levels, it never hurts to have something better to offer than simply initiating stance. I had to be careful. I was too close to Level 3 now to go backwards; I didn't want to risk being assigned any points. Who should I talk to? Who could I get to take the bait?

I moved through the small gatherings, nodding to people as they gave me way more respect than I'd ever gotten before, or probably even deserved. With Annabel's new hero status, it was like I'd gotten promoted, in a sense. My level rank was the same, but my social standing had clearly gone up. Almost everyone I saw made it a point to greet me. It was different than usual, and very interesting.

Before long, I had talked to pretty much everyone out in the commons except Janie. People whispered that she was too traumatized to join the community yet, that she wasn't doing well. Poor thing. The journals I read, with the descriptions of PODS, made my skin crawl. Of course, the medical leaders were stabilizing her before introduction; it was a lot for a person to handle, even in the best of health. I hoped that when the Select found her group, it would help her.

I made my rounds, taking mental notes of who was where. A few Levels on shift wanted to wish me well on behalf of my sister, and I chatted with them for a while. I let them talk, listening for anything that might be helpful, like an idea of what I needed to offer and to whom.

Our kitchen was filled with drop-offs of grateful loaf, roll-out cookies and tarts that people had left over the last day and a half. My grandmother wouldn't eat sweets and I didn't have much of an appetite with the stress. As I listened to my well-wishers, however, I realized I did know who would. Better still, this particular sweet tooth would be on ground patrol that evening. Perhaps, with a few pans of the good stuff, I might be able to buy myself a glance in the other direction.

I made my way towards the shadows near the patrol room. I was focused now, ready. I knew what I had to do.

Hot breath hit my neck. "What are you doing?"
I jumped, startled, and turned around. Reign Andrews stood there with his big, dumb smile.

"I should have expected it to be you. What are *you* doing? *Lurking? Creeping?*"

I spit, stepping back. Reign slid into view, too close for comfort, his uniform hat pulled down so low all you could see was his great big grin. He was missing his top two front teeth. Reign and his twin, Regal, were always in competition with each other, and I'd been lucky enough to witness the one that took his teeth. Stacking bins to see who could jump over the highest stack probably seemed like a brilliant idea at the time. Too bad it had led Reign to lose his teeth and his rank for some time.

Reign leaned in close. "Looks like you're doing the same thing," he said in a loud whisper, gesturing towards the patrol room.
"What are you talking about?" I bluffed, a little thrown off that he may have noticed what I was up to.

"Mmmmmm-hmmmmm," he said, dragging out the sound as he circled me. "I know a thing or two about lurking and creeping, and you are definitely creeping. Maybe even lurking."

"I'm bored. I was strolling," I lied, shrugging him off. Reign sure did know about lurking; he was demonstrating it now by walking that way with his hands in his pockets. I wondered how long he'd been watching me, and I wondered why. The only thing Reign and I had in common was our ability to rack up points. Sure, we'd sat through retraining sessions together and got assigned to the same extra detail when we needed to shed points. It didn't mean we were friends.

Reign acted as if he didn't believe me. "You're bored, huh?"
"Yeah. What of it?" I snapped defensively. "Things are always boring when they're off on sweeps."
"Yeah, me too," Reign admitted. He let out a big breath of air, like he was glad to be doing anything other than waiting around. Whether or not I wanted to, I understood. I felt the same way.

He continued. "My house is full of ladies planning our brother and sister's wedding. And there hasn't even been a proposal! Sheesh," he mocked, tugging his hat down as if it could possibly get any lower. Then he looked at me. "You wanna go over there and ooh and ahh over what might look best on your sister? As if it were even possible to clean that girl up," he teased, smiling deviously as he crossed his arms.

I knew he was waiting for a reaction to his stupid joke, so I didn't give him one. Instead, I looked around, observing posts and checking to see if they'd added any with the Select out. They hadn't. Reign was an idiot, but he was giving me the perfect opportunity to look like I was doing nothing, while I made my plans.

Reign must have realized I was ignoring him because he got really close again. "You know," he said, getting right in front of me and blocking my view, "come to think of it, Annabel's the one that's *not* so bad on the eyes. It's *you* I can't wait to see cleaned up." Reign laughed like this was the funniest thing he'd ever heard. "You, all dolled up!"

"Yeah. Clean dolls," I muttered. Was he trying to flirt with me? Whatever it was, it wasn't worth my time. I did my best to look around him, continuing to think about logistics. Reign didn't seem bothered. "What are you even looking at?" he asked, shifting around behind me and looking over my shoulder as if to get a better view. He looked around, then gasped dramatically. "You wanna leave again?"

"What? No! What are you talking about?" I stumbled over my words, my voice coming out two octaves higher than normal. And I thought Reign was dumb. "Anyway, I didn't leave. I almost left. Everyone knows that."

Reign smiled, but he didn't say anything. He didn't need to. It was obvious he was pleased with the rise he got out of me, and with whatever he seemed to know that I did not.

"Ugh," I spat, my frazzled nerves showing. "What do you know?" I started to walk away, but Reign stepped in front of me.

"I know that you're up to something," he grinned.

I gave him a cold look and pushed past, making it a point to bump him aside as I walked by.

"Take it easy, sis," Reign called out behind me. I didn't answer. Instead, I kept walking, not letting him get the satisfaction of knowing how much he had gotten under my skin.

I returned home to determine which baked goods and food could be sacrificed. I didn't want to take any of Grandma's or Annabel's favorites, but there were plenty of options. Most Select families were large, but there were only three of us. We could hardly get through the food we were given and always ended up sharing. This time, there was even more than usual, so we had food to spare.

Once I found the right bribes, I returned to the patrol room, casually handing out thoughtful snacks and asking the posts questions disguised as nice conversation. I left the room with empty hands and a full-fledged plan.

I'd scarcely gotten out when I heard a voice behind me.
"Uh huh. I knew it!"
I practically jumped right out of my skin, swinging
instinctively before I'd recognized my "attacker." I pulled
my punches with a groan.

"Reign Andrews! What is wrong with you? Seriously,
how bored do you have to be to go around sneaking up
on people?" I whisper-screamed.
Reign smiled really big. That's all he was really; a stupid
smile in a hat.
"I know what you're doing," he said, the smile staying on
his lips.
"You don't know nothing," I spat back.
"I know Royalty must've taught you a thing or two."
"Yeah, as if *Royalty* could teach me anything," I scoffed,
ignoring my discomfort. Reign was way more observant
than I'd ever given him credit for, which wasn't good.

Reign laughed. "You should be nice to Royalty." A little
sneer appeared on his face. "He's your big brother. He
worries about you."

I immediately lost my temper. "I'm fine. I don't need
your worry. What I do need is for you to shut your
mouth." I jammed past him, bumping him harder this
time as I left. Until now, I thought Royalty was the
Andrews that bothered me most. Well, I stand
corrected. All the Andrews brothers favored one
another with their pale skin, dopey doe eyes, and dark

hair, but Reign was like a miniature version of Royalty—
without any of the charm or skill or rank.

"So, you're fine huh?" Reign's tone was antagonizing.

"You mean, you're finely aligning the pieces."

I should have kept going, but Reign had my attention
now, and he knew it. I turned around, keeping quiet as I
looked back at him. Not that my silence mattered;
stopping in my tracks said more than enough.

Reign's expression was shadowy and vague, but his
body language was alert. "You only give Millie cookies
on her birthday or if you want something from her, and
it's not her birthday." Reign scratched his head and
rubbed his chin, exaggerating his movements. "What
could you possibly want from her, other than for her to
'not notice' when you sneak past later?"

That was the final straw. I knocked Reign's hat off his
head so I could look him in the eyes. "You know what,
Reign? You're doing way too much. Why don't you take a
seat somewhere?"

Reign scrambled for his hat. "I'm only doing as I was
asked," he confessed. I paused. Maybe it was how he
said it, or the fact that his stupid hat was no longer
covering most of his face, but he sounded sincere.

"Asked?" I asked through gritted teeth. "Who asked you
to go out of your way to annoy me?"

Reign picked up his hat and dusted it off, smiling slightly.
With his hat in his hands, I could see his expression. It

made him slightly more tolerable. Reign looked down, and he looked a lot more like Royalty standing in my kitchen a few days before. I narrowed my eyes.

"Did Royalty ask you to mind me?"

"Sort of." Reign shrugged. Then he began to explain. Apparently, Annabel knew I would try to step out, and she told Royalty, who asked Reign to keep me from getting in trouble.

"They knew you'd leave," he added. "I've been watching you and even I could tell it was your plan. It looked like a good plan, too. You put all your pieces together, except for one little thing…" he trailed off as if he wanted me to beg him to tell me what I'd forgotten. He was really infuriating and I was over it.

"Is this little game some lame attempt at flirting, Reign?" I demanded. "Because I'm about done."

"You're not my type." Reign laughed, rolling his eyes. Then he paused. "Consider this a negotiation."

"A negotiation?" I repeated, puzzled.

"Yeah." Reign grinned. "You want… something, and I want something… plus, I know something… you don't know. So, we negotiate. I help you… and you help me, ---- ---then maybe I share that information with you."

"Stop pausing so dramatically between words," I snapped. "It makes you sound like you don't know what you're talking about."

Still, I knew that at this point it didn't hurt to listen to Reign, even if he was annoying. He told me that the leaders had assigned a new post that came on after

241

everyone else in the late evening. The post was Given, a newly ranked Level 4 who liked being liked. Reign went on to explain that being nice to Given and promising that one of our siblings thought he was cool would probably get us a free pass—well, that and a pan of cheesy biscuits.

"Us?" I raised an eyebrow. I was seeing Reign's value, but that word "us" was a little concerning.

"Well, you can see how helpful I am," he began, dragging things out the way he did. "One might even say you couldn't do it without me..."

I was getting fed up. "Spit it out, Reign," I demanded.

Reign braced himself. "Look, I won't say a word about you leaving, but you have to take me with you."

I looked at him: "Okay."

Reign looked like he was going to fall over. He clearly never thought I would agree without hesitation. But I knew he was going to make everything more difficult if he couldn't come. It would be pointless to try and convince him to stay behind. I hated the thought of him coming along, but I wanted to activate the map more than anything. If it meant putting up with Reign Andrews, then that was simply the price I had to pay. I did want to know why he wanted to come though, so I asked.

He countered with, "Why do *you* want to go anyway?" I couldn't answer that, not without revealing too much of my family's weird story. I could tell Reign was keeping something hidden as well, but it was easier not to pry. Instead, we both shrugged and agreed to meet back in the same spot in an hour.

In the next hour, I managed to slip in a cup of tea with Grandma. I told her I was going to be spending time with Reign Andrews. It was nice to be mostly honest for a change. I did not mention the part about stepping out on the surface to reprogram a dead map.

I was beginning to find teatime to be more of a pleasure than an obligation. I knew Grandma was worried about Annabel, but she seemed to be keeping it together. It was evident that Mrs. Andrews' cheery attitude had rubbed off on her. I liked it on Grandma; happiness suited her. If this was how she was going to be if Annabel and Royalty got married, then Annabel might very well have to say "yes."

After Grandma left the table, I left home. I didn't bring much besides the cube, a journal for reference, and (of course) a pan of cheesy biscuits. I'd even rewarmed them so they would be even more enticing.

"Oh, great you brought them!" Reign exclaimed, appearing out of nowhere to snatch the pan from my hands. I hated that he did that, coming out of nowhere. "Reign! Do you walk around tiptoeing? You ought to wear a bell or something."

Reign opened the biscuits and shoved them into his mouth, moaning and making smacking sounds as he chewed with his disgusting mouth open. I went to grab them back when he pulled away. "Full disclosure," he said with his mouth full, "these were for me. You try getting the best of anything with five brothers ravaging the kitchen!" Pieces of food flew out through the gap in his smile as he continued, "Anyway, Given is easy. I'll promise him a play date with Royalty, and he'll do anything we want."

"Hey! You're eating them all!" another voice screamed. I turned around to find Regal. He pushed past me and greedily grabbed the biscuits, shoving some into his mouth as well. They ate savagely from the pan, making horrible sounds and getting crumbs everywhere.

"Look how big a bite I can take," Regal announced, stuffing most of a large biscuit into his mouth.
"Not as big as me." Reign took an even bigger biscuit. The twins went back and forth, shoving the biscuits in their mouths without chewing. With full cheeks, they looked at one another and started to laugh and choke in unison. I was so put off by their insanity, I forgot to question why Regal was even there in the first place.

Reign handed me the empty pan they'd practically licked clean. Then they simultaneously wiped their hands, first on their pants and then on each other. The twins laughed, sounding so much alike.

"I hate to interrupt this brotherly moment and all," I said sarcastically, "but can I talk to you for a minute, Reign?" I said as I waved him over.

"Not if you're going to talk about me," Regal cut in. He was a copy of Reign, younger by three minutes and eighteen seconds, with the same scrawny build and the same smile—except Regal still had teeth.

He looked at me through bushy dark eyebrows, smirking the same devilish way Reign had earlier when he unveiled his "master plan." Regal smiled, the ends of his mouth curling up and highlighting a giant scar on his right cheek he'd won from another failed twin competition.

I glared at him, then shot Reign a look that made him jump. "Reign?"

"Nor?" he stammered back.

"Reign said I'm coming too," Regal proclaimed, letting out a disturbingly loud burp then laughing hysterically.

"Yeah, makes sense. Because you're so *discreet*." I was trying not to punch the both of them, so I let my voice drip with sarcasm.

Reign looked defeated. "I know," he admitted, "but when Regal found out, he put me in a bind."

"I know the feeling!" I stared at him pointedly.

Regal walked over between the two of us, putting his hands on our shoulders and pulling us close as if he was about to tell us some big secret. "We've never had a sister before," he whispered softly. I couldn't tell if he was being facetious. "So, sis, tell us how it's done."

I hated the idea of Regal coming, but I began to explain the plan, anyway. We had precisely thirty minutes to walk past conveniently turned heads, get our information, and get back without getting caught. "No problem," Regal grinned. He gestured to Reign. "Shall we?"

I got to watch the Andrews twins using their doe eyes and their famous older brother as leverage, turning heads I hadn't even thought about. Before I knew it, we were out on the surface.

The first thing I did was take about ten extra steps, to make it further than I had before. Then I stood there and let myself absorb everything for one glorious moment in time. I pulled the air deep into my lungs; it felt amazing.

The sky was different than before. The nature room in our community imitated the sky in different phases of sunrise; high noon and sunset, but the simulation didn't come close to this. The glow of the sinking sun was astonishing. The purples were deeper, the oranges softer and the red hues were so much more intense. I looked behind me to find the boys wide-eyed. They were stuck in place beside each other, breathing in the air as deeply as I was. I smiled. For the first time since they finished the cheesy biscuits, Reign and Regal were completely quiet.

I walked over and playfully punched them both. "Be careful out there," I said. "We don't have much time."
"Thirty minutes?" Reign confirmed.
 "Twenty-eight now," I clarified. "We should set a timer for twenty-five and meet back here."

Reign nodded, turning to Regal. Their goofy demeanors vanished as they became two trained soldiers, crawling away on their bellies in the tall grass.
It was time to do my job.

As I walked, I understood what my sister meant when she'd described her feelings about the surface. The land was breathtaking, though I was not yet in a position to appreciate it because of the constant danger. I moved back and forth, hoping that was all I needed to do to get the cube map to sync.

Suddenly, something grabbed my leg. I looked down to find the twins at my feet. They were both shaking, drained of life. I dropped down beside them. I didn't need to ask what was wrong; their faces said it all.
We were on a POD's radar. How had this happened? My heart collapsed into my stomach as I came to terms with reality. We could be living our last moments. Although I hadn't caught sight of the POD myself, I thought I knew what to expect from the journal entries and my sister's

tales. I wasn't prepared for the true horror of what society had really become.

My ring flashed as it caught a reflection of something stirring nearby. The twins and I tried to move through the tall grass, but we were unsure of where to go. Which direction was safe? With nothing to lose, I pulled out the cube and quickly opened it. To my surprise, the translucent sheet was more of a map now. The area around us was marked clearly, the green light steady as it showed our location. The purple light still flickered slowly, but now there was something else—a red dot. That red dot was not far from our green light. We needed to maintain that distance.

The twins watched my every move, following my lead as I went. The red dot—the POD---chased after us without hesitation. The boys were sweaty and paler than normal, and they were silent. That left me to figure out what, if anything, could be done. My ring reflected the setting sun, flashing here and there as I did my best to play a terrible game of avoiding the PODS and getting to safety. We were down to eleven minutes, and we were getting farther away from home.

I glanced at the map. A sound of dismay escaped my lips as a second red dot flickered onto the map. The twins shifted behind me; they knew that couldn't be good, even though they couldn't see what was on the map until they were programmed in. I signaled and we ran.

We couldn't let the PODS catch us, but also could not risk leading them back to our community.

An emaciated looking body with saggy skin and sunken yellow eyes burst into view, running toward us at full speed. The POD was far worse than what I imagined when I read my Granddad's descriptions. I would have gagged if I hadn't been so desperate to pull away. The POD was too fast; there was nowhere I could go.

I was going to die.

I thought about sitting at my kitchen table over a cup of tea with my grandmother and sister. I would never see them again. They would never see me. I closed my eyes tight and waited for the impact.

It never came.

I opened my eyes. The POD lay on the ground a few feet from us, still and lifeless, as if it had been powered down. The boys were staring at my hand, their eyes and mouths wide. Then I saw my ring. It was still glowing, lit up from inside in a way that seemed powered up, rather than reflecting the light.

"We saw it." Reign stammered as he pointed at my ring. "It let out a force field. It protected us and disabled the POD in the process."

I had nothing but questions. We had survived certain death. It was overwhelming…so much so that the twins and I hugged each other for a few seconds. Then Regal pulled away. "Three minutes," he said, and we ran for home.

We managed to sneak in and run to the nature room. There, we sat quietly, appreciating the room for its safety, not its accuracy.

Regal broke the silence. "You dropped this." He held out his hand with the cube in it. I went to grab it, but he closed his fist and pulled back. "I think we should talk," he began, but Reign gave him a heavy look.
"Leverage is not the way to make her talk," Reign said, swiping the cube and handing it to me.
"Fine," Regal shrugged. He turned back to me, batting his eyes instead. "You might as well tell us what happened. After everything we've been through, what do you have to lose?"

"You only have something to gain, sis," Reign added, his smile creeping across his face as he raised his bushy eyebrows at me. "Namely, us: Two allies."
"What are brothers for?" Regal affirmed. They both nodded, laughing the same laugh at the same time.
I did not want to admit it, but they were right. It was all out there now.

I started from the beginning.

It was day four of Annabel being gone, and day two of my newly acquired double friendship. The twins and I had spent the day before idle, recovering from our near-death experience. As we talked, we filled each other in on our real reasons for being on the surface. Reign and Regal's reason was far less complicated than mine. They had simply wanted to see a POD—mission accomplished.

Unlike Annabel and me, the Andrews brothers were much less transparent with each other. The twins only knew what they had overheard from Royalty's conversations. I quickly figured out they did not have reliable information besides bits and pieces they had strung together. I cleared things up for them.

After almost dying together, those two idiots who had made everything into a competition had become my instant best friends. I almost hated to admit how quickly I'd come to like them, even though they brought out the worst in me. I was naturally competitive, so the way they made everything a competition both annoyed me and pulled me in. I ended up encouraging them so I could win, or at least try. It was a vicious cycle.

When the twins and I weren't getting lost on a tangent of foolish contests, we did a lot of talking. To my surprise, I found they were good listeners. They even competed over it, bickering about who listened best or heard the most details. It turned out we had a lot more in common than our tendency for collecting points and demotions. How had I been around these boys my whole life, but was only now getting to know them? Reign and Regal balanced one another. Separate, they were individuals; together, they were simply two halves of a whole.

As we talked, I explained everything I found during my suspension, including my family's journals with descriptions of PODS and my Granddad's old-timey book, which proved to be anything but normal. I told them how Annabel and I solved the code and unlocked the mysterious cube. There was something about the twins that made them easy to talk to. They could spot a lie or a half-truth immediately, and they would call me out if I tried it. I liked it when they caught me. It forced me to be myself.

After almost dying, sharing things I had never told anyone except Annabel felt natural. As the boys put it, we had nothing to lose, only something to gain. Now I had help working in my favor in the form of two extra pairs of eyes and the ol' Andrews' charm, even if we were not really going to be siblings. In the spirit of friendship, I confessed how I had played Royalty, but the twins didn't seem to be put off. Perhaps they understood it was simply the means to an end.

Or maybe not.

"You never know right?" Regal teased me. "Enjoy the moment, sis."

"I'm enjoying it for what it is," Reign shrugged.

We had formed a lifetime friendship in about twenty-four consecutive hours, then slept for about ten. Both the friendship *and* the rest were necessary. Now fully refreshed and with the epic protection on my pinky, we were unstoppable.

Our siblings were not back yet, and we were antsy. I had an itch to do something, anything! The twins and I had almost died the day before yesterday, and it still felt like the boredom we suffered from was worse. To distract ourselves, we theorized what the map might lead to.

Both Reign and Regal attempted to use their charm to see if I'd let them have time with the map. It was a good effort, but they failed. I wanted to give them time—especially Reign—but we knew it wasn't safe. We needed to keep it hidden until absolutely necessary.

Reign, Regal, and I were a good team, even if I hadn't realized their skill sets before. Reign was observant. He could figure out what anyone was up to based on their body language, and he had a brain for puzzles and patterns. Regal could memorize anything instantly, and he had a silver tongue that metaphorically (and sometimes literally) opened doors. Behind the twins' crude humor and excessive enjoyment of bodily functions, they were likeable and sometimes even funny.

I guess I wasn't surprised when I learned the twins *meant* to be annoying. It was part of a long running competition between them to see who could drive people the craziest. I did not let it work on me, not anymore. I let them know I was their annoying equal, so they could let the game go when it was the three of us. They did—mostly—and it allowed me to like them even more.

We prepared ourselves for another surface run. It was easy for me to take the reins of our mission and give the boys assignments. I had always assumed the twins' dad, Rarity Andrews, was the one who ran things and whipped the boys into shape. The twins told me their dad was a softie, despite his towering height and intimidating size. He might have appeared large and in charge, but when it came to discipline and order, it was peppy-sunshine-and-rainbows; Mrs. Andrews that kept them all in check. I picked up a few things from her, finding that if I was sweet yet stern, the boys fell in line quite easily—that and a snack. The promise of food made Regal and Reign go from playful to serious in a moment's notice.

The prep was easy enough. I sent the twins out to talk to the right people and use that charm of theirs to put the pieces into place. I banned Reign from wearing his hat off duty. He was more relatable when there was a face behind his words. I also tried to beat it into the twins that sneaking up on people was not the way to gain their favor.

Both were able to do more than they were assigned. Regal came back with the news that he was able to safely buy us a full hour instead of thirty minutes. Apparently, there was going to be some kind of community meeting. We would pretend to be on detail for the event and Given would cover for our absence in return for promised time with Royalty.

Reign came back with a training tool—a demo map Level 4s used as part of surface certification training. This one belonged to Cali Richard. Reign was not sure of the map's abilities. Cali was supposed to master it in order to get a real one assigned to her, but she seemed less interested in how it worked than she was in Reign's (false) promise that Royalty would eat lunch with her. Still, Reign showed us things we had not yet realized we could see. He was not exactly sure how to activate it, but we meant to find out.

The nature room gave us more solace than ever before. The twins and I used to look at it as a tease, a terrible sample of what we imagined to be so much more amazing. Before, every time we sat in there felt like we were settling for less. It was different now. It was not about how realistic it was or wasn't. We knew our indoor sun paled in comparison to what it actually felt like out there. The real sun beaming down on you radiating warmth and goodness. I will give it the credit it deserves. Our imitation was close, but it was not the original.

That was not what mattered any more. The twins and I did not appreciate the indoor sun for how lifelike it was. We loved it for what it represented—safety. Those 30 minutes of time we experienced on the surface had been poor Janie's whole life. All our basic needs were met by the community; needs like food, water, and shelter. We didn't worry about *whether* we would eat, but rather if we'd get enough of our favorite foods.

The twins and I realized how easy we had it. We were guaranteed safety, which meant we could live and not only try to survive. We could enjoy the indoor sun without feeling our impending doom. Thinking we would never see home again gave us a different appreciation for both the nature room and our community. It was a place so safe you could get bored... and we were bored.

With our siblings still out on surface sweep, and still no lessons, the three of us together could set our sights on anything. I thought I was ingenious when it came to coming up with schemes, but the three of us together were flawless. The twins and I sat undisturbed in our own corner, snacks close by. Two of us played lookout while the other attempted to discover more about the demo map. We were less worried about getting caught with it. Yes, it would be confiscated, and we would get points, but we could eventually make up for points. We could not make up for it if the real thing got taken away.

Neither Regal nor I could find anything about this demo map that was different from my own. We were slightly discouraged but Reign still had time with it. We knew he was the one who stood the best chance of finding something. While he worked, I thought about the surface. We had sixty minutes above. It was exciting. With double the time, we could cover more ground. Having the ring to protect us would let us do what we needed to with less worry.

I wondered if my grandmother's ring was the same as mine. Did she know Granddad's ring had this ability? There was no way. Surely, if Grandma knew she would have given it to Annabel to ensure her safety during sweeps.

The ring didn't respond again, though we tried everything. Reign thought the ring was self-activated, sensing when PODS were around. Regal had memorized the flashes it made when we thought the ring was reflecting the sun. He was sure he would recognize it if it happened again. To me, it was so much more than a ring. It was a chance for survival.
There was a part of me that wanted to share it with our community. Then again, we did not know much about it. What if what happened out on the surface was a fluke? I

knew I couldn't make any moves without Annabel. After all, I may have let the twins in, but this was still *our* mission.

Regal and I decided we would let Reign get time with the demo map when we snuck out. We had an effective team. I would calibrate the real map, Regal would be lookout, and Reign would master the demo map undisturbed. It was going to work out perfectly. All we had to do was get up there.
We were ready.

The twins and I went over the details, committing everything to memory. It wasn't long before we were interrupted by a public announcement.
"Gathering in common hall in ninety minutes."
"This is it," Regal said excitedly. We all nodded. It was time.

We needed to meet Given in forty-five minutes, but before that we had to be in uniform and make it a point to be seen on detail. Detail workers did the grunt work, including clean up service or anything that needed to be done for the meeting. This was a community gathering, which meant Levels on detail would be prepping food and a sit-down atmosphere. If we showed up early, we could be seen before Given "assigned" us our special task. As soon as that happened, we would take off while the rest prepared. Sixty minutes later, the community gathering would only be half over. We could slip back in, clearing plates and things as if we had been there the whole time.

It was failproof. No one would think twice about what we were doing with the angelically trustworthy Eric "Given" Parker cosigning for us. We called him Given because it was like he had given up. After losing his dad to the surface, Given had tried to up his level several times, only to fail. The failure got to him every time. Given would get sad and try to fix his feelings with food, and at his next attempt, he would be ten pounds heavier. That went on for a while, till we hardly recognized him. Then Given fell out of sight and stopped being a part of community events that were not mandatory. I had no idea how he made it to Level 4. Maybe people took it easy on him because of his loss, or maybe his mother's hunting certification had bought him some favors. Either way, no one would question Given. We knew we were in good enough hands.

We didn't have much time to prepare. I ran home, practically bursting through the door. My grandmother was at the table, sipping tea with Regina Andrews. I scrambled to assume stance.
"Oh, Nor. At ease!" Mrs. Andrews laughed. " I see those boys of mine have contagious energy."
My grandmother joined in her laugh. "Having fun with the twins, are you, Nor?"
"Yes," I answered, heading towards my room.

"Wait, Nor! Sit... sit." Mrs. Andrews beckoned, pulling out a chair for me.

"I... uh," I started, then paused. I really *did* love teatime, and I had some time to spare. "Okay."

"Why the hesitation, Nor?" Mrs. Andrews asked, smiling sweetly as I sat next to her. "Are we holding you up from more playtime with the boys?"

I decided to tell the truth... mostly. "We're on detail for the gathering."

My grandma sat up straighter. "You're shedding points on your own accord?" She sounded intrigued.

"Yeah. It was Regal's idea," I said, staying as truthful as possible. Mrs. Andrews cried out, "Well then, there it is! My boys finally have a reason to be a good influence... having a sister." She pulled me close, smothering me in her bosom as happy tears dripped onto the top of my head. My grandmother laughed. "Regina, you're giving the child a shower."

"Oh. Perhaps I am." Mrs. Andrews freed me and we all laughed. "Nor, you should still stay and sip tea a moment before you suit up." My grandmother stood up and grabbed the kettle.

I stayed; I could not resist. I really did enjoy Mrs. Andrews and her light-heartedness, and I loved the influence she had on my grandmother. It was nice to sit with the two of them, even nicer when my grandmother talked about me the way she normally talked about Annabel. My heart melted, and when Grandma told a rare story about us that involved my mother, I cried. Then Mrs. Andrews broke the mood by asking me to choose which twin I would marry, and I laughed.

Was this what having family was like? If so, I was now on board for Annabel and Royalty's marriage. Getting used to the idea of six brothers seemed like a lot, but I liked sitting like this. I sipped my tea and listened to a few baby stories about the twins, mostly so I could make fun of them later. Then I hugged Grandma and Mrs. Andrews tightly and suited up.

I met the boys in the common hall. They were having a head-standing contest and didn't even realize I was late. "Aha!" screamed Regal. "I win! Again!"
"You cheated," Reign protested.
"He did cheat. I saw him," I chimed in, and immediately assumed my own headstand. "But I can do it for longer. Watch!"

We'd fallen over each other into a pile when Given interrupted us softly. Regal grinned at him. "Who won?" he asked, putting Given on the spot. Given looked at us, turning red and sweaty. He clearly wasn't sure what to say. When I realized how flustered he was, I punched Regal and claimed the victory. "I won. It was obviously me."
Given looked so relieved. "It's time to go," he started, but our laughter drowned him out. It took me a moment to realize he was trying to say something, but when I did,

261

I elbowed the boys. We stood up and got serious. Reign tugged his hat down and Regal stood in good posture. I was impressed by how they could go from fools to Select material in seconds.

"Um," Given began. I pitied him. He was a Level 4 with a Level 1 attitude; he did not seem in charge of himself, much less anyone else. He tripped over his quiet words. "I'm going to... if you would walk, I'll walk you out, please." We followed him.
"What's the meeting for anyway, big guy?" Regal asked. I elbowed him, and Regal corrected himself. "Sorry. I mean, Level 4, what is the gathering about?"
"To properly meet our new community member," Given answered, breathing louder than he spoke. That interested us, and we were glad we would be back in the middle of the gathering to catch at least a glimpse of the newbie.

"Have you seen her?" Reign asked.
Given nodded. "She has been through an awful lot, but she is doing better." He walked us toward our burrow's entrance, timidly reiterating the plan we already knew by heart. I nudged the boys, and we all assumed stance. Showing Given some respect was the least we could do. He was really coming through for us.
I was not sure if it was the odd lighting by the entrance or if Given's eyes actually got watery. "The only thing is," Given hesitated, choking on air, or maybe nerves. "Um, one of you has to stay behind for now. I have to loop the

cameras, so we don't get caught, and someone has to be at the internal entrance point."

He swallowed hard then continued, "I will be back, but Freely is on roaming post, so if you see him, ring me stat." Poor Given. He looked sick at the thought of getting caught.

"Good plan, my man," Regal surprised Given with a hug. "My brother is going to be so happy to know that this whole time you simply wanted to hang out. He has been saying the same." I wanted to shove Regal, but Given seemed to be enjoying it, so I let him have the moment. "Thank you, Level 4 Eric Parker," I said. I assumed stance, and the boys followed my lead.

Given left us at the entrance. The twins and I decided it was smartest to leave Reign behind so he could work on the demo map without much distraction. I would move around to try and sync more to the map, while Regal insisted, he'd still be lookout in case our tech failed. That was fine with Reign and me; we grew up knowing better than to solely rely on tech.

Then Regal grabbed us close, the way he did when he had a secret that was not really a secret. He took a deep breath, and we waited for whatever crazed pep talk he had planned. Instead, Regal let out a massive burp and cracked up. Reign and I punched him at the same time. It was a fantastic way to start a mission.

Regal and I stepped out. There we were. We swore we wouldn't get lost in it, but that was easier said than done. The sun was higher in the sky than it had been before, hiding off-and-on behind grey clouds. Even hidden, the sun beamed down hot through the moist air. Regal gazed up. The sky looked like it went on forever.

"Admire it as you walk," I reminded him. Regal snapped out of it. "And don't look directly at the sun up here. It isn't like ours. You'll blind yourself, and then you won't be a very good look out." Teasing, I pushed him down and ran in the other direction. I had to cover ground to give the map more details, and running through the tall, dewy grass seemed like the perfect way to do it.

Regal easily caught up with me, pushing me back. I tripped and fell on the soft mounds of grass. The meadow was so similar to our nature room, and yet so different. Everything was vibrant. Each blade of green and individualized. Foolishly, we rolled around for a minute before we shook it off. Having the ring was making us careless. We knew what we risked by playing around.

I pulled out the map, seeing nothing but a green dot and the very rare purple flicker. For the moment, we were clear. Then I noticed something new flicker onto the map. It was a red dot, but something was not right. The dot was right where we were standing.

"I told you we would need a lookout," Regal stated. "Tech fails and we hardly know what we're doing to rely on it fully."

I nodded and held out my hand. The ring was quiet. No spark, no light, no signs of charging up. We watched it out of the corner of our eye as we knelt and peered through the tall greenery.
"Come on." Regal took the lead. "We've been this way before."
"Wait," I whispered. I pointed to the map again with the flickering red light.
Regal dismissed it. "Is that even accurate?" he asked.
I wasn't sure. The green was accurate, but we couldn't know about the purple. Now, with the inconsistent red, we didn't know what we were looking at. I restored the map into a cube and packed it up. Regal was a good guide at least. He had memorized the lay of the land the last time, and now directed me to cover new areas. We covered wider and wider sections, making sure we never went too far. It helped that we weren't distracted by fear. We had the ring; we were protected.

Regal alerted me that he'd seen movement. It was Reign. "Guys, I am so close. I know there's more to it." Reign glared at the map as if it were his enemy. Then he paused. "Oh, and I snuck a peek."
That got our attention. "The newbie?" I asked.
"Yep." Reign sounded like he was purposely being vague.

"And?" I encouraged him.

"She's a little girl like any other, really. Small, thin. I think she was hurt pretty bad. She had scars, like a lot."

We were silent for a moment, thinking about Janie. Then Reign asked, "Where's the map?"

"On the fritz," Regal responded.

I handed the map to Reign, showing him the red dot that went in and out in different spots nearby and beside us, even though there weren't any PODS in sight. It didn't make sense. It did however, gain us more details so we were doing something right.

"I wish I knew." Reign handed me back the map. "I told Given I would be back. I'm gonna master this demo thing by the time you come back."

"Bet on it," Regal challenged. "You use that one and I'll use Nor's. When we meet back up, I'll show you how it works."

"Oh yeah? Well, I bet you dessert for a week," Reign declared, invigorated by the contest. The twins looked at me for approval.

"Oh alright," I caved. "I'll be the lookout." That made them both happy.

Reign ran for home as we took to the shade. I surrendered the map to Regal. I knew we could have joined Reign, but this way we could take advantage of our last fifteen minutes. I didn't mind being the lookout.

It let me observe instead of walking around trying not to trip over piles of dirt and things that ran over and under my feet. Regal was quieter than I had ever known him. I circled him, keeping an eye out in every direction as he sat on the grass, legs crossed and concentrating.

Then he shouted. "It's layers! There are layers! Take that Reign!"

"What is it?" I asked, resisting the urge to get lost in it. I wanted to see, but I was doing my job. Still, I glanced over. Regal had opened the map and expanded it into 3D. It was in layers, exactly as he said.

Regal handed the map to me, and we traded places.

The top layer seemed to reflect what used to be there. I could see a more detailed version of what was there before; a little open land, a small house, and a barn off in the distance. The next layer reflected us: a green dot glowing against the lay of the land where we had been. It was more detailed than before.

Then the red spark flashed.

"There!" I called out, switching my attention to the bottom. The bottom layer was our home community. It was not a blueprint, but a basic sense of the space, including a general idea of the common places. The red flash became more consistent; it was in the bottom layer. I made a horrible realization. "Regal," I managed to say. Regal had seen it, too. We ran towards home.

Three or four steps from the entrance we lost our footing. The ground was trembling under our feet. We fell hard, the earth shaking through our whole bodies. We composed ourselves enough to stand and run, unsteady and scared, toward the entrance.

There, we saw a figure. It was Given. He was helping Reign, who was limping. Regal and I ran to them, hoping we were wrong about what we thought had happened. We knew better. We could see the life drained from Given and Reign. Regal and I hugged them; we didn't know what else to do...

Grandma. I went to run home, but Given grabbed me. "No," he whispered.
"We have to help them!" I screamed at full volume, forgetting where I was. I thought of a POD being loose in our community. How had this happened?
Given held me tighter as Regal pushed past him.
"Nor, we can't," Reign cried out, tears streaming. He was shaking and breathing heavily. "Everything shook... there was a loud bang, and everything shook. I think I saw fire in the distance. I don't know. Things started collapsing. Everything was blocked and we could hear screaming... terrible screaming! We only got out because we were by the entrance."
Regal shot back, "There's got to be a way in. There has to be. Mom is down there, and Dad..."
"Stop," Given said softly.

"You weren't down there." Reign spoke in a way that chilled me to the bone.

"We have to help them! My Grandma... her ring. She might be okay." I was crying now.

"We can't," Reign was pleading with me.

Regal was on my side. "There has to be a way."

"Please, stop," Given whispered.

"We were down there. Even if someone is alive, we could not get to them. It is blocked. Completely blocked!" Reign was screaming now. "I tried with all my heart and soul to get back through. It almost killed me, but Given pulled me out in time!"

"Please," Given cried.

Regal ignored him. "You didn't try hard enough; I know *I* could get through!" he yelled back at his brother.

"STOP!" Given belted out, startling us all into silence. "The way is blocked. There is no way through from either side." He paused, then continued in his normal tone. "Now stop. I've never been out here, but I do know we shouldn't be screaming."

Neither the twins nor I had ever heard Given speak in anything above a whisper before. Now, he was giving us a reality check.

"Given is right," Reign began.

Given cut him off. "My name is Eric," he pointed out sternly. It seemed almost dying gave him a backbone. "We need to find somewhere safe to be. Then we can talk about what we can do to help anyone who survived."

My knees were wobbly, and my head was spinning. I needed to be somewhere we could sit because I was not going to stay upright for long. We could not go too far; Eric's energy was already spent, and Reign was limping pretty badly.

All of us walked silently in disbelief and shock. We were out here for real this time, not for thirty or sixty minutes. We had nowhere to return to and nowhere to go. We were unprepared, with only a little water and a few snacks. We chugged the water, not knowing we'd come to need it soon.

My grandmother had to be okay. I wanted to reassure the others that Grandma—and her ring—was probably with the Andrews, and if the POD got close to her, it would be disabled. Everyone had to be okay; structures were the only things damaged. I wanted to say all of this, but I couldn't. I wasn't even sure I believed it.

It wasn't long before we had to rest. Reign was too injured; he desperately needed to be still. We stopped as the sky turned purple, and sat beneath a few trees. "This looks like the nature room," Regal observed. It did look similar, but maybe it seemed that way because I was homesick already. The boys seemed to agree. We all wanted to be home so badly.

"I don't know if I can walk anymore," Reign admitted.

"Me neither," Eric muttered desperately. I was surprised he had made it this far. We had all seen Eric lose his breath when simply standing still, and we had been walking for a long time now. He had kept up though without complaining. I let myself fall to the ground. I did not think I could stand if I tried.

"Rest," Regal told us. "I'll take first watch." Maybe we could rest. Regal had the map for a second set of eyes; it might prove reliable yet.

Suddenly, without words, Regal ran off into the distance. I sprang to my feet in time to see him fight... no... *hug* someone. Before I knew it, my legs were carrying me in that direction.

"Annabel!"

For a moment, I forgot that everything was terrible. Annabel grabbed me, hugging me tight and hard. Then she paused, pushing me back by my shoulders, and looked at me. "Wait. If you are out here, that can't be good. Is everyone...?" she trailed off as she saw Reign and Eric behind me.

None of us could speak as the reality of the situation hit her. Then Royalty stepped into view. He had a wide gash splitting his face from his eyebrow to his ear. Annabel looked back at him. "It was an ambush, Nor, a setup. There was no family to save. The rest of the Select...."
She trailed off again.

Something moved behind her; it was a woman. The woman's head was shaved on the sides. Only a thin strip of blonde hair ran down the middle of her head. She was tall and broad and dressed in layers, even though it was sweltering out. The woman looked young, but it was hard to tell with the big, dark glasses she wore. She had symbol-like markings on her face.

Then, a small, round, dirty face appeared from behind the woman's legs. Warm light-brown eyes peered up at me from behind messy tangled hair.
"This is River and the little one is Ash," Annabel told us. River nodded in our direction while Ash hid. "Their community saved Janie, too. They are all that's left." It took us a minute to understand what Annabel was saying. *Their community saved Janie, too....* Annabel continued. "River was tracking the set of PODS that trapped us. She saved us."

Without a word, we joined Eric and Reign. There was nothing we could say. The brothers held each other, and I was with my sister, but that did not mean that Eric was alone. He was part of our group now, our rag tag team— our new family.

River stayed standing as the rest of us sat under the trees. She knelt down and picked up Ash, placing the child in the tree above us. Then she stood guard. Although River said nothing, we knew she was taking watch. I leaned on Annabel while Regal monitored the map. Royalty tended to Reign's injuries. Eric lay snoring louder than he ever spoke as the sun disappeared. I wanted to ask what we were going to do now, but I knew no one had the answer.

DON'T PUSH BUTTONS

2063

I glared at the gift basket sitting on the table that the realty company had sent. It contained an odd variety of fruit and an array of muffins encircling a bottle of wine, all wrapped up with a big gold bow. I said it was unnecessary but she insisted and in a grand gesture, placed it in the middle of the table.

I was sweating and could feel my throat tighten.

I dragged my feet over the worn-out floor in the kitchen, snagging my sock on a loose piece of vinyl that had lifted. The once bright yellow linoleum was more of a faded dull brown now from the years of wear and tear.

This place didn't have the same sentimentality with me as it had with my mother. It was never home to me and somewhere I never really wanted to be.

I enjoyed city life until Mom seemed to have lost touch with reality and forced us to isolate from the world. It happened right before my freshman year of high school. I never really forgave her for taking away those most important years, ripping me from my friends and everything I knew, to live in the middle of nowhere.

Nothing about this place had changed, not a single thing, and I imagined it was the same long before I could remember it. I hated being here, it made me feel trapped and helpless. I looked out that giant window into the green nothingness that extended far beyond what my eyes could see. There was nothing here for me, there never had been.

"Well, it could use some work but it's a classic so there's some charm in that, which will definitely help. I mean yes, we have hurdles," the annoyingly squeaky voice reminded me I was not alone, "but we're not going to focus on that. Nope, we're not; instead, we're going to focus on the good."

As she continued thinking aloud, I wondered what the hell I had done to deserve this. I'd walked right out of the funeral straight into the closest real estate office and hired the very first agent I saw. It was going to be a bar, but when I saw that sign, it was simply that: "Sell Property Fast & Easy," which was all I needed. I went straight in, literally bumped into her and gave her the job.

I wanted to be rid of the house and never look back but now I was regretting it. It was the worst time for me to deal with an airhead, desperate for approval, try-too-hard attitude. I'd done this to myself, I should've hired someone else, but I simply did not have the energy.

She continued to tell me her ideas for selling the house while jotting down notes on her tightly held clipboard. "I think with the..."

"Yeah, let me save you some time," I interrupted, "do whatever you think is going to get it sold," I said flatly. I'd explained that to her earlier when I started the tour, then let her finish on her own. She kept asking me questions and awing over what a classic family feel it had. I left her on her own when I realized she was a touchy-feely person who needed me to cosign every little thought she eagerly scribbled down.

I didn't care about her techniques or strategies as long as I never had to come back here.

I was ready to leave. I'd been there two days already, and it was two days longer than I wanted to be there.

Every moment she took, standing there explaining something to me that I didn't care about, was one more moment she wasn't trying to sell it. All I wanted was to go home and put this all behind me.

In the dead silence of the country air, I could hear her pen scratch nervously on the paper, the same way she seemed to do everything, and it drove me mad.

"Well, looks like you've seen it all then? You're all set?" I asked trying to move things along. It had been a very long day.

"Oh, yes. I mean, there's quite a bit of property to walk, but now with it dimming, I'd like to come by earlier in the day and give it a proper once over if you know what I mean?" she said without taking a breath. She was taking more notes and I wondered what the hell she was still writing. How many notes could you take on selling a crappy piece of land with a hollow barn and an old house?

"So, yeah, do you need anything else from me?" I asked more to dismiss her than to assist.

"Oh, no, I'm okay. I mean, I will call you first thing to come by and to…"

Before she could continue, I butted in, "Yeah, so call me the minute you have an interested buyer. I'll talk to you then."

"Yes of course, I will, and I will call you to come walk the property and…"

I cut her off again, "Call me when you have a perspective buyer. You don't need to call me to walk the property, you have my permission. Do whatever you have to do."

I turned back around and stared out into the darkening sky and the only thing I ever liked about the countryside was the details the city lights hid.

I grabbed onto the counter, leaned on it and sighed.

"Should I show myself out then?" she asked, finally taking a hint.

I didn't say anything. I turned around, half smiled then nodded slightly, glancing in the direction of the front door.

She walked towards the door, and I called for her.

She was instantly by my side. "Yes?" she asked, looking up at me wide-eyed like a puppy waiting for a treat or to be pet.

"Take the basket with you," I said motioning towards the table and turning back around to look out the window.

"Oh no, I couldn't, that's for you. It was meant for you to enjoy, and you should…" she went on.

"I don't want it!" I spit out so loud I even surprised myself. I stunned her and she looked as though she might cry. I swallowed hard then lied, calmly saying, "I'm sorry, I'm on a diet and the muffins are tempting."

"Oh, yes, I understand," she said looking down, "but there is also fruit which might be a better option for you. I mean, I can take it if you really want me to? I'm sorry." She reached for the basket.

"No, I'm sorry, it was actually very thoughtful of you," I said because it was. "Leave it. Thank you, Cassie."

She nodded and attempted to tiptoe out, but did the opposite, clumsily stepping on every creaky floorboard and bumping into furniture, emphasizing her exit.

When the slamming of the screen door let me know, she'd finally left, I immediately loosened my blouse and threw my bra to the floor.

I wasn't a people person on a good day, but surely, she understood the circumstances well enough to catch on without any further explanation. Selling the property my mother left to me after she died, or more accurately hopelessly trying to rid myself of the place she'd held me captive in, the place she lost her mind in, the place she committed suicide in.

It would put anyone in a bad, not very sociable mood. Cassie wasn't my cup of tea. She had way too much frantic energy and she overcompensated for it by being ridiculously peppy. She was constantly fishing for compliments and always touching me, which is a huge pet peeve of mine. All in all, I didn't care because she was simply the means to an end. I would tolerate her if she could find someone to make an offer. All I wanted was to pawn this place off on someone else and disassociate myself from everything that came with it, or the lack thereof.

Without warning and without realizing it I was suddenly, savagely punching the kitchen wall; my knuckles were bloodied, which left stains on the dingy wallpaper. Not far from the smeared blood was a growth chart on the doorway frame. It had been carved into the wood, my mother was there, measuring in shorter than her father, whose height and age was also tracked along with his brother and their father.

I hadn't experienced family memories and things. By the time I got here, I was basically fully grown. There was no need to add myself to some tradition I'd never been a part of.

I tried to clean the stains off the wall though it only smeared them, so I gave up and washed my hands.

I was told it'd be a week before someone could clear the stuff off the property. Most of it was trash anyway. I planned on using the next few days to sort things out myself to hurry along the process. Everything in there was original so I thought at the very least I might find some antiques to compensate me for my travel, the service and every other burden I was currently facing as a result of my mother's selfish behaviors.

It had been a very draining day, and I was running on little to no sleep. I'd barely slept the night before. I wanted to stay at a hotel to avoid the triggering scenery, then I realized it was probably best for my pockets and for selling the property that I be at the house and readily available. In the meantime, I would go through what I had to.

I was hoping to break a record for the quickest sale or offer on the market because I had a life to return to. Perhaps not a life of glamour but it was my life, and it was far, far away from here.

It would have been easier to sell the property off to someone who would level it and turn it into a parking lot or something, but my mother made it a condition with the very few neighbors in the area, that if I sold it, it would be to someone for personal use. Everything in the area was being bought up by big businesses and she couldn't bear the thought of that happening to her beloved childhood home.

So far, that had shortened the list of potential buyers to none. She had to have known I was going to sell it. It was no secret I despised the place, plus, who else could she leave it to?

We immediately received quite a few offers; a factory, strip mall and a space for a storage facility, none of which I could accept, or believe me, I would have.

The outdated appliances, the unreliable electricity, the choppy reception, the unbearable silence, the entire atmosphere was testing me in a way that was jeopardizing my sobriety. It was bad enough that since I'd gotten here everything seemed more intense. It was probably the lack of background noise that allowed me to hear my own thoughts and there were so many because I had nothing to do. Maybe I was reliving the moment I broke. Every second I spent in this house I lost myself. I could feel myself losing all the progress I'd made. I'd come so far from being the person this place made me into. I was finally getting things together.

Things weren't always broken between my mother and I; we were once inseparable. It was us against the world. I never had a big family but I was happy. I have vague, inconsistent memories of my dad. He and my mother separated early and I can't remember them together. I recall blurry occasions of pick-ups, drop-offs and holidays spent with one or the other, but never both. One day I walked down an aisle tossing petals and was promised a whole new life if I were to go live with him instead. Then there's the hazy arguments of clashing parenting I overheard but hardly understood. Over time I saw him less and less and then not at all.

My mother was sure he hadn't a clue how to raise me properly and he made it clear that her problems were beyond him, so he moved on and started a new family. A family I didn't fit into anymore.

I couldn't blame him for wanting to start over. He became "Dad" in a perfect family with 2.5 kids and a dog living in the suburbs. A big house with a manicured lawn and a tire swing where they hosted barbeques and game nights. The kind of family that has siblings, cousins and grandparents. The kind of family that consists of more than stories of people who died before you even existed.

It was only us, my mother and I and I was content with that. She owned a floral shop, and she collected a few friends along the way. Those friends had kids of their own and by default we became friends.

That was the closest thing I had to real family. There were four of us, Johnathan was a year older than me, and Mina was a few months younger than me, and her sister Michelle was a year younger than her. Johnathan's mom worked at the shop with my mom and one of the girls' moms was a frequent customer turned employee and the other was quite handy and helped my mom out around the shop.

We were more family than friends since we were forced to be together in close quarters in the back room of the shop to do our homework after school. Whenever large floral orders took our moms hours to arrange, we would hang out back there and play. I was never good at getting along with people, but with the three of them I didn't have to try. We'd known one another since we were about four years old. Six years later, we had no secrets and spent very little time apart. We met up in the morning to walk to school together and helped out at the shop even if it was only an excuse to keep hanging out after school.

I watched my mom flourish in city life and I enjoyed the scene. She was in her element. Unlike me she was a natural people person. She was right where she needed to be. She had a green thumb and could very easily read a person. She had this beautiful way of knowing what they were looking for and exactly what they wanted. The shop was always booked up with weddings, funerals, quinceñeras, bar mitzvahs, and any other occasion flowers were needed.

The four of us got stuck with the overflow; miniscule tasks like clean up and sorting. I wanted to help making the bouquets and set ups, but I was never quite as good as she was, no one was. That left the tedious tasks for us and that was where we bonded.

Things were steady, nice and predictable, and when the space above the shop became available everything fell into place. I was happy and I felt safe. I cherished that feeling. That was the last time I felt stability because overnight everything took a turn. My mother lost her uncle, and she was never the same. In fact, nothing was ever the same again. It changed her, she never recovered. He raised her and though he hadn't been himself in some time, it hadn't softened the blow of the loss.

I only knew him as "the guy who'd raised her," another story about a relative before my time. He wasn't the funny lighthearted guy she'd described. He had become someone I had to reintroduce myself to several times in one sitting. He was that part of her family she spoke of that I'd never had a chance to know. She told me about him, her mother, and even her dad whom she'd never met. She always spoke of them as if they were still alive.

She lost her dad before she was born and her mother when she was about ten. Her uncle was all she had left, so I understood even at a young age what a loss it was to her, but I never knew that his passing would alter everything.

When he passed it was really tough on her. I was eleven and I remember it vividly because it was two days before my twelfth birthday. We had to cancel my party and we spent it here in this house without even a signal to reach home.

The property fell to her and at first it was nothing more than her making a few phone calls to a neighbor's son and a bi-weekly payment, and he handled all the maintenance. Once he moved out of town, the responsibility fell to the elderly Mr. Ackles, who although he considered himself spry, was far from it.

More of the upkeep became my mother's direct problem as Mr. Ackles became capable of nothing more than a simple mower ride over the new growth. Once in a while he'd glance over at the house and barn to see if they were stable looking enough. That meant we visited a little more often to handle what he could not.

The more time we spent there; the harder it was to go back home. Whenever I got back, I'd missed so much I always felt like the odd one out. We used to be a four pack, a quad and now with my consistent back and forth, I felt like I hardly knew the three of them. With my mother running such odd hours, the shop was closed more often than not, which meant we saw each other far less.

When Mr. Ackles passed, we went from sporadic visits to every school vacation including summers. Which meant my school breaks were no longer spent with Johnathan, Mina and Michelle, and instead I was slaving away tending to yard work and maintaining the barn and farmhouse. Coming home highlighted all the ways I'd been left out of the loop. A few weeks away is nothing to an adult, but to a twelve-year-old it was all the difference in determining friendships.

My best friends had done as my dad and had started over. They added a new version of me to their group. She knew all the inside jokes they'd shared while I was away at farm prison.

Then one summer we never even went home, and I had been phased out enough to where no one seemed to notice.

When summer came to an end so did life as I knew it. She tore me from my home, my friends, my school, and everything I knew. According to her that life was not meant for us.

She tried to convince me that it was for the best, that the city was dangerous, and people couldn't be trusted and that we were all each other had and needed. I hated her, she didn't even give me enough respect to explain it to me, to ask me, to warn me. She acted as if anything before then hadn't really happened. Whenever I brought up our past: our home, the shop or anyone from it, she changed the subject. I finally accepted the new life thrust upon me, but when I mentioned school and the commute, she said nothing. My freshman year began in a new town, and I was on time to class, early even; homeschool in my kitchen.

That year I discovered an appreciation for my uncle through his extensive collection of moonshine. It was that moment that changed everything.

I tore into the plastic of the gift basket, tossing aside an apricot and a blueberry muffin. I grabbed my keys off the counter. Fourteen months sober, yet I still carried a bottle opener/corkscrew on my keychain. I opened the bottle and the sound of the cork popping echoed through the quiet.

2065

"Top it off," he told the waiter.

I grabbed his hand softly and he knew it meant, "should I really have another?"

"Eulalie, you're fine. You doubt yourself," he said shaking his head. "Don't do that, you're strong. Bad habits are for the weak."

"Top it off," I confirmed. I *am* strong, I'll be fine.

Apollo Levin, the love of my life. I hated cliches and yet everything about the way we met was one; me on the side of the road helpless and him coming to my rescue.

He knew me better than anyone and unlike everyone else, he never judged or limited me. He embraced all of my destructive tendencies and my rebellious nature, and as a result I became my best self.

It wasn't because I'm not a people person, it was that I was in the wrong position, on the same level. He taught me that elevated was the best way for those like us to live. It didn't matter if you were easy to get along with when you were in a position of power. When others wanted to please you, you didn't even have to try. I used to say please and thank you before he taught me that those words could easily be replaced with currency. When you paid for a service, it wasn't a favor it was their job, so the niceties were pointless.

Any friends I made were loyal because they had less and were honored to share everything that came with knowing me. Being my friend made their life better so they accepted me exactly how I was, or they would cease to exist to me.

Apollo showed me that the biggest mistake I made before now was that I didn't hold myself to the high standard I deserved.

"This bread is not warm," he said shoving the basket into the waiter's chest. The waiter stammered, then apologized and ran to correct it.

I thought it was warm, but I didn't want to second guess him, instead I grabbed his hand again.

"It was warm, very warm," he agreed with me aloud. "I wanted to see if he'd tell me that. If he'd stand up for himself and say that it was warm and fresh, but he was weak. I don't even want bread; the bread is beside the point."

I nodded and eagerly absorbed his life lessons. He was molding me to be the highest version of myself.

"Ah, my poppet," he said in that way that made my heart skip a beat. "You have to decide how you want to be treated. It is not conceited to think you are better if you are---and we are." I felt my cheeks redden so I looked down.

He lifted my face gently and said, "Don't blush, take the compliment and look me in the eye. Blushing is for those who cannot control their emotions. You know better."

He was right. In the last two years I learned what I hadn't or couldn't in the twenty-four that preceded it.

I wasn't depressed or an alcoholic or a drug addict. I didn't need to repent for my sins or beg for forgiveness. I wasn't weak, I was misinformed.

My mother had failed me; she did not teach me what mattered most. As much as she spoke of the past, she never spoke of my heritage: where I came from.

I was made to believe I was damaged; sent to rehab and was told I was out of control. I was responding to life the only way I could, unsure because I was uninformed. I hadn't known my true origin and the fact that my mother mentioned everything but that, baffled me. It added to the list of reasons why I despised her.

I was enamored with my new life; I didn't have to be a people person because I felt I was hardly a person at all. Now, I was learning my capabilities and Apollo led the way.

The reason for my lack of control was because I never learned to manage the most critical side of myself. My oversensitivity to touch that set me off was normal, something I could master, use even. People tend to respond well when you know them, everything about them, even what they don't want you to know.

My whole life my mother told me to ignore my sensitivities. Therapy, prescriptions and self-medicating all to push down everything I thought made me crazy.

Apollo knew how to truly live in this world. He had such a gift. He executed better than me, but he had a lifetime of practice.

The world bows before you when you come up with flawless, innovative inventions. It became effortless when you could attend business seminars and pick the best ideas from the minds of geniuses. Then before they could trademark those ideas, you claimed them as your own, then used them unapologetically, even selling them back to them if they were so inclined.

Apollo made a living that way, it was an art form, and it came with a fortune. He was tech savvy yes, but he went beyond that by taking bits and pieces from all the most talented minds around and combining them to create the very best, the elite. It was working smart, not hard, using what we had, to advance ourselves in the way we deserved.

Before now, physical touch entailed what I thought to be overactive empathy and it left me at the bottom of a bottle to quiet both my own emotions and theirs.

Within less than two years I had become a different person. I felt powerful and strong. I was only still learning and hardly the master Apollo was, but I was happy with my progress.

"Finish your glass," he reminded me. The waiter had filled it up, left to fetch warm bread and brought it back, and I hadn't even taken a sip.

I grabbed the glass and when I heard the clink, I understood. I gasped so loud it was as if I inhaled all the air in the room. I plunged my hand into the glass pulling out a ring worth more than the restaurant we sat in. I made a mess, red wine splashing all over the table.

He grabbed the dripping ring from me and dried it on a napkin. Then got down on one knee and slid it onto my finger where it fit perfectly and looked like a dream.

"I know we can leave a lot unsaid between the two of us, but this needs to be said; will you let me make it official?"

No hesitation. He knew, but I screamed "yes" anyway because I was so excited. I kissed him passionately and wanted him right then and there, I knew he felt the same.

He got up beckoning the waiter. The red wine on the white cloth made the table look like a murder scene, but that wasn't our problem.

"This table is a mess," I said firmly. "I don't like this table anyway; I want a seat by the window."

"Of course, madam, right this way," said the waiter showing us to a clean table with a better view of the city skyline in the setting sun.

"She will also take a new glass," he told the waiter who was walking on eggshells at this point.

Apollo smiled; he was proud of me. *I* was proud of me.

2068

"Stop trailing off," he said in that firm but tender way that was so inexplicably attractive. He wanted me to know my worth. I tended to not finish my sentences because I spent my life with no one listening to me.

"I'm sorry," I said even though he hated when I apologized.

He cupped my face softly and pushed my hair back and kissed me until my toes curled. He then turned me around so I was facing the mirror while he stood behind me.

"Look at yourself," he pointed to my reflection. The more I'd come in touch with the other part of myself, the more it showed. Intense emotions would set me off and to full humans it would look like I disappeared. However, with my own human genetics factoring in, only parts of me would vanish. Imagine the shock and awe when part of an arm or torso became visible and floated through the air.

"Calm yourself," he said standing behind me.

I was worked up; I could see it and he could as well. To us it was like a shimmer, I thought it looked pretty.

"You should see true form," he sighed as he ran his hand down my body.

I was self-conscious as it was, but now he was comparing me to a form I'd never even seen.

"They're all starting to adapt to become more like, well you," he sighed.

I wasn't sure how to take that because he sounded so disappointed. Without realizing it, tears ran down my face. Still standing behind me, we made eye contact in the mirror then he wiped my tears. He corrected me, it wasn't that he was disappointed, he was honored. I confessed that I often felt inferior because he was in the habit of saying things like "tainted" and "hindered," when referring to humans.

I turned around and cried into his chest, I knew that he couldn't make out most of my words, but he knew what I was trying to say.

"No," he told me, stopping me from rambling any further. Softly stroking my hair, he reassured me, "I'm talking about them not you. *You* are not them. Humans are worthless."

"But I *am* human." I reminded.

"You will become less so in time; we will awaken what has been dormant in you," he promised. "We are better, don't you see that?"

I never saw myself as better than anyone, but he had a way of making me see things differently.

He turned me around to face the mirror again. He kissed my neck and pressed against me. I closed my eyes and breathed in completely calm. Suddenly I could see my mother sitting in my uncle's chair.

"Did you know my mother?" I asked out loud without meaning too. As soon as it escaped my lips, I realized I'd killed the moment.

"What? What? I'm kissing you, touching you and you're thinking about your mom?"

He sounded disgusted and stepped back. I reached for him, I wanted to fix it. I wasn't sure what happened, but I wanted to put it out of my mind and go back to the moment right before I stupidly mentioned my dead mother amidst our foreplay.

I pulled him in and standing on my tip toes reached up to kiss him but had this overwhelmingly sick feeling that I couldn't breathe. It felt like my throat swelled up and closed off. I kept gasping for air, I felt like I was drowning.

I dropped to the floor and Apollo panicked, "please, please, I cannot lose you." He exclaimed.

As he rubbed my back, I fought past the feeling, whatever it was. I caught my breath, though barely. I think it was anxiety. My heart was racing and I was sweating.

"Oh," he exhaled. "You're okay after all. Simple human afflictions I suppose. Anxiety, was it?" He helped me into bed then placed a damp washcloth on my forehead.

"Here." he said handing me a purple pill. "Please, my love, so you can get a good night's rest tonight. You know how you get after one of these attacks?"

I did sometimes lose myself for hours after a panic attack trying to regulate my breathing and stop whimpering. I probably wouldn't sleep at all if I didn't take the medication. He handed me water and I swallowed the purple pill.

He took such good care of me. He kissed me softly and the world started to fade away.

2071

We got into a place where it became annoying how much better he was at our abilities. With a simple touch he knew everything I was thinking, and it wasn't the same with him, he could block it. Which meant he could keep things from me.

Once I said I do, it was as if my role became less his woman and more his girl who needed guidance and direction.

In a way he had been doing it the whole time, but it became condescending. I understood it may not have been purposeful. After all, he had much more experience than me. The age gap was greater than it appeared. His physical form did not account for his actual years because we don't age as fast when we're not mixed with human DNA. Unlike me he wasn't mixed, although he called it pure and often said I was "tainted by human genetics." It cut deep when he said that even if he didn't mean to be offensive. He meant that my human side hindered me, but I couldn't help that. I knew about my human family, but what made up the rest of me was still a mystery to me.

Apollo taught me that my true family history began when a scout was sent to Earth to mate and create a half breed that they could then use to determine how humans survived under the intense heat of the sun. They also wanted to replicate their short gestational period.

Loosely translated, we were considered *Echoclairvoyanites* or *Echoclairs*. My other half, well not technically half because my mother was three quarters, which made me merely about a third myself.

They scouted planets, different ones that might sustain them because their temporary home was running on borrowed time. After many disappointing attempts, they came across Earth and sent a scout to land and investigate.

He came back with a mixed review. It was an odd location with the direct heat of the sun, but most of the various species adapted pretty well.

There seemed to be a most dominant species: humans. They were slower and primitive in both intellect and technology and they were wasteful and destructive. They seemed to be causing irreparable damage to the same planet they expected to support them. However, what they could do that we couldn't was multiply in one third of the time. That was intriguing because our species was on the brink of extinction following a brutal war. The few that remained, lived on a desolate planet abandoned by the former dwellers due to the lack of resources.

They were curious, but hesitant because of human ignorance and hostility, but they had an upper hand due to intellectual advancements. Our kind needed to learn how to reproduce at a rapid pace so they could repopulate. They planned to study the humans closer and if possible, prepare the planet to become their new home.

The mission was to send out a female who would mate, have a child, then return with the child when it was of a more capable age. Although human pregnancies were much shorter, the development of their young was painfully slow.

The theory was to combine both DNA's and when the child was older, return for study and an exchange of information. Unless of course there was a reason Earth was truly uninhabitable in which case a certain signal marked in the crops would warn them to stay away.

The first scout sent out in that regard was my great-grandmother; my grandfather Elias' mother. She gave birth to my grandfather. According to Apollo my great-grandmother was weak and had *Stockholm's Syndrome* so to speak because she betrayed her home by not fulfilling her mission and lying, proclaiming it was unsafe. I understood what he meant in that she sacrificed the good of many for one, but I also empathized, not because I could understand being a parent, but because I was part of the result of her betrayal.

From the moment she landed, she was meant to find a mate, make a child, then use her abilities to advance and become popular, rich or in power... then sell an undeniable piece of technology to the masses. Something their dull species had yet to invent. The humans would basically worship its newness and it would easily and quickly become a trend. When everyone was on board, our people would put into play the ultimate move, which would prepare the planet for them.

My great-grandmother Norma on my father's side wasn't the only scout they sent. She came first but warned others to stay away for years by her message imprinted in the crops. As pollution worsened, visibility became limited and the warning signs were not as clear.

Desperate, they decided to touch down again as a reattempt. They sent my maternal grandmother Violet, who came and failed as well. She fell in love with the very person she was meant to capture and return with. She tried to convince those back home that their baby, my mother Ellie, would be the better specimen. She was trying to buy herself time while attempting to also use the signals to warn them to stay away.

Unbeknownst to her, her location was barely visible, and others had touched down, signaling safety and forming numbers on Earth.

They lost track of my mother when her uncle moved her to the city. During that time, they successfully sent out a few more pairs to establish a network and stay informed while they tried to find the specimen, my mom.

2072

I basked in the glory of being a celebrity. I loved it; everyone bowing before me, and cleaning up my spilled droplets of the finest champagne. My husband is a tech genius.

He did it, well, we did it really. I gave some silent suggestions. I was not the master he was, but I did contribute a certain skillset. I was expelled from college for changing my grades. I changed a friend's too, who later confessed, hence the expulsion.

Before I met Apollo, I used to make money hacking into emails for jealous husbands. I'd get paid to completely clear the search history of someone trying to avoid blackmail. Every so often, I'd still help someone change a test score or two.

Now, I found myself standing alongside the man who headed the largest global technology industry. We were an instant success; we had no competition.

It had not even been released, and yet the hype was beyond any other premiere. There was a waiting list to get onto the waiting list. We had constant free advertisement thanks to all the influencers and eager celebrities we'd given VIP passes to. Media coverage was constant and not by mistake either.

Apollo was right, grubby humans would happily purchase the newest, coolest thing. They considered it a status icon and would pay anything to obtain it. If they thought it would make life slightly easier, they were invested. It was way too easy.

ThinkTech had turned me into royalty and I relished in it.

Everything I had was exclusive or custom made, and whatever I wanted was handed to me. As a result, I become really spoiled and impatient. Apollo had only the best help at my beck and call.

I was better than them. You had to be crazy to accept this level of a technological upgrade; one that involved a brain implant. But they were eating it up.

I stood on the top floor penthouse balcony. I loved looking down on everyone. It was a literal representation of my new day-to-day and it brought me great pleasure. My robe blew open in the wind and I didn't bother to close it. Modesty was for the weak.

"There's so much more to come, my poppet," Apollo said joining me on the balcony. "The world is ours. Now drink up." He handed me a glass of champagne. We clinked our glasses and sipped while overlooking a world of consumers.

2075

"You did it on purpose! It's different with you because you're tainted," he said sharply, grabbing his head and losing his camouflage. (I'd never seen that happen before). "This cannot happen! You do realize that, don't you?" He grabbed me roughly by the collar of my night gown.

I hadn't been sober nor awake long, so I thought perhaps I was still dreaming or more so; having a nightmare. I wasn't. I stood stunned; I don't know how I expected him to react.

"This is awful timing. You parade in here with this like it's some kind of gift."

"I didn't parade, I..."

He shook me and the test strip dropped from my hand as the door of his office swung open without warning.

"I hope you don't mind that I let myself in." He stopped in his tracks when he saw the two of us together. My nightgown was disheveled, and Apollo was breathing heavily.

Mike Peters, a very important business partner began: "I didn't mean to interrupt. Apollo you old dog, you," he chuckled assuming he'd walked in on something completely different than what was actually happening. Apollo rolled with it, embracing the idea that we'd been intimate instead of argumentative.

Mike looked down and noticed the pregnancy test at our feet. "Were you celebrating? Oh congratulations!"

I smiled awkwardly and scurried out of the room.

"A family man is a great look for a company in the spotlight. Makes you trustworthy, dependable…"

That's when I knew Apollo would tolerate the pregnancy.

2076

Apollo attempted to appease me saying: "I know you're bored. I'm sorry. I can send Gerri back to sit with you."

"No! I'm tired of staff, it's not fair," I knew I sounded like a spoiled child, but I didn't care.

"You must rest, Eulalie," he said.

"I'm not sick, Apollo," I snapped at him.

Sometimes I think he played into his role so well he forgot I was pregnant, not ill. My problem was that the pregnancy and hormonal changes were not allowing me to control my camouflage reflex, so I couldn't be seen out in public. Staff saw it, but they were programed to forget. Outside the manor, not everyone had been chipped yet so we couldn't risk it.

"I'm bored! I'm so bored!" I pounded my fists into the bed.

"I know, I know my dear, what can I bring you? What can I do?" He asked. He had become quite the doting expectant father, much more so than I'd expected him to be, given his initial reaction.

"You can't do anything for me if I have to stay here," I pouted.

"Please," he said putting his hand on my belly and looking at me, "who knows the toll it might take on him, with you having to concentrate so hard on holding it together."

He was right, this pregnancy was different so he had the right to be hypersensitive. I eventually composed myself, remembering that I wanted what was best for my belly fruit.

"We have to call him something other than belly fruit, don't you think?" He asked smiling that gorgeous smile of his. For a moment I actually forgot how upset I was.

"Yeah, you might be right," I said reluctantly.

He kissed my belly, then my forehead and left me to go take care of some business.

Still restless, I put the weight of the third trimester on my feet as I strolled around. I demanded that staff stop tending to me as if I was the child instead of the one having the child. They played into me being sick also, whether it be to please Apollo or due to their programming.

"I'm fine," I spit out at Gerri as she walked right behind my waddle as if she was expecting to catch me if I fell.

"Back up some would you," I said elbowing her.

"I'm sorry," she said, but did not back up.

I liked her well enough when her programming wasn't overriding her. I liked her better before she was chipped, but I had to remind myself of the goal. I didn't want to chip any of the staff at first because they were trustworthy and nice. Apollo reminded me they were merely staff, human staff, and I had to start accepting my superior position. It was for a better world. People who followed commands without question did not start wars nor commit heinous crimes.

That's why I stopped letting myself get close to the staff, to anyone really. I hadn't met others outside of Apollo yet, but I would soon and I decided to wait until then to form real relationships.

"I have to name the baby, Gerri," I announced. I was walking down the hall needing to stretch my legs because I had been pouting in bed for hours.

"You're going to name the baby Gerri?" she asked playfully.

I laughed a bit, "Funny Gerri."

"I try," she said dryly as I made my way to the table.

"I need chocolate Gerri. Tell Marcus, I can't get up again," I was out of breath.

"Of course, Mrs. Levin," she said and headed off.

She returned with chocolate pudding and chocolate milk both of which I pushed aside.

"Marcus is making cookies now," she soothed me.

"I'll wait for the cookies," I sighed.

"About the baby's name Mrs. Levin?" When I looked up at her she continued, "I say a namesake speaks volumes, starting with yours I suppose."

I scoffed, "I'm named after a stupid poem in a collection of crazy stories my mom adored, probably because she was crazy too."

"You've never read the poem yourself?" She asked.

"No," I said feeling judged. Everyone always asked that when they said how different my name was and they couldn't pronounce it.

"That's interesting," she said softly.

"How is that interesting?" I asked irritated. She was emphasizing why programming was perfect because I didn't have to think about answers to her stupid questions.

"Five, alpha, thirty-one, seventeen, solid, two, beta demonstrate," I said to override.

She instantly became someone else; rigid and vacant, but at least she wasn't going to judge me.

"What can I do for you Madam Levin?" Even her tone was different.

"Fetch me that book that was with my mother's things and have the cookies brought to my room. Now help me back upstairs," I demanded.

2078

"You must calm yourself my poppet," Appollo walked toward me trying to get me to embrace his touch.

I snatched away. "Don't," I said through clenched teeth.

He shook his head as if I was a child throwing a tantrum. I felt it coming from him, that "there, there, you'll be okay," attitude and it was patronizing.

"That can't be the plan, it's cruel and it's not what I agreed to," I contested.

"I keep trying to explain the difference to you between cruel and necessary. It's what we must do in order for our species to have a future," he said with indifference.

"If we have to kill in order to live; is it worth it? How is this right?" I asked, though I knew his answers would only further infuriate me.

"It *is* the right thing. Think of it in the long run. The big picture, a proper future," he said as he grabbed both my hands and looked me in the eyes.

I didn't pull away. I loved him, but I hated this. How else had I really expected the arrival of a new species to go? I was being emotional. Of course, it made sense and it was the right thing.

"Get out of my head!" I yelled pulling away from his grip, "you said you wouldn't do that. I'm not being emotional. You can't possibly think this is right, Apollo?" I was asking because I needed to hear him say it wasn't. He was silent. He turned away and looked out the window.

"They dominate by murder and capture, whether it be towards each other or inflicted on other species. We're simply doing the planet a favor by giving the other species we plan to coexist with a chance to repopulate themselves," he said. He really believed he was doing the right thing.

"It's genocide!" I screamed. His calm demeanor regarding something so brutal and horrifying was enraging me.

"Genocide is a term you learned in human school. Humans had to define it after they invented it. They hunt to extinction instead of simply taking what they need. But if you want to live by human education standards, then let me refer you to Darwin and his theory of survival of the fittest: and my dear, we are by far the fittest. The world will not mourn them. Now, calm yourself, stop overthinking," he said patting me on the head dismissively.

"Is my human showing? You say them. You call *them* weak, useless, pathetic, but I am human! Your son is human! What will happen to us?" I was upset, but I had a valid point.

"You two will always be protected," he said embracing me. "I don't mean to dismiss you. Come, I'll hear your concerns over lunch," he said as he kissed my forehead. "I'll have the staff prepare something nice and set up the patio."

2079

"This is my mother's handwriting," I said. Cassie nodded as I flipped through the pages of the journal, she'd handed me.

Day 16

The space is becoming much more habitable, we've done a lot in a short time. I'm proud of our progress. I work in private and although I hate lying to Uncle Ev, I'm doing this because of him. I knew the plan involved the extinction of the human race, including me due to the fact that I'm mixed. But this isn't for me, it's for everyone I've met along the way. For my uncle who raised me to the nice lady at the coffee shop who always gave me extra caramel in my latte. We're doing this for every child that waved or smiled at us and anyone who held a door open or donated to a charity. It was for the good of all humanity, but most importantly it was for Eulalie.

Day 23

I sent my uncle on a wild goose chase for a color of paint that doesn't exist. He wants to paint Dad's old room for

Eulalie so she can have a place of her own whenever we visit.

I really need to finish up some details. I'm grateful for Cassandra, she's been able to upgrade my tech and speed along the process. I have a few ideas I would like to test with the new technology but my days are numbered, and I can't seem to get enough done.

Day 41

I've given Casandra permission to finish while I flee. I cannot risk Eulalie. I have confidence in the small team we have formed. She promised to help work towards my theory. I don't doubt that her connection will provide her tech that will make it all possible, but I feel bad for what she has to do. She has an important role to play, and I must let her, even at the risk of losing her as I know her.

I'm not worried about Uncle Evan; he doesn't know anything. He isn't even on anyone's radar. I couldn't involve him for his own safety and sanity. Especially with his constant stockpile of moonshine. He started a little moonshine business that was picking up. I love that he was trying to have more money on hand to be helpful to me and the baby, though I worry that he may be tempted to dip into it himself. His intentions are good though and he really is the best Uncle. I love him. All he wants is to spoil his great-niece. She can hardly hold her head up yet and he's talking about buying her first bike.

I became lost in my mother's words...

"What is this? What is she talking about? Working on what?" I wondered, but I could envision it all at once before Cassandra answered. "It's here, isn't it? This whole time you knew? You always knew?"

"Kind of," she said. "At first, I knew, I worked with Ellie and helped it all come together but," she paused.

I grabbed her. I knew she was being honest. She liked Earth. Apparently quite a few of them did, though not for the arrival. They liked it the way it was.

They agreed that keeping up form was exhausting, but humans were interesting, and she had fallen in love with one herself and understood the appeal.

Not all of the Echoclairs sent to Earth wanted to follow through with the next part of the plan. They liked living among humans and thought a better way to survive would be to blend with them and make families.

Their approach was a nonviolent one: befriend and love humans. Make families and intermix so much so that if they did decide to step forward in the future, they would simply be an additional race among the diverse human population.

They prepared an underground establishment, a place to live safely if the next part of the plan happened. They decided humanity was in fact worth saving and she paid a price to make it so.

Everyone who was in on assisting a group of humans who were not ThinkTech chipped, knew the next step.

They secured their plan by using an additional ability I didn't know we had: the removal of memories.

Cassandra had my mother remove any of the information she knew concerning the secret project, which even included knowing her. It was a safety measure in case she was read by anyone who supported ThinkTech's next move.

When my mother was gone so was her hold on Cassie's memories, so they came flooding back. She wanted to tell me everything immediately, but she also knew the hand she'd had in my mother's death and hated herself, fully expecting I would hate her too.

Cassie knew Apollo; she worked with him. Her mind had been wiped so clean that she didn't even remember she was rebelling against the original plan. When Apollo, who was in charge touched down, she naturally fell in line.

First, Apollo senselessly pulled all the thoughts and memories from my uncle ruining him for nothing because he hadn't known a thing.

Then he came searching for us. My mother knew we were in danger. She isolated us by hiding us at the farm, believing it to be safe, not understanding the true cause of Uncle Evan's demise. So, she lived there even after I took off. She stayed protecting something I knew nothing about and that's when Apollo came to her.

At first, he came in peace because he'd misjudged her strength. He assumed he'd easily be able to read her or push her thoughts. She was much stronger than me so he failed. He sent others to read her in order to locate the button. Every night they stole memories from her and forced mad thoughts into her mind. She'd call me sounding insane, begging me to come because she couldn't protect the fate of the world if they ate her mind. At the time however, I was too high or drunk to even care.

The deeper they went into her mind to determine the location, the weaker she grew. She did the only thing that made sense to her; she killed herself before they could completely break her.

By then she wasn't making enough sense to leave a well-thought out, meaningful letter. What she left read: Eul don't push buttons.

I had no way of knowing it was literal. She sacrificed her life to stop arrival preparations and I handed it to Apollo so I could sit beside him on the throne.

"I have to do something; this is all my fault!" I should've never given Apollo that button. I had no idea what I was doing!" I said crying.

"It isn't your fault at all," she tried to calm me.

She reached out and touched me. I knew she was trying to read me, but I was so lonely that I hugged her. I barely had any peer interaction with anyone who wasn't paid to tolerate me.

"It is my fault. I was blind. Teach me, teach me everything Apollo has withheld from me to weaken me," I cried out. I began to weep.

She hesitated then spoke softly, "You need to start with sobriety." She flinched, bracing for my response.

I was calm and honest. "I've been sober since the moment I found out I was with child," I said proudly.

She did this thing where she floated her hands over my shoulders and back, close, but not touching. It was like she was miming a massage.

"We have to be transparent to do this," she hesitated. "I can tell there's something in your system."

"What?!" I scoffed. Now I was offended. "I'm not lying, what would I gain?" I asked.

"It's dissipated though," she walked around me hands out like she was warming them on a fire. "Days old maybe," she finished.

And we realized at the same time: it was Apollo.

Every time I asked too many questions, we'd sit together for a meal. If I was furious, he'd convince me to sip tea he'd brought me. He was drugging me to keep my abilities from piquing, making me less aware. He wanted me sedated so I wouldn't realize what was going on because he knew I was not on board with the plan. Pregnancy distracted me, but I had become more present since becoming with child. I had been asking him questions instead of simply taking him at his word and he needed to control that.

"Teach me everything!" I demanded and pleaded with Cassandra.

"How much time do you have?" she asked agreeing.

Apollo was overseas on business. I intended to call this place home during that time. I would take Polly away from the chaos in the city.

2081

"You cannot leave me here! You're crazy! Do you hear me Apollo?! You cannot leave me here, I swear! I want to see my son! You cannot keep him from me! He's mine! He's not a PR stunt!" I screamed at the top of my lungs. Then I shrieked over and over until my whole body ached.

"I'm sorry Polly," I choked out as if he was in front of me.

Apollo was scared of me now. I learned some of the history he'd left out, some of which he hadn't even known himself.

I kept it from him, I learned how for my son. Nothing before he was born had ever made me want to be sober more. I'd never had a reason and now that I did, I couldn't maintain my sobriety at no fault of my own. Alcohol and pills were Apollo's way of controlling me, to keep me in check and my son was his leverage.

I screamed myself into exhaustion, I laid on the floor of a room I used to adore. I wouldn't touch that bed, the bed he fed me lies in, laid beside me all the while poisoning me, using me. The room was bigger than the size of the studio apartment I once called home and yet it felt like I was inside a shoe box.

I couldn't catch my breath. I yelled so loud my lungs were throbbing and my heart was beating so fast in my chest I thought it might jack hammer its way out. I still wanted to scream, though I had no more energy to do so, plus it was pointless.

I knew from the moment I started, that my cries for help would be for nothing. The staff had learned their lesson about interfering and when they still couldn't resist my pathetic pleas and felt tempted to help, their programming kicked in. Then they did as they were supposed to; ignore me, secretly drug me, keep my son away from me, lock me up, whatever he said.

I was suffering. Apollo was using visits with my son in exchange for me agreeing to be sedated. Sometimes before my visits to keep me from saying too much, but Polly knew. Young as he was, he was bright.

Apollo thought Apollo Jr. to be nothing more than a public relations stunt so he could present himself as a prime example of fatherhood. He needed to be seen as an honest, standup guy. A good dad and attentive husband who tended to his "sick" wife. They had to paint that picture of him because the truth would've gone against the ThinkTech brand.

Out of the spotlight he was cruel and murderous, cold, calculated, abusive, and an absent parent. He considered Polly to be inferior like me; damaged by human genes.

His one care in the world was to set into motion *Operation Clean Up* so that Earth would be prepared for the arrival. Now that he had what he needed from me, I was expendable and so was Polly. I long ago gave up the thought of my life having worth, but Polly would begin the next world. I simply had to get him there.

2085

His plan had failed, part of it anyway.

He was wrong about humans. I was human and no longer brainwashed to believe it was a disadvantage. I had never been misled, until I met him. I may have been uninformed about my genetics, but it was not only that which made me who I was. I am flawed and at times weak, but that didn't make me expendable. Who was he to determine if we were worth exterminating?

I, a lowly human, was one step ahead of him. He could still keep some things from me, but Polly knew, he always did, and Apollo underestimated him. He told me the plan then we prepared accordingly.

The night came where Apollo had callously activated the staff to kill both me, and his own son, laying in my arms.

We all played along.

Polly was safe, but the fact that I could have lost him fueled me with more rage than I'd ever known.

Apollo had too much of an upper hand for me to come at him halfcocked, so I suppressed my fury and channeled it into a master plan. I couldn't do it alone though, and lucky for me, I wasn't the only one who despised him, everyone did.

After I awoke from his spell, I realized I wasn't the only tortured soul in that place. We were all his prisoners, trapped, and at his beck and call. We had all been abused by him in some way. He considered us inferior. The only difference between them and me is that he had to pretend to consider me his equal, at least until he had what he wanted.

When I knew what was coming, I secretly had every staff member's chip removed, but they continued to behave according to their programming, whenever in his presence.

Apollo barely spent time at the manor in those days. If he came by it was because he was a control freak and wanted to verify that I was still being managed. He needed me to know he was still in charge.

When he was there the staff pretended to keep me locked in the room, to keep Polly from me, to keep me sedated and agreeable for when he did wish to interact with me. I pretended to be trapped, to be kept from my child, to be under the influence.

We were like playthings to him now; pets in a cage. He only came to us when he had nothing better to do or needed to keep up the image of a doting husband.

He'd come see me and attempt to push things into my head and I'd let him think he had. Unfortunately, sometimes he still could. He'd use me to suppress his boredom and I never let on despite how degrading it felt.

He would have his way with me then he would sentence me back to solitude at least until he was ready to dispose of us.

He didn't notice anything was off because he was blinded by his own arrogance. He thought himself far too perfect to make a mistake and me far too incapable of such a grand scheme, so he hadn't a worry that anything was out of the ordinary.

I needed that button so I could stop what he had set in motion.

The night came and he was ever so predictable, it was so obviously a goodbye, but I faked being far too loopy to realize of course.

He had us both dressed up nicely, matching each other, matching him. He spoke to me sweetly as if we were tip top. We shared a lavish family dinner, as if I had an appetite, but I played along. He sent Polly to get ready for bed and danced with me, telling me how he wished things could have worked out and how much potential I had. If I didn't know him better, I might have thought he was having regrets.

After he convinced me that I wanted him, I endured his forced touch one last dreaded time and then he ran me a hot bath.

He chose navy blue silk pajamas and laid them out for me. I put them on and climbed into bed. He kissed me on the forehead and gave me the biggest privilege of all: access to my Polly.

He allowed me the rare occasion of approved one-on-one time with my son, even going as far allowing him to sleep with me that night. I held my son close in his matching pajamas.

Apollo stepped out. I knew he wouldn't go far. Of course he would want to revel in the result. I knew him well enough to know that he would need the satisfaction of seeing his request fulfilled. He could never get his own hands dirty and do it himself, but he would want to bask in the glow of the aftermath of it being done.

I relied on his need to appreciate his well-executed plan because that's when I would execute mine.

I stayed awake all night. How could I sleep? We had mastered slowing our breaths and heart rates, but we practiced some more anyhow.

The next morning, Apollo eagerly ran into the bedroom like a child on Christmas morning only to find us both unresponsive in bed. We lay there still and lifeless. I held my breath and although my eyes were shut, I knew he was smiling. He stood over us gloating, proud. I felt it.

I could feel his breath as he got closer and I prepared myself, holding tight to the knife Gerri had snuck me. He leaned in to be sure, and I pushed the blade against his throat and slid it across. It cut like a hot knife through butter. I tried not to choke on his blood as it rained down on me. Polly jumped from the splatter, and I tried to hide how much I enjoyed seeing the life drain from Apollo.

I may not have said it out loud, but in his last moments as he fell quivering on top of me, I looked him right in his eyes. He knew what I was thinking: we may not live the same, but we die the same.

I took over ThinkTech. I tried to do what I could to save who I could by removing their chips and it worked for a while until it didn't. We were really only prolonging the inevitable. Unless we found the button, we could not do much. Things were still moving forward in preparation for arrival.

I was also in danger of Apollo's team. The chip removal had not been part of the plan, and it was only a matter of time before someone came to stop me from interfering. All I could do in the meantime was work on a map that might help me locate the button and do everything I could to get it back.

2086

Apollo was gone, but we still hadn't made any progress on locating the button. We were working on a map to help us narrow down its location. I had a small team of Echoclairs that assisted me at the manor, Cassie included. We tried desperately to do as much as we could but we had targets on our backs. We knew our time and resources were limited.

I sent most of my staff to live with the Opt-Outs, though some refused to leave me, and against my better judgment I let them stay. I begged Gerri and Marcus to leave but they refused, and I both loved and hated them for it.

I still couldn't convince myself to send Polly away yet because I knew I couldn't go with him, and I was not ready to say goodbye.

I never knew what I was handing Apollo. What my great-grandmother had come down with, what my mother found and protected and eventually died for.

I didn't need to say anything to my son as I hugged him. He instinctively knew I loved him. He knew why I had to stay and that he had to go. He did not protest.

I gave him the book and inserted the map into its spine. It would be safe there until the chaos of the surface calmed. When the time was right, he could pursue it.

I slipped a dull band on his finger and handed him the second one, and though I didn't need to speak, I did. "These are the prototypes my mother, your grandmother Ellie was working on. Keep them on until you're safe." I wasn't sure if they worked, but if they did, I wanted him to have them.

"No one can know who you are. You are not Apollo, you are nothing like him, or me..." I trailed off.

I ached in my soul knowing these were the last words I'd ever say to him. I didn't have much time now that we had been breached.

"You can never tell anyone where you come from. You can be whoever you want as long as you're a good person. Polly, call yourself something different and save whoever you can."

"Montresor," he said, he seldom spoke aloud. "I will call myself Montresor."

I knew why. He was not leaving me as Apollo Levin Jr. he was beginning a new world as Montresor West.

I hugged and kissed him one last time, then I shoved him outside as I heard Gerri scream.

www.ingramcontent.com/pod-product-compliance
Lightning Source LLC
Chambersburg PA
CBHW060945030726
47503CB00003B/741